Beco

Mua

Becoming Mila

ESTELLE MASKAME

INK ROAD

First published in 2021 by Ink Road
INK ROAD is an imprint and trademark of
Black & White Publishing Ltd
Nautical House, 104 Commercial Street
Edinburgh, EH6 6NF

1 3 5 7 9 10 8 6 4 2   21 22 23 24

ISBN: 978 1 78530 332 6

A CIP catalogue record for this book is available from the British Library.

Typeset by Iolaire, Newtonmore
Printed and bound by CPI Group (UK) Ltd, Croydon, CR0 4YY

For the two brightest stars in the sky,
baby Buchan & Jensen Buchan.

1

So, I messed up.

Like, *really* messed up.

It's all I can do to keep myself steady while I struggle under the weight of my regret and fight this throbbing headache. But after last night's mistake, I deserve to suffer.

The room is silent except for the sound of the AC purring, and my eyes fasten onto a smudge that's blemishing the white marble of our dining table.

"How are we going to spin this?" Ruben sighs, seething with frustration. He's at the end of his tether with me. He couldn't make it any clearer just how tired he is of these impromptu damage-control meetings.

"It's *your* job to spin this," Mom snaps at him, her nails tapping frantically on a cell phone. "So, start thinking."

"Marnie, there's only so many indiscretions we can sweep under the rug," Ruben counters. "The showbiz press is fast latching onto the fact that your daughter is turning into a reliable revenue stream."

I suppress enough nausea to steal a peek up from the table. Ruben has his back to me, focused on a MacBook on the kitchen countertop. Mom is engrossed in her cell phones. She keeps switching between two devices: one for business, one for personal use. Even at this ungodly hour of the morning, she has somehow still had time to blow-dry her hair and apply full makeup in between dealing with the latest publicity crisis. There are two women here from the production company; executives of some sort, but I don't know their names. All I know is that they look entirely furious.

"Can't we pass it off as an episode of vertigo?" one of them suggests. She catches my lingering gaze and I look away.

"Oh yeah, *sure*, that'll work," Ruben drawls. He spins around, jaw clenched. Ruben has been in our lives for the past decade, but he still scares the hell out of me sometimes. He sets the laptop down on the table in front of me and tilts the screen back. "Look," he says, but I'm too ashamed to read the headlines. "Mila, *look*," he demands.

With heat spreading across my face, I reluctantly glance at the screen. Several windows are open, all minimized into small boxes that cover the screen; a blur of words that squeezes my chest that little bit tighter in their clutch.

EVERETT HARDING'S DAUGHTER TURNS WILD CHILD?

MILA HARDING CREATES A SCENE AT THE
"FLASH POINT: NO RETURN" PRESS CONFERENCE

DOES EVERETT HARDING SLACK OFF WHEN
IT COMES TO PARENTAL SUPERVISION?

"I'm *sorry*," I whisper, my voice hoarse from dehydration, making me sound weak and insincere.

"Apologies aren't going to shut down those hacks," Ruben snaps, then strides off with the laptop again. He perches it back on the counter, then directs his aggravation toward the production executives. "And which liability of yours thought it was a great idea to give Everett's sixteen-year-old daughter champagne at such an event in the first place?" he demands of them. "Someone who should no longer be working for you, that's who."

"No one *gave* me the champagne," I quietly cut in, mostly because I feel bad enough as it is without dragging someone else through the mud with me. Besides, no one else was actually at fault. It was all my own actions and decisions, which means it's all my mistake. "The flutes were already poured. I just grabbed one whenever no one was looking."

Ruben casts a look of disgust over his shoulder at me. "Mila, you're at an age where you *know* exactly how the tabloids spin the slightest trip-up. Their eyes light up with dollar signs. They've not a shred of sympathy for a kid who makes mistakes, especially when that kid is Everett Harding's daughter."

Someone's phone rings. One of the executives leaves the room, barking orders.

"I'm sorry," I say again. I don't know how many times I've apologized since last night, but it doesn't feel like enough. And, besides, what else can I say? I suck in my lower lip and cast my eyes down to the table, fighting back tears.

"I know you are, honey," Mom says. She places her two

phones down next to me and angles in close, putting an arm around my shoulders. She smells like blossom, fresh flowers in the spring. "In the grand scheme of things, it's a rite of passage as a teenager to experiment, so I'm not angry at you. It's just that …" She rests her chin on my shoulder and exhales, her breath tickling my neck. Her voice turns low. "Other kids can afford to mess up every now and then. *You* can't. Not when we're in the public eye, and right now of all times, the spotlight is shining just that bit brighter."

In her warm, scented embrace, I start to cry.

The other times I messed up recently, they were mild in comparison. When I gave the paparazzi the middle finger from the passenger seat of our Range Rover because I forgot that the windshield isn't tinted, Ruben nearly throttled me. And last month when I got into a spat with a Z-list model on Twitter, Ruben dealt me a blanket social media ban for two weeks. But now those stunts don't seem like such a big deal, because last night's antics were in a different league altogether.

Imagine this: it's the glitzy press conference for one of the biggest blockbuster releases of the summer, and the publicity run for the long-awaited third installment of the *Flash Point* series is in full swing. A luxurious Beverly Hills theater packed with journalists who have an abundance of questions lined up. The majority of the main cast is in attendance, but the lead, Everett Harding, and his glamorous co-star, Laurel Peyton, are the names on everyone's lips. On stage, the cast laughs with the audience, answering their questions and sharing their passion for their latest movie. Meanwhile, backstage, the production company celebrates. The champagne flows a little too freely. Everett Harding's chic wife floats elegantly around, engaging in animated discussions with executives and snapping behind-the-scenes candids for her husband to share later on social media.

And then there's me, their daughter, who makes the rookie teenage mistake of swiping champagne at a showbiz party that is already subject to so much scrutiny. I should know better than to try out something new, but I'm backstage, and I figure no one will notice.

I figured wrong.

The event wraps up to thundering applause. Mom pulls Dad into a giddy hug when he emerges backstage, and Ruben calls our driver to bring the car around because Dad is too exhausted from a full day of press to stay and mingle. Ruben hunts me down, steers me out the back door behind my parents to the dazzling flashes of the waiting paparazzi and their cameras. *Like sparkles in the night sky*, I used to think when I was younger. But now, it's just blinding.

The fresh air hits me too hard. I stumble over my own feet, knock into my mother, then crash against the barriers that are keeping the paparazzi at bay. Dad hears the commotion and turns to reach out for me, but Ruben shoves him into the waiting minivan. Mom disappears inside the vehicle behind him, and by the time Ruben comes back to marshal me, I am on my knees on the concrete, fighting to stabilize myself. A surge of nausea washes over me, and it's too intense to suppress. I throw up just as I'm trying to recall exactly how many champagne flutes I tipped down my throat.

The cameras flash brighter, the click of their shutters echoing in my dizzy head. A clash of voices yells different things all at once, some screaming my name in hopes that I'll glance up and look straight into their lens for that perfect candid shot, others screaming gross questions in hopes of triggering an even more inappropriate reaction.

Ruben grabs me by my elbows and hauls me off the ground. With a raised arm, he shoves cameras out of our way as he pulls me to the minivan, guides me inside, then slides the door shut with a slam. The chaos of noise outside is muffled, but hands are still banging on the windows.

"Mila!" Mom gasps, sliding into a kneeling position on the floor and cupping my face in her hands as my head sways. She looks up at me, her makeup still perfect, wide-eyed, and shocked. "Are you okay? What have—"

But Dad is the one who finishes that question. With a thunderous look of disbelief, he snaps, "What the hell? Have you been *drinking*?"

I'd completely messed up.

And now that it's the morning after, everything seems a hundred times worse. Headlines drag the Harding name down. Photos are all over the internet. I've made a fool out of my father.

"This is happening far too often," Ruben grumbles from across the kitchen. I can understand why he's upset. He's dad's manager, so *managing* our lives is what we pay him for, but I don't make it easy when I keep accidentally stirring up the hornets' nest that is the gossip press. "There's four weeks until the movie's release. Stories about a drunken Mila Harding on her knees throwing up at a press conference hitting the tabloids are *not* doing us any favors."

"Negative publicity surrounding our main lead is not what *we* need to be dealing with either in the lead-up to this release," the sole remaining production executive adds. She folds her arms over her chest and stares me down. She doesn't have any personal interest in us as a family – all the production company cares about it is how many dollars this movie will rake in at the box office.

"Plus, school just let out for summer, which means you, little lady, will now be in the public eye more often," Ruben says, rubbing at his stubbly chin as though he's thinking hard.

I wipe tears from my cheeks and pull out of Mom's cradling hug. Sitting upright, I sniff and look Ruben straight in the eye. "How can I fix it?"

Ruben shrugs. "Ideally? By not being here over the next few weeks so that no one has to worry about you becoming the tabloids' new best friend."

"Ruben," Mom hisses, placing a hand on my arm and squeezing tight as though to protect me from his words. The look she fires him is nothing short of disgusted.

"What? You have a better idea, Marnie?" he remarks dryly.

There's a creak at the kitchen door. Through swollen eyes I spot my father leaning against the doorframe. He's wearing his favorite sunglasses, his eyes most likely tired and sensitive after yesterday's hectic schedule, and his hands are stuffed into the pockets of his jeans. We all remain silent, unsure of how long he has been listening in the hallway. Mom takes my hand in hers.

"Mila," Dad says, clearing his throat. His voice is low and husky – part of the reason why he sells the whole global heartthrob thing so well – but even more so in the mornings. He reaches for his sunglasses and lifts them slightly so that his dark eyes meet mine. They are bloodshot and heavy from lack of sleep. "I think it's best if you go home for a while."

"Home?" Mom echoes at the same time as my heart sinks halfway down my chest. "*This* is our home, Everett. And Mila's home is right here. With us. Let's talk about this properly before—"

"Ruben, arrange travel," Dad says, riding roughshod over Mom's protests. Gaze still locked on me, I catch the flicker of remorse in his eyes before he drops his sunglasses back down and quietly says, "Mila, start packing. You'll be spending the summer back in Tennessee."

2

THE HARDING ESTATE.

The words are engraved in gold on a slab that's bolted onto the heavy stone walls that surround all fifty acres of the ranch's perimeter. The entrance gates are electric, and access appears to be granted via a keypad which I don't have the code for, so I call the help button and stare up into the security camera, waiting for something to happen.

My personal airport chauffeur has already made his getaway, leaving me abandoned in the middle of nowhere to stand in the sweltering heat with my luggage. It's eerily silent out here on these country roads – the neighboring ranch is at least a mile down the road – and the lack of noise pollution is jarring. Silence like this simply doesn't exist in LA.

I wipe a bead of sweat from my brow, not realizing there's also a speaker on these gates until I hear a buzz and the sound of someone clearing their throat.

"Mila! You're here! Just give me one second."

Aunt Sheri! It's been *ages* since I last heard her voice in person – with its comforting, unmistakable twang – so a happy grin spreads across my face.

I wait a minute longer, sweating even more with each second that passes, and continue to study these towering walls.

When I was a kid, the ranch was open to the road – no fencing, no walls, no gates. No *security*. Just a weather-beaten wooden signpost with the name of the ranch hand-carved into it. There was no need for anything different back then, but once strangers started turning up, there was no other option. Super fans of all ages would come lurking every once in a while because, for some reason, visiting the ranch where Everett Harding grew up is a big deal or something. That's why Sheri insisted my parents secured the ranch – for safety reasons – and Dad called in a construction crew and took care of all the costs so that any hassle from unwelcome visitors would end. However, I don't remember the walls being *this* lavish during our last visit. The gray stone is pristine and looks entirely out of place out here in the open countryside, the ranch more like a fortress than a family home.

There's a loud shrill of a bell, and the gates slowly open, revealing Aunt Sheri waiting on the other side.

"Mila!" she exclaims, pulling me into the type of hug that I always associate with the friendliness here – a bear hug that's suffocating, my body pinned beneath her grip while she sways from side to side with me. "Oh, let me look at you!" She pulls back, hands on my shoulders, and examines every inch of me like I'm a rare artifact.

Aunt Sheri, despite being Dad's sister, looks nothing like

him. Dad has dark, intense features, while Sheri's face is much softer, her cheeks round and rosy, and her blonde hair is a mass of natural curls. She's the younger of the Harding siblings, and she has the fresh face to prove it.

"Hey, Aunt Sheri," I say, offering up a goofy grin. It's been almost four years since we last saw one another in person, and although Sheri looks as though she hasn't aged a day, I can understand why she's studying me in fascination. I'm not quite that scrawny kid with the overbite and the pink glasses anymore – dance classes, braces and contact lenses took care of that.

"Aren't you a sweet grown-up thing?" she says. "So good to see you for real instead of on that laptop screen." But then she frowns as she pinches my cheek. "There's no need for all this makeup, especially not here with us …"

I know she's right, so I just lift my shoulders in acceptance.

But at this point in my life, I never know when someone with a camera will spot me, and the need to look picture-perfect at all times is ingrained in me, thanks to Ruben – and also my mom's immaculate example. I puff out a breath, feeling that makeup melting the longer we stand here.

"It's so hot out here," I say.

Sheri chuckles and swings an arm over my shoulders. "Welcome back to Tennessee!"

Fairview, Tennessee, to be exact.

I guess it's what my father still thinks of as home, and I suppose in a way it *is* home. I was born out here, and that sort of defines *home*. But the reality is, I have spent most of my life in California and it's pretty much all I've known, so

LA seems more like home than this place does. I don't have that level of attachment to Tennessee, but how can I expect to feel differently when I left Fairview at the age of six?

That part, I remember.

The leaving part.

I was only halfway through first grade when I packed up my favorite toys into cardboard boxes, hugged my tearful grandparents one last time, and boarded a one-way flight to Los Angeles. I didn't understand what leaving meant back then, but my parents kept calling it "our little adventure", and I had no idea how much our lives were about to change. All I cared about was getting to live near a beach.

The reason for our move right across the country was simple – to chase Dad's dreams.

Dad was always acting up as the class clown in his teen years, but one pesky detention where he had to help out in the drama department altered the course of his life forever. Painting sets for the winter play soon led to the "discovery" of Dad's natural talents – plus the movie-star looks and charisma that soon became apparent – and, before long, he was a certified drama heartthrob. So much so, he surprised everyone by pursuing this passion in college where he met my mom. By his mid-twenties, he was starring in low-budget independent movies, slowly building up his filmography, his name appearing in more and more credit sequences. And then, out of the blue, he nailed an audition for a movie that was pitched to be the next big Hollywood blockbuster – and it was. Landing that role was Everett Harding's stepping-stone into a world of stardom and fame.

So off to California we went. Mom quit her job and took on the role of Dad's personal assistant at first, supporting him every step of the way while readjusting her own career; brilliantly as it turned out, as she's now a much-in-demand movie makeup artist. To give them credit, my parents have worked *really* hard over the years to establish themselves.

So, we have lived out in LA for the past decade, moving from one house to the next, each one increasing in size and grandeur. For now, though, we are pretty comfortable in our home within a gated community in Thousand Oaks. My school is there, my friends are there, my life is there.

Long story short, California *is* home to me, and Tennessee is simply a blip in my distant memory.

Fairview, in my mind, became nothing more than somewhere we used to visit on vacation. The only real memories I have of this place are from the occasional trips we've made over the years to see family, and the last time I was here I was twelve.

But this time, it's not for the weekend. Dad wouldn't back down, and Ruben agreed it's best I hang around here for a while, at least until the initial hype of the movie release dies down. Surely, I can't do any more damage if I'm not in the vicinity of him or the Hollywood press?

"Lucky for you," Sheri says, "I've got the AC cranked up full. Let's get you settled." She grabs my suitcase and drags it down the dirt road that weaves a route to the house.

The ranch hasn't changed much from that last time we all gathered for our Thanksgiving get-together four years ago. It's just stretching fields that were once home to grazing cattle and sheep many moons ago when my grandparents ran this place, but now the only livestock are the horses. I can see some of those horses now, lingering in their field by the stables just beyond the approaching three-story family home.

I think the security around this ranch is probably its most luxurious, high-end feature.

Everything else is … normal. The grass is a little overgrown, the stables could do with some fresh paint, and the house shows its age with its old-fashioned windowpanes, slightly rusty ironwork, and a wooden porch. It feels humble and charming. No Hollywood glitz. Just a real, down-to-earth southern ranch.

"Are you sure it's okay for me to stay?" I ask as we near the house. This plan for me to spend the next month or so out here only came into existence two days ago, so it's last-minute for everyone involved. Sheri most likely hasn't even had the chance to fully think it through, and already I feel like I might be a nuisance.

She pulls my suitcase to a stop outside the front door. "Sweetheart, you're family, aren't you?" she says with a warm smile and a tilt of her head.

"Yeah."

"Then there's your answer!" She pushes open the door and gestures for me to head on in first. "Besides, we could use some young company around here."

I step into the house and the AC blasts cool air against my face, which is a welcome relief from the heat. Sheri drags my suitcase over the welcome mat and into the wide entryway, where a rustic wooden staircase leads upwards. The room ahead of me is mostly open plan, with structural archways separating the space, and I gaze in at the living room and then the kitchen, surprised by the sense of familiarity that warms me. Nothing appears to have changed since my last visit. There's the same well-loved furniture that's been here for decades and the walls are lined with family photographs in glass frames that are gathering dust. The kitchen hasn't been renovated in years, and although one of the cupboard doors is quite literally hanging off its hinges, I actually like that not everything is perfect. It feels real, like *actual* human beings live here even though there is way too much space for just two people to fill. Plus, there's that same glorious smell of Sheri's incredible cooking that I remember so vividly.

"Beef stew," Sheri announces, seeing me sniff the air. "And all the damn fine sides you can imagine. You deserve a real welcome home."

There's a loud creak from the top of the stairs, and my heart triples in speed and nearly bursts straight out of my chest when I hear the words, "Is that my little Mila?"

The voice belongs to my grandfather.

Slowly, he descends into view and instantly my mouth lifts into a grin that mirrors his.

"Popeye!" I run up the staircase to meet him halfway, throwing myself into his outstretched arms. We wobble unevenly, but Popeye grasps the banister for support, one arm around my shoulders, pulling me in tight.

My grandfather smells like laundry detergent and bales of hay, enough to tickle my nose. I hug him tight, fearing

I may end up crushing him, and pull back once I'm fully reminded of just how loving his embrace can be. Four years of video calls that Sheri helps set up aren't enough – seeing Popeye in real life again after so long fills me with such overwhelming warmth that my eyes dampen with happy tears.

I take his hands in mine, noticing the slight tremor in them. They are rough and well-worn from a lifetime of hard work. His face is a bit thinner and more sunken than I remember, but it has been years since I've actually stood face to face with him – and of course he has aged. His full head of white hair is enviably silky in real life, though, and I see the flicker of my reflection in the glass eye that replaced the real one he lost back in the Vietnam War. When I was a little kid, I thought Grandpa was just like Popeye, the cartoon figure. The nickname stuck.

"Those computers don't do you justice, little Mila," Popeye says, beaming brightly as he gives my hands a careful squeeze. "You are becoming such a beautiful young lady. Fifteen now ..."

I don't want to tell him that he looks more fragile in real life than he does on our Skype calls, so I just laugh and squeeze his hands in return. "I'm sixteen, Popeye. You sent me a birthday card, remember?"

"Growing up too fast, I tell you!"

After Popeye and I get caught up, Sheri insists on giving me a guided tour of the sprawling farmhouse to refresh my memory. We stayed for a week that Thanksgiving four years ago, so although I don't remember much about

Fairview in general, I do remember this house. Sheri even sets me up in the same guest bedroom I stayed in last time, with the large bay window that overlooks the stables. I bring my luggage upstairs, freshen up after spending ten minutes figuring out how to operate the old-fashioned shower, then head back to the kitchen to sit down with Sheri and Popeye for lunch.

There's so much food here for three people, dishes of home-cooked meat and all the sides you can imagine, and I don't want any of it to go to waste, so I load up my plate and dive in. Also, I am *starving*. The nauseous swirling of regret meant I could barely eat the past few days.

"So, like, what exactly is there to do around here?" I ask just as I'm finishing up. I'll lick every last speck of food off this plate if I have to, it's that damn delicious. Back home, Mom has us on a strict protein-rich diet at the say-so of my father, and I am *so* tired of salmon and steamed asparagus.

"You can help me clean out the stables. The manure really doesn't smell all that bad once you get used to it," Sheri says, then upon noticing my blank stare, she laughs. "That was a joke, Mila. Though I *will* need you to help out around here."

"I can help out with the laundry. And cleaning," I offer. I push my plate away as a clear signal that I'm done eating, and then rest my elbows on the table. "But seriously. What is there to do for fun in Fairview? Because I don't think the playgrounds I loved when I was four are going to cut it anymore. Is there a way for me to get to downtown Nashville?"

Popeye releases a throaty chuckle as he grabs his empty glass and stiffly gets to his feet. "The only way you are getting to Nashville is if you drive yourself there," he says with a sympathetic pat on my shoulder and moves toward the faucet.

Sheri leans back in her chair with an air of resignation, clasping her hands together in her lap. "Actually, Mila . . There are some rules that are in place while you're here."

"Rules?"

"Rules defined by Mr. Ruben Fisher."

"That shark," Popeye grumbles under his breath, filling his glass at the sink. Sheri watches him fondly out of the corner of her eye. "Horrible, horrible man ..."

"Oh, yeah. I know," I say, relaxing. Ruben has already covered this with me when he drilled the same phrase into me for hours and hours. "*Maintain a low profile and don't draw attention to yourself or your father,*" I quote with an eye roll.

"That's not all," Sheri says. She stares down at her inter-locked hands in her lap, then glances back up at me with a perturbed look. "Ruben's instructed me to keep you here on the ranch at all times."

"What?" My stomach sinks. "I'm not allowed to go anywhere?"

A smile creeps onto Sheri's face. "Who says we're *fully complying* with Ruben's instructions? You and I ... We will have our own rules."

"So," I say hopefully, straightening my shoulders, "I *can* leave the ranch?"

"Yes, but promise me, Mila, that you will do your absolute best to stay out of any kind of trouble," Sheri says, her tone serious with concern and her smile gone. "I need to know where you are, who you're with and what you're up to. As long as you keep me in the loop, you can have some freedom, and I'll take care of Ruben. Does that sound fair?"

"Yes! I promise. No trouble." I mock zipping my lips shut and blink innocently at her.

Popeye returns to the table with a fresh glass of water. A little spills as he steadily lowers himself back into his chair and asks, "Do you have any old friends here?"

"I left when I was six," I gently remind him with a sigh. "So no, not really."

"Then you go out and make new friends," he says simply, as though it's ever that easy. Maybe back when he was a kid, sure, but in the twenty-first century? Yeah … No.

Sheri nearly bounces straight out of her chair. "Oh! The Bennetts have kids. They own the ranch at the end of the road. Real nice folks." She taps her index finger against her lips, looking up at the ceiling. "The daughter's name is Savannah."

"Savannah?" I repeat. The name Savannah rings a bell, stirring up a vague memory of childhood friendship, sitting together at those low desks in the first grade.

"She would be your age, I believe."

"I *think* I remember her." I close my eyes to focus deeply, but nothing more comes back to me.

"Well, there's a start," Sheri says brightly. She stands from the table, gathering up the dishes. "I can take you over there so that you can introduce yourself again after all this time."

"Huh? Wait – no. What?" I stare at her in horror. What kind of insane idea is that? Introduce myself to a girl I haven't seen in a decade? Who even *does* that?

Sheri dumps the dishes into the sink with a tremendous clatter, then rummages around in a cupboard and pulls out a random baking tray. "Perfect!" she announces, spinning back around to face me. "I borrowed this from Patsy last week. I was attempting a new recipe for peanut butter brownies – they were a disaster, for what it's worth. But it would be oh-so-kind of you to bring it back to her for me. There, that's a nice excuse."

"It doesn't … It doesn't work like that," I stammer. She really wants me to turn up on a stranger's porch and hand them back a baking tray? This is not how the world works. "I can't just knock on someone's door and ask to be friends."

"You can in Tennessee," Sheri says firmly as she shoves the baking tray into my hands.

I glance at Popeye for backup, but he has a smug grin plastered across his face. They are *so* old-fashioned.

"Can't I at least go tomorrow?"

Sheri isn't giving me a choice. She gathers up the remaining dishes from the table, drops them into the sink, then grabs her car keys from the counter.

"No, because by tomorrow you'll have a list of a thousand excuses, and in order to have freedom, you need to have friends," she tells me. Then, "Dad, will you be all right while I take Mila along to the Bennetts'?" she asks Popeye.

"Go, go," he says encouragingly, waving a hand to urge

us out the door. Before we disappear, he reaches across the table and places his hand over mine. "Make some friends. We'll bore you to death if you don't."

I can't even laugh. Baking tray gripped tight, I rise out of my seat, heart thumping.

3

This is stupid. So, so, so stupid.

The Bennetts' home is the Willowbank ranch. It's a mile along the quiet, twisty country road and is easily walkable, but Sheri insists on driving me so that (1) I don't get lost – even though I fail to see how that's even possible considering it's the first ranch we come upon – and (2) so that I can't back out of doing this. Figuratively speaking, I'm being dragged to the Willowbank ranch against my will.

I press a hand to my forehead, wiping away a glaze of sweat. Even with the AC blasting through Sheri's van, the vehicle still feels like an oven. The leather upholstery is a heat trap, and my thighs stick to my seat. It's been – what? – an hour since I showered? Yet already I feel gross again. Maybe this really is the seventh circle of hell – Nashville humidity, miles from civilization, and Aunt Sheri forcing me to talk to the neighbors. I'm quickly realizing that being here on a quick visit is a lot different than knowing I actually have to *stay* here.

We've passed the ranch sign and have turned down the old dirt road that snakes through the property. Unlike my family's ranch, Willowbank isn't kept hidden behind solid walls that are eight feet high and there's no intimidating security gate holding us back.

We pass a tractor parked at the edge of the grass, then Sheri pulls to a stop outside the house. I'm sweating profusely now. Is it one hundred degrees outside or am I really this much of a loser? I interact with big-shot names in the film industry, from Oscar-winning actresses to studio executives, yet I can't say hello to some kid I went to elementary school with without turning into a useless sweaty bundle of nerves? What's wrong with me?

"Be nice and smile real big," Sheri says, her nod genuine and encouraging. But still, I think if I were to refuse to get out of the car, she would drag me out by my flip-flopped feet. Even if I have to keep my head down, having at least one friend to hang out with over the summer is as much a benefit to her as it would be for me. I doubt she wants a sixteen-year-old stomping around the ranch every day – even though that's exactly what Ruben has me ordered to do. "And give back the baking tray."

"Okay." I gulp back a breath of warm air and tuck the tray under my arm. "I'm on it."

Relaxing my shoulders, I climb out of the car and start for the house. I've walked a mere ten feet when I hear the crunch of tires against the dirt, and when I spin around, my jaw drops at the sight of Sheri's van disappearing down the road, kicking up dust. She's *leaving* me here? I was hoping I could simply hand over the baking tray, mumble a quick hello, then dive back into the safety of the boiling van.

Does Aunt Sheri seriously expect me to stay here and hang out with a complete stranger? What if Savannah Bennett barely remembers me either and thinks I'm a weirdo for ambushing her after a decade? Then I'll have to hang my head in shame and walk back home. It's not far, but still. This is so humiliating.

Sheri is *so* getting an earful when I make it back to the house.

I grit my teeth and head up onto the porch. My bare leg brushes against the wooden balustrade and it's so hot it scorches me. I flinch away, closer to the front door, and stand directly on the welcome mat.

"Grow up," I mutter to myself under my breath.

Okay, this is the countryside. Rural Tennessee. People are friendly here. It will be fine.

Just do it, Mila.

I swallow hard, then knock.

Long, agonizing seconds pass before I sense any movement behind the door. Finally, I hear the latch unlock and the door swings open.

"Hey there!" says the short, smiling woman in front of me, her eyebrows shooting up in a questioning manner. Patsy, I'm guessing. It's kind of strange to think that maybe I've met this woman before when I was six years old. Maybe my mom used to talk to her at the school gates. Who knows?

"Hi. Sorry to interrupt you, but I'm ... I'm Sheri Harding's niece," I start, but my voice is wavering. It feels strange to introduce myself as *Sheri Harding's niece* rather than *Everett Harding's daughter.* The words don't feel right on my lips.

"She asked me to bring back your baking tray, so … Here."
I offer the tray with what I hope is a polite smile.

"Thank you, honey," she says, stepping out onto the porch.
She runs her eyes over me from top to bottom, and I feel
like a lab rat in a cage, but I don't think she realizes just how
intensely she's scrutinizing me. I can almost see the gears
in her mind shifting as she pieces together the obvious.
"Sheri's niece," she ponders out loud. "So, you must be—?"

"Yes," I say a little too sharply before she can finish. Judging
by her smile of recognition, she already knew the answer.
It's not hard to make the connection – Sheri's one and only
sibling is my father. "That's me," I add with a shy giggle so
that she doesn't think I'm surly. I'm just sick of everyone
caring *so* much about who my father is. He's just … my dad.
He wears slippers with jeans to lounge round the house and
sings his heart out to rock classics in the shower.

"Oh, how lovely," Patsy says, but she doesn't sound entirely
sincere. She hugs the baking tray to her chest, leaning against
the door frame. Her lips are pulled into a smile that is so
clearly suppressing a frown. "Are y'all visiting? I hope the
press doesn't catch wind or else these roads will be clogged
up all the way to Nashville."

Maybe she remembers what happened when we visited
for Thanksgiving all those years ago. I don't quite understand
how word gets out, but both the media and the fans always
know exactly where Dad is. Celebrating his anniversary
with Mom in the Bahamas? The press is already waiting
at the hotel before their flight has even touched down. A
Thanksgiving trip to the hometown to be with family? The

Tennessee-based fans camp out around the walls of the estate, hoping to catch a glimpse of Dad, until the police ushers them away.

We barely left the house that trip, and when we did, it was to sneak off to Nashville in the early hours of the morning under the cover of dawn. Now that I think of it, I can imagine the neighbors around here didn't appreciate the disruption of their usual peace and quiet.

"No, just me," I reassure Patsy. In other words: *don't worry, I don't attract a paparazzi mob or hordes of stalker fans.* "I'm staying here for a little while to get a break from LA, so we're keeping it quiet."

"Oh." Patsy seems relieved. "I won't say a word."

"Thank you," I say, and I mean it. Once the new movie hits theaters and the hype dies down, I can go home – but not until the heat on my father is off. For now, none of us can afford to have the neighbors selling stories to the media.

I am about to say goodbye and part ways when I remember the real reason why I'm even standing on this porch. "I was wondering … Is Savannah around? I think we were in the same elementary class."

Patsy's eyes light up. "Yes, you were! Let me just grab her for you." She turns and disappears deep into the house. "Savannah!"

Thank God for the reassurance – I was worried I was imagining this link to Savannah Bennett, and *then* how awkward would this have been?

I play anxiously with my hands while I wait for either Patsy or Savannah to show up in front of me. The AC from the house cools my legs and I can't help but edge closer to the door, fanning my face. Even in the shade of the porch, the humidity is crazy. I stand there for a minute, maybe longer, listening to the faint sound of voices from somewhere inside the house. Maybe Savannah doesn't want to meet her childhood friend who has crawled, completely unexpectedly, out of the woodwork. Maybe Patsy is having to beg her to come and say hello.

This is kind of mortifying, actually.

"Eavesdropping?" a voice says.

I spin around, heartbeat rocketing, and lay eyes on a boy. "Who are you?" I say defensively.

The boy doesn't appear that much older than me. There's dirt on his face and his pile of blond hair is unruly. He's leaning against a shovel that he's dug into the ground, his rubber boots covered in caked earth.

"Sorry," he says. "We don't usually get strangers wandering in here. Are you looking for something?"

"I'm waiting for Savannah," I say, but I feel like an immense *idiot*. Waiting for someone, who probably doesn't even want to say hello to me, let alone hang out with me for the entire summer. "I'm not an intruder, I swear."

He plucks the shovel out from the dirt and tramps over to the lowest step of the porch. "Myles," he says, stretching up the stairs to offer me his slightly grubby hand. "The smarter, more good-looking one of the Bennett offspring."

Oh, Savannah has a brother. And her brother has hands covered in dirt. "Uhh," I mumble, staring at his outstretched hand.

Myles smirks. "Someone's not a ranch girl," he remarks. I guess it really is that obvious. "Where's that accent from, anyway? 'Cause you aren't from around here."

It depends how you look at it. Does being born here count as being *from around here*? I purse my lips and tell him, "California."

"Nice. I really want to learn how to surf one day," he muses. "How do you know Savannah?"

"We were in the same class back in first grade."

It's immediately clear that Myles thinks it's a bit bizarre for such an old acquaintance to be showing up out of the blue after all this time. Maybe he expected me to say something normal. Something like, "Oh, we met at a party a couple months ago." Something that would actually justify me being here.

But then I hear footsteps from inside the house and I turn my back on Myles, facing the front door to see who has turned up.

Savannah Bennett has decided, at last, to come and say hello. It's most likely just to satisfy her curiosity, but I'll take what I can get.

She's smaller than her mom – like, *a-tiny-smidge-over-five-feet* tall – and her scrubbed face makes her appear young for our age. Strawberry blonde hair frames her round, full cheeks and her eyes are big and bright, long eyelashes defining them. She's the only person I've met so far today who isn't wearing flannel; she's got on faded denim overall shorts with a striped tee instead. She offers me a smile that's warm and kind, and it eases the tightness in my chest a little.

28

"I thought Mom was pulling my leg," she says, stepping out onto the porch in front of me. She studies me up and down, head-to-toe, the exact same way her mother did. "But you're really here, huh?"

I wonder if she even remembers me, or if my name simply jiggled her memory a little the same way her name did mine. We were so young when I left Fairview that for a second it crosses my mind that maybe she has no idea what actually happened to me. I'm pretty sure we left without much warning, so was there even time for explanations? I can't remember if I gathered my friends on the playground and said goodbye. Maybe I just disappeared one day, and everyone forgot I ever existed by the following summer. Even those handful of times I've come back to visit over the past decade, I was too young to leave Mom and Dad's side. No catch-ups with old friends, just the constant ushering into minivans and sneaking into buildings via back doors to hide from paparazzi.

"Yeah. Alive and in the flesh," I joke.

"What are you doing back here? Don't you live in LA?" Savannah questions, her accent softer than her mom and her brother's. So, she *does* remember me to some degree. She catches the slight arch of my brow, then blushes. "I've kept tabs on you. Is that weird? It's only every once in a while when I see something about Everett Harding on Twitter and it reminds me to check in." Her face falls in horror, as though she can't stop the words from tumbling out of her mouth. "Oh, crap, I sound like a stalker now. I do, don't I? And why did I call him Everett to you? Why didn't I just call him your dad?"

"Savannah," I say, and she ceases her babbling. "It's cool."

She covers her face with her hands, unable to look at me now. She even groans a little.

I stifle my laughter. This is kind of amusing, mostly because I've never personally experienced any sort of freak out like this. At Thousand Oaks High, my friends couldn't care less who my father is. Because their mom is a model. Or their own dad is a rock star. Or their grandmother is a fashion designer. In Thousand Oaks, pretty much everyone has some sort of connection to the celebrity world, which means famous relatives is the norm. And that means no one cares.

"Ohhhhh." Myles takes a sharp intake of breath as he connects the dots and somehow his expression is one of both fascination and horror. "The ranch down the road. That's your folks?"

Warily, I nod. The fact that Sheri borrows baking stuff from Patsy Bennett leads me to believe that the two neighboring ranches get along just fine, but who knows? There could be some underlying resentment there. Maybe the Bennetts secretly despise us Hardings for being, you know, *Hardings*. It wouldn't be the first time. Fame can certainly have a downside – resentment is pretty common; I've learned that firsthand.

"So that guy from the *Flash Point* movies ... You're his kid?"

I'm also Marnie Harding's daughter, and Roxanne Cohen's best friend, and Mr. Sabatini's top chemistry student, but no one defines me as those. Only my father is important, like the sole reason I even matter in this world is because I share his DNA.

"Yeah, that's me," I say through tight lips. *I have my own name.* "Mila Harding."

Luckily, Savannah changes the subject – for her sake or mine, I'm not sure. "My mom says you're here for a while," she muses brightly. "That's cool. Missed Tennessee?"

"Yeah. I'm not sure how long I'll be here for, but I'm guessing a month or two," I admit. I glance at Myles, his head tilted to the side as he watches me in fascination, then move my gaze back to Savannah. "I know it's been *forever*, and it's super out-of-the-blue for me to show up like this, but the truth is … I'd really like someone to hang out with other than my aunt and my grandpa."

"Oh." Savannah's eyes narrow slightly. "So, you're just looking for someone to use for a couple months?"

"Oh God," I mumble, feeling my chest sink. I sure do have some nerve. "I'm sorry. You're right. I shouldn't have come here."

A singsong of laughter escapes Savannah's lips, dancing through the humid air, as she reaches out and grasps my wrist. "I'm kidding!"

"Oh."

Myles cracks up with his sister. I stare at the knotty wood of the porch beneath my feet. Have I always been this much of a nervous wreck? To be fair, this suddenly feels out of my comfort zone and I don't know how to navigate it at all.

"Yep. We can be friends," Savannah says reassuringly, her voice gentle once the laughter has died down. I look up to meet her eyes and she smiles, sweetly. "We already were once, anyway."

"Thanks," I say, so quiet it's almost a whisper. Well, that's something.

"Ohhh!" Savannah exclaims, waving a hand at Myles as though he will telepathically be able to know what she's thinking. Maybe he can – maybe it's a sibling thing. I wouldn't know. "We're heading to a tailgate party later," she says. "Super low-key. You should come with us! You can get to know all the Fairview locals – there isn't a lot of us."

"A tailgate party?" I can't help the surprise that crosses my face. "You guys really have those?"

In one of Dad's first straight-to-TV movies, I'm pretty sure there's a low-budget scene at a tailgate party where he finally gets the girl and kisses her in the truck bed. I cringed then and I cringe now. There's something super gross about watching your father kissing on screen – especially when it's not your mom he's locking lips with.

"Just for saying that, you're not coming," Myles says, shaking his head at me in disappointment. Then his mouth twists into a teasing smirk, making it clear that he's only messing with me since I'm clearly not the brightest at knowing when someone is kidding around. "You can come. I'll give Blake a heads-up."

"Who's Blake?"

"Our cousin," Savannah answers. "He's hosting."

Not only do I already feel sluggish from the early alarm and long flight this morning, it feels a bit risky to start breaking Ruben's rules on day one. Maybe I should stay at home with Sheri and Popeye tonight. But a tailgate party ...

"Sounds like fun." I wipe my brow. "But I don't know ... There'll be a lot of people there and I really shouldn't be—"

"You're in Fairview now, girly," Savannah says with a grin. "I know you only just got here, but when something actually happens around here for once, you don't even think about it. You just do it."

4

Aunt Sheri and I are out on the porch together, waiting for Savannah and Myles to swing by and pick me up. It's been a few hours since I walked home from the Willowbank ranch.

Darkness is rolling in, the sky a clear, gorgeous shade of deep blue with remnants of the summer sun lingering out on the horizon. The heat of the day is gone, replaced by a warmth that's comfortable and cozy. At night, the ranch is even more peaceful and silent. No car engines whirring in the distance, no voices floating by, not even the bark of a dog. Just a calm stillness that slows down the world a little.

"Try not to talk about your dad tonight."

Sheri is rocking gently on a wooden chair, running her hands up and down her thighs, scratching at the denim of her jeans. A nervous thing?

"I won't." I turn around to look at my aunt. "I never do."

"Good," she says. Although she seems worried about the potential repercussions of breaking Ruben's rules by allowing me to go out tonight, I'm glad she hasn't changed

34

her mind about our little pact. "Have you spoken to your parents yet?"

"Only my mom," I admit, turning back around. I rest my hands on the porch railings and stare out at the walls that close us off to the rest of the world. It's only now, gazing across the field, that I realize how much of a prison this ranch can seem. It feels claustrophobic despite the acres of land sprawling out around us. "I texted her, but I'm still annoyed."

"At least that's something," Sheri says from behind me. I hear the creaking of her chair still rocking back and forth. "I know she's worried about this arrangement. She checked in with me earlier too."

I know I should call my parents at some point, but I'm not in a hurry to talk to Dad. Mom tried to fight for what was best for *me*, but Ruben's job is to put Dad's career first. Every argument Mom presented in my defense was quickly shut down, and no amount of persuasion could make Dad change his mind. In the late hours of that night, I lay awake listening to my parents' raised voices from their room, but by morning Mom had gone quiet, defeated. The decision was final. From Dad's side, it was far too easy. No protesting against Ruben like Mom did, no offering alternative suggestions, no objections ... Good PR is obviously the priority.

"Did your parents mention your allowance?"

I glance over my shoulder. "No. They've blocked my access to my account, so ..."

Sheri nods and stops rocking in that rickety chair. She

stands up, sticking her hand deep into the front pocket of her jeans, then pulls out a few bills. "Here's some cash for tonight in case you need it," she says, offering the money to me. I swivel around to take it from her – it's fifty bucks. "I have an allowance to administer for you. I'm to give you some cash as and when. Though who knows how they expect you to spend anything if you aren't supposed to leave this place … I'll tell them you've been fending off boredom with shopping online."

"Thanks, Aunt Sheri."

I stuff the cash inside my phone case and my phone vibrates in my hand as I do so. It's a text from the most recently added number to my contact list.

> SAVANNAH: Hey girly, we're outside the gate. Do we come in or do you come out? I'm too poor to know how these things work LOL.

"Oh. They're here," I tell Sheri to appease her curious gaze. "Can you open the gate to let them in? Or how do I leave?"

To be fair to Savannah, even I don't know how this works around here. Back home, the security gates around our property are controlled by fingerprint access, the highest tech possible.

"Oh! Of course – the gate. We're having some technical difficulties with the remotes at the moment, so you'll need to open it manually from the inside like I did earlier. The big button on the control panel on the left," Sheri explains, then rocks back and forth on her heels. "Mila, if there's alcohol at this party, promise me you won't drink."

"After those headlines from Thursday night? No, thanks." I'm trying to joke, but a pang of shame sears through my chest. There's actually a *video* of me throwing up all over the TMZ website. And the images circling around the magazines are just as gross. I've learned my lesson – no more "experimenting".

Sheri frowns and says quietly, "Just remember who you are."

Ugh. The mere sound of those words has me clenching my fists by my side. I get it – I'm off to a tailgate party with strangers who have zero loyalty to me, but surely no one will care enough to go out of their way to talk to a journalist or sell photos to some sleazy celeb site? All things Everett Harding must be pretty boring by now to kids who've grown up in his hometown. I bet everyone is sick of hearing the name.

"And you'll need the code for the gate for when you get back! There's a keypad on the outside – take a note of this code," Sheri says quickly as I'm moving toward the steps. She gives me a string of numbers that I punch into the notes app on my phone.

"Okay, got it. Bye!"

I run down the porch steps and do an awkward jog toward the looming gate in the distance – if I were to walk, I'd feel rude for making Savannah and Myles wait so long. When I reach the gate, I spot the control panel, open it up, then push the button that seems the most obvious – the giant green one. A loud, long buzz rings as the electric churns and the gates move. I retreat, allowing them to open wide, revealing me to the outside world as though I'm something special. Truly embarrassing.

Outside, a truck is idling. The black paintwork, most likely freshly washed and waxed for tonight, glistens under the spotlights that shine down from the walls. The windows are all tinted black and Savannah lowers hers from the backseat.

"Hop in!" she says, beaming.

I dash around the back of the truck and climb in the other side, careful not to scuff the paintwork with my sneakers. I'm not sure Myles would be happy if I damaged his car.

"Sorry to keep you waiting," I apologize. I'm not sure how long they were sitting out here before Savannah texted, but I hope it wasn't a while. I pull on my seatbelt and check out Savannah's outfit to ensure I'm dressed appropriately.

I'm wearing a pair of ripped jean shorts, white Nikes, and a crop top. I straightened my hair and applied a generous amount of makeup, my lips sticky from the gloss. Luckily, Savannah is almost identical, except her hair is loosely curled and she's wearing a denim mini skirt.

"We just got here, don't worry," Myles says, and it's only when I glance up to look at him that I realize he's sitting in the passenger seat.

Which means he isn't the one driving. This isn't his truck.

"Uhhh ..." I shoot Savannah a questioning look, then subtly point to whoever is behind the wheel. They haven't turned around yet nor have they spoken.

"Oh!" Savannah says, bolting upright, as if suddenly remembering that introductions need to be made. "This is our cousin. Blake. And Blake, this is Mila Harding." Savannah puts a slight emphasis on my last name, or maybe I'm imagining it.

I look up and catch the gaze of the driver in the rearview mirror. He's watching me, brown eyes narrowed slightly, shining from the spotlights encircling the ranch. Then he twists in his seat and looks at me directly.

"Hi, Mila," he says coolly. "Your first tailgate party, huh?"

"Yeah. They don't really happen in LA."

"Of course they don't," he deadpans, then turns back to face the road.

Unlike his strawberry blond relatives, Blake has dark features. His hair is a warm brown and naturally tousled, his eyes shadowed beneath thick brows. His face is angular, his jawline sharp, and he seems much more aloof than his friendly cousins.

I swallow and lean back against the seat, suddenly aware of my heartbeat. I can feel my skin tingling. Off to a tailgate party with strangers ... But this is what normal teenagers in Fairview do, right? Except, as my parents so often remind me, I'm *not* a normal teenager.

"Let's head over and show Mila some reality then," Blake says, and he bumps up the music a little and sets off down the quiet roads away from the ranch. There's something slightly off with his tone. Mocking. Something that if I wasn't so nervous I'd ask him to explain.

Instead, I let it slide.

The music choice isn't really what I'd expect, because instead of R&B we're listening to acoustic country. Not exactly the kind of tunes to get us into the party vibe, but it's chill and relaxing as the sky continues to darken outside the tinted windows. The sunset has fully disappeared now.

Myles and Blake talk between the two of them, so Savannah turns to me for our own conversation in the backseat. However, every once in a while, my eyes wander to the boys in the front, observing Blake's hands on the wheel, Myles's more animated gestures and their unfamiliar profiles as they turn toward each other while speaking.

"Are you excited?" Savannah asks, tucking her hair behind her ear. That's how I notice the funky earrings she's wearing – dangling horses.

"Nervous," I admit.

"You'll maybe remember some people from our elementary class," she says in an effort to put me at ease. Considering I barely remembered Savannah, my *best friend*, I highly doubt I'll remember any of the others in our class. "There'll be some people from the grade below, and some from above, like Myles and Blake."

"How many people will be there?"

Savannah smirks, then rolls her eyes. "We're in Fairview. Like, twenty of us."

"Oh," I say, staring down at my Nikes.

A small crowd is even *worse*. A small crowd means it's harder to blend into the background. A small crowd means everyone will most likely sit together and be part of one big easy conversation. Until right now, I was imagining plenty of parked trucks, dance music blaring through the darkened countryside, and lots of different people milling around and doing their own thing. Instead, I realize this "party" is actually more of a casual get-together. Maybe huge parties don't exist in a town as small as Fairview.

I glance back over at Savannah. "Wait. Are we going to a sports game or something? Isn't that what tailgate parties are for?" It's summer, so there's no football. Maybe we're going to a baseball game?

"That's the tradition," Savannah says, "but they're fun to host on your own, anyway. You'll love it."

I hope so. I admit, I like the idea of trying new things on my own without my parents as my entourage, because I've never had freedom like this before. Of course, I've had some amazing experiences, like walking the red carpet of the Oscars, but maybe it's time to branch out and do things for myself. Maybe this little break away from home will be good for me. A chance to be my own person without Ruben ordering me around, a chance to figure out who exactly Mila Harding is. And she *isn't* just Everett Harding's daughter. She has to be more than that.

Doesn't she?

I stare out of the window, watching Fairview unravel around me. There's a whole lot of *nothing*. Just the open road and the trees that circle around us with the occasional flicker of light from an oncoming car. With the quiet musings of Myles and Blake and the lull of music, it almost feels as though we're off on a road trip. It's also kind of eerie, all this emptiness. There's barely any other cars, only the occasional house, and definitely no other people.

I'm not sure I like how alone Fairview makes me feel, so disconnected from the rest of the world. But maybe, I tell myself, that disconnect will turn out to be a good thing.

After five minutes or so, I begin to spot streetlights which can only signify that we've left the deserted countryside behind and are entering the Fairview metropolitan area – or at least whatever sort of downtown area a town like Fairview might have.

"Do you remember anything about living here?" Myles enquires.

Blake catches my eye in that rearview mirror again, awaiting my answer. It makes me wonder just how much Savannah has filled him in on … But given that Blake has just picked me up from the famous Harding Estate, I'm sure he can figure out for himself who I am.

I sit up a little and squint outside. We're heading down a long stretch of road that's home to enough familiar establishments to reassure me that Fairview, Tennessee is more than just some town out in the sticks. There's the usual McDonald's, a Dunkin' Donuts – oh, thank God, because I'm *addicted* to their hazelnut iced coffees – and a Walmart, from what I see in the dark. A street sign lets me know that this is Fairview Boulevard. It's a bit livelier, with more traffic and a few pedestrians on the sidewalks, but still – I remember none of it. I'm so used to LA now that small-town life tends to feel too restricted, though I'm sure it has its perks.

"Not really," I finally answer, shaking my head. "I left when I was super young."

"You probably think we're just a bunch of country bumpkins," Savannah says with a chuckle. "But I swear it's not that bad here. We have high-speed internet these days and everything."

Myles and Blake stifle a laugh. I get that Savannah is just kidding, but it makes me kind of paranoid that they all believe I'm some west coast city girl who's going to shrivel up and die out here. I was born here; I can survive in Tennessee. Hell, I'll maybe even like it.

"Blake, drive by Fairview Elementary first," Savannah instructs, leaning forward to tap him excitedly on the shoulder. "Let Mila see."

On the left, we pass a sign for Fairview High School, and on the right is the elementary school. We pull into the small parking lot and Blake slows the truck to a crawl, circling around and shining his headlights upon the red stone building. There's an air of expectancy in the car, like they're all waiting for the nostalgia to hit me.

"Do you recognize any of it?" Savannah asks, eyes wide and encouraging. She's like a puppy that's finally got its favorite chew toy back – she seems so happy to have me around. "We used to play tetherball in the yard *allllll* the time!"

I take a good look at the building. It's familiar in a déjà vu kind of way – I *know* I've seen this before, but I can't really associate many memories with it, and I certainly don't recall playing tetherball with Savannah Bennett. I can barely remember the house we lived in, let alone the school I attended.

"Sorry," I say with a hopeless shrug. Maybe Savannah wants me to remember so that I feel like less of a stranger to her.

"Well, that was pointless," Blake mutters, then pulls back out onto the road.

I wonder where this tailgate party is being held, but the answer becomes obvious when Blake cuts across the road to the high school. It's summer, school is closed, there's no one around, but still ... A tailgate party on school property?

We draw closer to a parking lot out by the sports fields where a handful of other trucks is already parked, and a small bunch of people is milling around. There's a girl standing in one of the truck beds, setting up a huge pair of speakers on the truck's roof, and another guy is kneeling by the ground, rifling through a cooler.

My palms feel clammy as it becomes real to me that I'm going to have to talk to all of these people at some point. I'm usually a sociable person, but it helps that everyone I interact with back home already knows what my deal is. Here, though? Here, I wonder who knows and who doesn't. A stranger wouldn't be able to figure out who I am just by looking at me. It's only Dad's super fans and the press who pay me any attention, so to the rest of the world I look like any other teenager ... Except this is Fairview, Dad's quaint little hometown, which I'm sure must mean the locals here know all about us Hardings. But so far, the only people who know I'm Everett Harding's daughter are Savannah, Myles and Blake. No one else knows I've arrived here from the Harding Estate tonight.

Maybe I can pass myself off as someone else. A new girl in town whose parents have bought a home here ...Normal. Nothing gossip-worthy.

We park in the next available gap, adding to the wide circle that all of the trucks are starting to form. Blake kills the engine and throws off his seatbelt, already sliding out of the vehicle.

"Nervous?" Myles asks in the new silence that has formed inside the truck. When I look up at him, his cheeky smile is directed at me. He's kind of goofy, but in an attractive way. He playfully purses his lips. "Don't worry. They'll like you."

"You'll fit right in," Savannah adds.

Really?

The Bennett siblings climb out of the truck and I follow suit, tugging at the belt loops of my jean shorts to keep my hands busy. My naval piercing shines under the lights, the aquamarine gemstone glittering – my birthstone. My parents still don't know about it, but for once they aren't around to see it. There's a kind of thrill in knowing my parents are a thousand miles away and have zero control over me for however long I'm here. It lets me do things like flash my piercing to the world without fear of repercussions.

"I like that."

My eyes slide over to find Blake acknowledging my piercing with a clipped nod.

I hug my arms around myself and look him up and down in return. I feel oddly weird about Blake noticing, mostly because I fear he's making fun of me. I let his remarks in the truck slide only because I'm trying to make some friends, but he strikes me as being ... Well, maybe not the nicest person around here. Not as welcoming as his cousins, and definitely harder to read.

Blake scoffs at my protective stance. "Why get a piercing if you're going to hide it?"

He turns away, moving to the back of the truck to help Myles lower the tailgate. I flip a strand of hair away from my face in irritation as he effortlessly springs up into the truck bed and hauls different items around, slabs of muscle shifting in his arms.

Luckily, Savannah appears by my side as a distraction. She grasps my wrist. "Let's go say hi to Tori."

I let her guide me along through the circle of trucks. A couple more pull up, filling in the remaining gaps, and everyone gets set up. People are lowering their tailgates, dragging out chairs and coolers and snacks. I spot someone unwrapping disposable grills and lining up packets of hot-dog buns on the bed of their truck. The atmosphere is lively, and I enjoy the buzz of voices that gradually grows louder and louder. Everyone seems to be in good spirits.

"Tori, come down here for a sec," Savannah says as she brings me to a halt by the truck with the girl who's setting up the speakers.

"Hang on," Tori says over her shoulder, fiddling with notches on the speakers with one hand and scrolling through her phone with the other. After a second, music echoes through the speakers, a nice R&B groove, which is a welcome change from the country we were listening to on the drive over here. She lowers the volume to a respectable level, then spins around with a proud grin plastered over her face. "There. Call me the tech wizard."

"I need to introduce you to someone," Savannah tells her.

Tori jumps down from the truck, pulls Savannah into a hug, then faces me, arm still slung around Savannah's shoulder. So, they're best friends.

"This is Mila," Savannah explains. "She was in our class in grade school."

"Ohhhh," Tori says with a knowing wink. Her hair is dyed a bold pink that pops brightly against her bronze skin and there's a stud piercing in her nose. "Mila Harding. Hey, girl. You're back." She steps forward and draws me into a tight hug, enveloping me in a luscious scent of perfume, and I awkwardly embrace her in return even though I have no recollection of ever knowing her.

Is this how it's going to be? My childhood peers can all remember me because *of course* they'll be well aware that once they went to school with the kid of an A-lister, but I can't quite recall any of them because in the last decade my childhood memories have been somehow overtaken by more exciting, glamorous ones. I can remember every peculiar detail of meeting the Kardashians, the super-luxe thrill of taking a private jet to Paris. But I'm struggling to unearth memories of Savannah and Tori from first grade, of playing tetherball in the schoolyard. How shallow does that make me?

For a second, I feel guilty. But it's not like I forgot my life here on purpose. I was just too young.

47

"Yeah, I'm back," I tell Tori with an unconvincing smile.

"For good?"

"At least for the foreseeable future."

Tori and Savannah exchange a look, using silent communication as their secret best-friend language, one that perhaps I'd understand if I'd actually grown up with them. But I didn't.

Suddenly, a loud clattering echo rings out around the parking lot. I startle at the sound, then relax when I look over my shoulder to see Blake standing in the back of his truck, banging barbecue tongs against the floor of the truck bed. The buzz of voices trails off and everyone instinctively congregates in a semi-circle around Blake. Tori turns down the music to play as background noise.

"All right, guys, thanks for coming to the June tailgate," Blake says, flopping down onto the truck bed and hanging his legs over the edge.

I haven't figured out much of the group's dynamics yet, other than the fact that Savannah and Tori are obviously best friends, but it seems Blake is the one in charge. He totally seems like the type who would be.

"Y'all can thank Barney for the cookout this time. Tori's got the music. If anyone's got beer, just don't be a jackass and don't drive home," Blake tells the listening crowd, like a homeroom teacher delivering the morning announcements. It's kind of fascinating how civilized this all is. "And some of you might have already noticed we have a new face here tonight."

Oh, God, no.

Obviously, everyone *has* already noticed, because their

gazes have all landed on me without Blake even having to point me out. I shrink into myself, hunching my shoulders and wishing I had a jacket to shield myself behind. Dad might love having all eyes on him, but I hate it.

"This is Mila," Blake says, his twang clear and pronounced over the vowels in my name. His eyes lock on mine and I glower back, cheeks flaring with heat. I swear, just for a split second, he smirks as though he's getting a kick out of embarrassing me like this. Then he blinks and looks away. "So, everybody make sure you make Miss Mila welcome."

Miss Mila? I grit my teeth and glare at him even harder, wishing I could scorch him with the power of my eyes alone. What exactly is this guy's problem? Because it sounds like he's making fun of me for being here, which is ridiculous considering he doesn't even know me. I only met him two minutes ago! Maybe I should have emphasized back in the truck that I'd like to fly under the radar, because *this* is not maintaining a low profile.

There's a couple *whoop*s and *hell yeah*s as everyone returns to their conversations, though I notice a few lingering stares … Blake might not have said my last name, but I don't think it will take a genius to make the connection.

Blake leans back on his hands, still perched on the tailgate of his truck. His eyes are on me again, focused through the crowd, lips curving into a crooked smile. There is devious amusement dancing in his gaze. There is no way he's just being friendly by introducing me. I can see it written all over his face, the pleasure he takes in making me uncomfortable …

I glower straight back.

5

Savannah touches my arm in an attempt to get my attention. "Are you okay?" she asks.

I tear my eyes away from Blake and lock them on Savannah instead. "What's the deal with your cousin?" I ask, my tone sharper than intended. "Is he, like, the captain of the football team or something? The student body president?"

Tori busts up with laughter and Savannah bites her lip to stop herself from joining in, the two of them sharing one of those knowing glances that I can't understand. Tori excuses herself to get back to her DJ duties, leaving Savannah to fiddle with her earrings in front of me. I raise an eyebrow, prompting her for a reply.

"Our school is small, so we don't really have cliques. Everyone is kind of friends with everyone," she explains with a shrug, her gaze wandering off over my shoulder. "Blake is just good at getting things done and making sure things run smoothly, so he tends to be at the forefront of stuff like this." She scoffs quietly. "It's kind of in his blood."

Okay, good. So, I can go talk to him without fear of getting on the wrong side of Fairview High's top dog, since there isn't one, apparently. Which I don't buy for a second. In what world does a high school hierarchy not exist?

"Thanks. I'll be right back," I tell Savannah, then spin on my heels and stalk off.

Blake's still in the back of his truck, bent over a cooler and rummaging through its contents. I stop by the side of the truck, then knock my knuckles hard against the paintwork to get his attention. He glances over but doesn't straighten up.

"*Miss Mila?*" I challenge, crossing my arms over my chest. I feel patronized and, therefore, defensive. I don't think it's cool for a complete stranger to call me *Miss Mila*, and I don't believe either that it's down to southern etiquette.

"Well, you're not married, are you?" Blake says matter-of-factly, finally straightening up from the cooler having retrieved a can of Dr Pepper. "You *are* Miss Mila. I simply assumed that you're addressed with a title."

"Are you messing with me?"

Blake pops the tab of his soda and gives me a flippant, disinterested glance. "Now why would you think that?" He takes a sip, exhales loudly, then awaits a response from me.

"Because I didn't want to be *addressed* or introduced. And especially not as *Miss Mila*."

"Oh, I'm *sorry*. Would you have preferred to have been introduced as Mila Harding, the daughter of that guy … What's his name again?" Mockingly, he cups a hand to his ear and angles toward me, listening for a reply that never comes. "No, I didn't think so."

Stunned, I shake my head wordlessly at him. What a jerk.

I press myself against the truck and hiss through clenched teeth, "Who do you think you are?"

Nonchalantly, Blake jumps down from the truck bed and closes the distance between us. He looks straight into my eyes. "Blake Avery," he says with an infuriating smirk. "It's nice to meet you, Mila."

Ugh. I can't take another second of his obnoxious self-confidence. Fixing him with the most intimidating look I can muster, I turn and stomp back over to Savannah, who seems to have been watching the whole thing.

"What was that about?" she questions, glancing between Blake and me. He's talking to some guy now, casually waving his soda can around as he speaks.

"Nothing," I mutter, ignoring the quick beating of my pulse. "Your cousin is—" I start, but as rattled as I am, my voice trails off when I remember it's probably not a good idea to talk trash about Savannah's relatives.

"You'll warm to him," Savannah says with a teasing smirk, but no, I definitely will not. "C'mon, let's sit down."

I don't know whose truck it is that Tori is working from, but I help Savannah drag out some lawn chairs from the back of it and set them up. We sink down into them and I take the opportunity to really study the crowd.

There's a mixture of ages and equal amounts boys and girls. Myles is sprawled out on a lawn chair with some girl in his lap who's biting at his earlobe, and I give Savannah a sidelong glance to see if she's noticed, but I'm pretty sure she's actively avoiding looking in that direction.

I pay attention again to the truck from before, the one

with the packets of hot-dog buns laid out on the tailgate. There's a guy setting up a trio of the disposable grills and I assume that must be Barney.

"Any boys caught your eye? Or do you already have a boyfriend?" a voice from above us says, and my eyes fly upward to find Tori leaning over us from the back of the truck. She sticks her tongue out, upside-down, and then jumps down and gets comfy in the chair next to me. She passes out cans of soda to us, and I figure she must be satisfied that her playlist is now set up and running correctly.

"No and no," I say. "What about you guys?"

"Savannah has a *huuuuge* thing for Nathan Hunt. That guy over there helping Barney with the food."

"No, I don't!" Savannah protests, catapulting forward in her chair to lean over me and whack Tori's arm. "I only said he was cute *one time* and now Tori thinks I'm obsessed with him," she tells me.

"Oh, please," Tori snorts. "You stalk his Insta feed daily."

Tori goes on to tell me about some guy she's been seeing, who isn't here tonight, and then they fill me in on everyone who *is* here. They give me the low down on who's dating who, who was on the prom court, who's on the football team (surprisingly, *not* Blake), and who went skinny dipping in the lake last month. Maybe there's more to Fairview than meets the eye.

Barney and Nathan dish out hot dogs to everyone but I decline when they offer me one – when I was a kid, Dad bought me a hot dog from a food cart at the beach and I got sick with food poisoning, so I've never been able to stomach one since – but Savannah and Tori both wolf them down.

The "party" is more of a chilled get-together among friends than the wild night of debauchery I was worried it might be, so I'm pleasantly relieved. People are relaxed, lounging on chairs, on truck beds, sipping on sodas and seltzer, though I do spot the odd beer every now and again. The scent of hot dogs wafts through the air and Tori's music is the heartbeat of the night. It's nice, and I feel at ease with Savannah and Tori with no one else bothering me, until Blake starts banging those tongs against his truck again.

"Everyone well fed?" he asks, arm propped up on the edge of his truck. The small crowd nods and holds up their drinks. "Good. It's time for Truth or Dare."

Okay, so maybe this is where the "party" kicks in. A hush of anxious whispering and giggles ripples through the group and people shimmy their chairs forward to form a closer circle. I follow suit with Savannah and Tori, edging in to the point where the proximity to everyone becomes a little uncomfortable.

To the surprise of no one, Blake leads the game. He steps into the middle of the circle and sets down an empty Pepsi bottle, holding it steady under his foot. The music is still playing, perhaps a little too loud. He summarizes the rules of the game as though there would ever be a possibility that any teenager in the world doesn't know how Truth or Dare works, then spins the bottle and leans against his truck. The white polo he's wearing stretches tight across his broad chest.

The bottle points at Savannah.

"Truth," she says anxiously, pursing her lips and giving her cousin her best puppy-dog eyes. Maybe she's hoping Blake will go easy on her, but I doubt it.

"Is it true you dip fries into your milkshakes?"

Okay, point *not* proven.

"Laaaame," someone drawls.

Savannah sighs audibly beside me, her face lighting up with a relieved grin. A lucky escape thanks to blood connections.

No one else is as lucky.

Poor Barney opts for a dare and Savannah orders him to streak across the baseball field. He laps it up, entertaining the troops with a faux striptease, then sprints around the field butt-naked. He returns, hands shielding his crotch, and bows to a round of applause that even I participate in. I get the feeling that this is something of a party trick. He seems like the kind of guy who's destined to become the joker of any friendship circle.

The game continues and there's a mixture of both dares and truths being chosen. The truths are the usual, obvious kind of questions, like who was the last person you hooked up with? And the dares are relatively tame in comparison to the one Savannah delivered – kiss someone in the group, post an embarrassing photo to your Instagram feed, chug the last remaining bottle of Bud Light that someone has found in the bottom of a cooler. Every time someone spins the bottle again, I stare at the dark sky and pray it points to anyone but me. So far, luck has been on my side.

Until …

"Ah Mila," Blake says as the bottle slows to a stop in my direction. "Truth or dare?"

My heart beats faster and everyone's gaze is on me, waiting to see if the new girl is brave enough to go for the dare. But even a truth is a scary choice when I'm with strangers who know nothing about me. They could ask anything since there is so much to find out. But I can lie, right? How will they know any different?

"Truth," I say, swallowing hard. *Of course* the bottle has to land on me when it was Blake's turn to spin it.

He sits on a chair now, across the circle from me, a fresh can of soda in his hand. He runs his finger around the metallic rim, pretending to think hard. Then he glances up and smiles. "Who's your father?"

Now my heart stops. *What?*

I stare at him with an icy look, wishing I could smack that smirk off his smug face. He knows exactly who my father is, but he obviously wants everyone else to know too since his introduction earlier clearly didn't cause the stir he was hoping for.

Confusion passes through the group, eyebrows furrowing and murmurs tainting the stilted silence. Expressions perk up with curiosity, but the small handful of people who already seemed to connect the dots earlier are now lighting up in an "I knew it!" sense of joy.

"C'mon … it doesn't matter," I whisper, groveling pathetically, appealing to Blake's better nature. That's if he even has one. Can't he tell I don't want to talk about this? That if I wanted everyone to know who my father is, I would have found a way to work that into conversations already?

Blake glances around the quiet circle, purposely drawing out the tension. "Did you guys know we have a celebrity in our midst? Sorry – the *daughter* of a celebrity."

My lips part, shocked that he's throwing me under the bus like this. We only just met – what could I have possibly done for him to act this way toward me?

I'm not oblivious to the power of celebrity – the truth was bound to come out eventually, but Blake is making every effort to shine the spotlight on me and, right now, it is burning far too bright.

Barney is the first to say it out loud. He hunches forward in his chair, the buttons on his shirt still waiting to be done up. "Wait. Mila ... Harding? Everett Harding is your dad?"

I close my eyes, inhaling deeply. Here it comes. Everyone bursts into a clatter of noise, questions flying through the air, both to me and to each other.

"Who?" someone asks.

"The guy who plays Jacob Knight in *Flash Point*!" someone else tells them.

"Is he here in Fairview right now?" an animated voice questions at the same time as someone else remarks, "I knew it was her!"

I open my eyes and search through the jostling group to find Blake. He relaxes back in his chair, swigging his soda as though he hasn't just created total chaos in my life. I shake my head slowly, angrily, and mouth, *Why?*

People have stood up from their chairs to shuffle closer to me, gathering around in hopes that I'll answer their random questions or spill some gossip. The entire night, no one has batted an eye at me other than to say friendly hellos. But now that Dad's name is out there? Suddenly everyone thinks I'm *so* cool and interesting.

"Should we act as bodyguards?" Tori jokes with Savannah as they remain on either side of me. To be fair, even Savannah freaked out a little over Dad earlier today. Tori is the only one who remembered who I am but doesn't seem to care all that much about Dad – and if she does, she certainly doesn't show it.

The girl who's spent most of her night in Myles's lap pulls a chair up in front of me, eyes wide. "Is it creepy to you if I say that your dad is hot? Do you think you could get me an autograph?"

"Do you have any pictures of you and him together?" Barney asks, towering over my shoulder from behind. "Can we see?"

"I guess," I mumble. What's the point of being secretive now that everyone knows?

I pull out my phone and swipe through my camera roll, painfully aware of everyone's eyes latched onto my screen, all of them subtly edging in closer and closer so that they can get the prime viewing angle. There's only six people cornering me, but it feels like a thousand. Everyone else at the tailgate is keeping their distance for now, though I can hear the hum of their voices.

I find a picture I took of Dad and me last month. A selfie of us on the beach in Malibu as the sun was setting over the ocean, casting a golden aura over us. My wet hair sticks to my cheeks and Dad's million-dollar gaze is even more smoldering than usual. Ruben posted this sunset picture on Dad's Instagram to remind the world that Everett Harding is a proud and loving family-man. But yet, he wasn't exactly conflicted when it came to making the decision to send me here.

Then, suddenly, as everyone coos over the photo, my phone is plucked out of my hand.

"Hey!" I yell, jumping up from my chair.

But Barney has already made his getaway, barging others out of the way, and slipping through a gap in the trucks. He has my phone in his fist, eyes locked on it as he runs. I give chase – because *he has my damn phone!* And with my phone he has access to a lot of different things, like my social media accounts, and my contacts list, and my private photos of Dad and me that haven't ever been made public but which plenty of gossip columnists would love to get their hands on. From the moment I first got a phone, Ruben has been one hundred percent clear that I'm never, ever to let even my best friends near it.

Savannah and Tori and the others follow behind me, a total ruckus as we all squeeze through the trucks to follow Barney. His hands move across my screen, scrolling, then he presses my phone to his ear. He's laughing as he moves fast and agile across the concrete, one hand held out like a true football jock to keep me at a distance whenever I get near him.

"Give it back!" I beg, both arms outstretched to try and claw my phone from him. He's calling someone and panicked, hot tears spring to my eyes. "Please, don't! Please!"

"Oh, hi!" Barney says brightly into my phone. "How do you do? Is this Everett Harding?"

No!

"Give her the phone back, Barney!" Tori demands as she gets close enough to kick Barney hard in the shin.

"Hey!" he barks, lowering the phone from his ear to reach down to rub his leg, and I steal that chance to snatch my phone. "What the hell, Tori?"

I cup my phone tightly in my hands and then rush to safety with it, kneeling down between two trucks to shield myself from view. I'm panting, my heart's beating fast. There's an active call ongoing – a call with the contact saved as *Dad*. I was praying Barney was just kidding, but he wasn't. He seriously called my father. Nerves rocking me, I force myself to press my phone to my ear.

"Dad?"

"Mila?" Dad snaps across the line. "What the hell is going on?" I can't blame him for being angry, but his abrupt tone still makes me flinch.

"Someone took my phone and—"

"You've been home for five minutes and already you're letting people mess around with your phone? Why aren't you at the ranch? Goddammit, I thought there was an emergency." I hear him groan and then exhale deeply. "Look, Mila, I'm at a business dinner. Please can you just behave?"

"Okay, I'm sorry! I—"

But he's already hung up.

I shove my phone into the pocket of my jean shorts and

press my hands over my face, trying to steady my breath. I'm still crouched down between two trucks, but a moment later I force myself to stand and walk back out into view, my whole body pulsing with adrenaline. Barney is arguing with Tori, and Savannah has stepped in as backup. The three of them go quiet when they spot me.

"Why the hell did you do that?" I demand, eyeballing Barney, my hands on my hips. A few others are still lingering nearby, while some people, like Blake, haven't even bothered to get up from their seats back at the social circle.

"It was funny," Barney says sheepishly, stifling a laugh when he makes eye contact with those who witnessed it. "You know – a joke?"

Before I flip out on this guy, I decide to remove myself from the situation. This party seemed like a cool idea, but it's spun out into something that's pushing the boundaries too much too soon. Blake has publicly taunted me, everyone here knows I'm the daughter of Everett Harding, and now Dad will be frustrated at me *again* ... I can only hope Ruben doesn't find out.

It was meant to be fun, a chilled evening ... but I really don't want to be here anymore. I want to be back at the ranch, tucked up in my new bedroom for the summer, doodling in my bullet journal. Which, ironically, is exactly what Ruben expects of me.

Turning away from everyone, I stride over to Blake's truck and try the door, but it's locked. He must notice me tugging on the handle, because he appears next to me, raising an eyebrow.

"Unlock your truck," I demand. "Please."

"Why?"

"So that I can hide inside until you take me home."

Blake presses his lips together and fishes his keys out from his khaki shorts, then unlocks the truck. As soon as I hear the *click*, I wrench open the door to the backseat, climb in, then slam it shut again. He peers in at me through the window, studies me for a second, then saunters back to his friends. I'd like to think all of this is his fault, but the truth is it's mine for agreeing to come here in the first place.

I sit back and bask in the silent privacy of the truck for a minute. Everyone seems to have calmed down, and have slowly congregated back inside the circle of trucks. I can hear music and voices, a muffled chorus through the glass. That was some finale to their game of Truth or Dare. Note to self: Be more careful with my phone in the future.

A moment later, the door on the opposite side of the truck swings open and Savannah clambers in to join me.

"I'm so sorry, Mila," she says, eyes full of guilt even though she hasn't done anything wrong. "That was so shitty of Barney to do that. Did he really call your dad?"

"Yes!" I throw my hands up in exasperation. "I'll be in *such* deep shit with my parents, and now you'll all just think of me as Everett Harding's daughter—"

"That's not such a bad thing, though," Savannah interrupts in an effort to cheer me up. "Everyone thinks it's super cool."

"That's not the point!" I snap.

Savannah looks a little hurt, like she's not sure how to navigate me. "Oh."

"I'm sorry," I say, rubbing my temples. I don't mean to

take out my frustration on her. "I just need to keep a low profile while I'm here. I didn't want anyone to connect me to my dad. It always makes life so freaking complicated."

"But ... Everyone would figure it out at some point, right? It's a small town. Not many Milas. Not many Hardings."

"I know, but I really, really need for it to *not* be a big deal. Between you and me, my dad's control-freak manager doesn't want the press finding out I'm here."

"Why?" Savannah asks. "What's so scandalous about spending your summer back in your hometown?"

I look at her kind, innocent face and it feels pointless to do anything other than tell her the truth. "The fact that I didn't want to," I say.

"Ohh." Savannah draws in a breath. "Are you here as a punishment or something?"

"Preventative measures," I correct.

"Okay. I'm on it!" Savannah says confidently, straightening her shoulders. "I'll head out and do damage-control." She holds up her pinky finger to me. "I promise I've got your back. I'll make sure everyone stays cool and collected, and I'll bodyslam any crazy, obsessed fans out of your way as and when required."

This finally gets a smile out of me. I guess I can understand now why Savannah Bennett was my best friend in grade school, because she looks out for others and still makes pinky promises at the age of sixteen. That, and the fact she believes her tiny frame could ever bodyslam anyone.

With a nod of agreement, I interlock my pinky around hers.

6

The party draws to an end an hour or so later. I watch as everyone gathers up trash and stacks away chairs and coolers. Tori shuts down her music and packs away the speakers, and soon people climb into trucks and disappear. There's not a single trace left behind of anyone ever having been here tonight.

All this time, I have remained in Blake's truck. I'm exhausted from this morning's flight, so it's actually been a welcome relief to sit in silence and close my eyes for a half-hour (mostly in fear of seeing an angry text from my parents or Ruben pop up on my phone). And now, finally, it's time to head back home.

Savannah and Myles climb into the truck first, the pair of them bickering loudly about something. I sit up and rub my tired eyes.

"How was the rest of the party?" I ask, taking a wary peek at my phone. Still no calls or messages. That's a relief.

Savannah yanks her seatbelt around her, annoyed. "Great, except Prince Charming over here wanted to sneak Cindy back to the house with us. So gross." Myles scoffs in the passenger seat, but Savannah ignores him and turns to me instead. "And I made sure everyone knows to stay cool about the fact that you're here."

The driver's door swings open and Blake slides into the truck, whistling a low tune to himself. Even the mere sight of the back of his head annoys me. He starts up the engine, turns on his country pop, then drives off school property.

"So, Miss Mila," he drawls, eyeballing me in the rearview, "do you think you'll be around for the July tailgate?"

"Hopefully not," I say through clamped lips. Why is he still bothering to even speak to me?

"What – you didn't have a good time?"

"Blake, shut up," Savannah snaps. "Can all of us in this truck right now please agree to make Mila feel comfortable while she's here?"

"Sure," Blake says with a stifled laugh. "I promise to be nothing but nice to Mila."

Savannah shoots me an apologetic glance. "Thanks," I mouth. I appreciate her effort, but it seems her cousin is determined to be a jackass. At least he turns his attention to wisecracking with Myles and doesn't say anything more to me as we head back along Fairview Boulevard and north into the spread-out landscape of the town.

It's nearing midnight, so there really is no one else around by now. We don't pass a single car on the ride back to the ranches, and there's nothing to look at besides the dark void. Eventually, we turn down the twisty road I recognize from earlier, and I spot the lights of the Bennett farmhouse appearing in the distance.

Which makes me realize that Blake is dropping his cousins off first, meaning I'll be left alone in the truck with him. *Why, why, why?* I assumed I would get dropped off first, because that makes sense, right? You *always* drop off the people you know the least well first, so that this exact problem is avoided. I don't *want* to be alone in the truck with Blake and I'm surprised he's willing to be alone with me. I don't need him antagonizing me, especially without Savannah there to put a stop to his fun.

My mouth feels dry and I try to focus on the crunching of dirt beneath the tires as the truck bobs its way down Willowbank's dusty driveway. Blake pulls up to a stop outside the house, and Savannah and Myles climb out.

"Blake will drop you off," Savannah whispers, her hand resting on the door. "You're only five minutes down the road." Then she raises her voice and directs her attention to Blake. "Be nice to Mila."

"Order received," Blake says firmly, saluting her.

The Bennetts say their goodbyes for the night and creep inside their house, wrestling silently with their elbows to be the first through the front door. They disappear out of sight, and Blake does a U-turn, driving off the property and back onto the road.

I feel ridiculous being in the backseat while he's up front, chauffeuring me, so I unbuckle my belt and climb over the center console.

"Hey!" Blake protests when I *accidentally* whack him in the side of the head with my elbow.

I collapse into the warm passenger seat that Myles has

66

just vacated, then pull my seatbelt on. Now that I'm alone with Blake, I have two options – I either act like a loser and allow him to walk all over me, or I stand up for myself.

"So, what's your deal?" I shoot at him, arms crossed, body angled toward him.

Blake flashes me a look of disdain, unimpressed with me clambering all over his upholstery. "My deal?"

"Yeah. What's your deal?" I ask again, firmer this time. "Because you seemed to love watching me squirm out there tonight. Are you the class bully or something? Who crowned you King of Fairview High?"

Blake throws his head back and softly laughs. "You're the one being a drama queen. I introduced you and I got you involved in the game by offering you a talking point. Tell me again how that makes me a bully?"

"You weren't doing me any favors. Why did you have to tell everyone who my father is?"

"Well, personally, I reckon your dad's acting skills could do with some fine-tuning. The *Flash Point* movies majorly suck, but a lot of people think otherwise," he says, shrugging. He drives with one hand slung over the top of the steering wheel, the other mindlessly fiddling with dials on the center console. "So, it seemed a shame to keep everyone in the dark. Besides, I didn't know it was some kind of big secret."

"Oh, give it up, Blake!" I nearly spit his name at him. "Don't act like you didn't know exactly what you were doing. You're a jerk. You ruined my night."

I turn to stare out the window, sending a prayer out into

the dark sky that Savannah doesn't hang around with her cousin all that often, because I really don't want to be in close proximity to him for the time that I'm here.

Blake doesn't bother to respond, only chuckles under his breath, and we sit in silence for a minute until, finally, the Harding Estate comes into view. The spotlights running along the walls light up the road in a cool, blue haze. I tug off my seatbelt before Blake has even reached the front gate, ready to make my getaway and hopefully never see him again.

"One Mila Harding safely delivered to her prison – sorry, home," he states, putting the truck into park.

"Prison?" I echo, bewildered. I mean, sure, the walls are intimidating, and the thought of the ranch being like a prison *did* cross my mind earlier. But still, the walls are there for a reason – to protect Sheri and Popeye.

Blake dips his head and peers through the windshield. "Well, yeah. I imagine it feels that way."

I haven't been at the ranch long enough to feel locked in yet, so I ignore his musings and get out of the truck. No way does he deserve a *thank you* or a *goodbye*, so I grab the door to slam it shut.

"Do you have a key for that gate?"

"I have a code," I say, shoving the door of the truck closed. "*Obviously.*"

I make for the gate and pull up the notes app on my phone to find the code I wrote down earlier, but I become aware that Blake's truck is still idling behind me. Why hasn't he left yet? I hate this feeling of his gaze following me.

Twisting around, I yell back to the truck, "Do you have to stay there and watch me?"

Blake rolls down his window, hooks an arm over the door, then smiles sweetly. It's the nicest smile he's given me all night, but it doesn't hide the steeliness in his voice. "Just making sure you get home safely, as promised. Surely you'd be worth a big chunk of ransom money? If you disappeared right now, I'd be the prime suspect."

"Go home, Blake," I order, disregarding him with a flippant wave of my hand. "Bye. Goodnight. See you never."

I turn back to the gate and take a deep breath, tuning him out, then punch in the numbers Sheri gave me. A shrill *beep* emits from the gate and the keypad flashes red, but nothing else happens.

Huh?

I try again – pressing each number on the keypad slower this time to ensure I've entered the code correctly, but another *beep* and a flicker of red light tells me otherwise. Did Sheri give me the wrong code? Did I note it down wrong? I *was* rushing to leave at the time.

Anxiously, I tap my foot the same way I did when I first arrived at the ranch this afternoon, thinking hard. I don't want to turn around and admit to Blake that I'm currently locked out, so keeping my head down, I swipe through my phone's contact list.

I am horrified to discover that I do not have Aunt Sheri's number.

My eyes widen as I check my list again, panic searing through me. Why don't I have her number? I wrote mine down on a sticky note in the kitchen earlier, but I didn't think to ask Sheri for hers in case of, you know – *emergencies like this.*

"Is there a problem with that big expensive security gate?" I hear Blake call.

"I told you to go home," I mutter with my back to him. I'm feigning confidence, but right now I am racking my brain for a way to get inside this ranch.

"But aren't you glad there's someone here to help you?"

The engine cuts out and I hear the click of his door closing, then footsteps. He stands alongside me and places his hands on his hips, head tilted to one side as he stares at the looming gate before us. Meanwhile, I stare at *him*, mortified. Could tonight get any worse?

"Maybe you should – I don't know – call someone?" he suggests.

"Well, yes," I'm forced to agree. "But ... I don't have my aunt's number."

He gives me a sideways look and the spotlights from the wall shine over the dimple in his cheek. "You don't have your aunt's number?" He grins like he can't believe anyone could be that dumb.

"Shut up!" I growl, still scrolling frantically through my contact list in case I've got the ranch's landline in here, but it's hopeless – whenever I call Popeye, I call from our own landline back home. I don't have anyone's numbers saved in my cell phone. "I only arrived today."

"That's unfortunate," he says, then turns to the stretching darkness behind us and jokingly calls out, "Does anyone out there have a tent Mila can borrow?" His voice booms in the night, echoing far in the distance. "And maybe a sleeping bag?"

"Stop it. This isn't funny."

I tilt my head back and run my eyes up the height of the walls. There's a reason they are eight feet tall – no one's going to scale those babies. I groan and press my palm flat to my forehead, mulling through my limited options.

"You seriously have no way to get inside?" Blake asks.

"What – you think I *want* to be stuck out here with you?"

He smiles, then reaches into his pocket for his phone. "Look, I'm going to do you a real favor this time."

I wonder what he can possibly do to help me get inside, but I'm willing to give him the benefit of the doubt. I may be angry at him, but right now I *am* secretly pretty glad that he didn't follow my orders to leave.

Blake dials a number, then presses his phone to his ear and walks away from me. He stuffs his other hand into the pocket of his shorts and paces silently by his truck, not making eye contact with me. I remain where I am, watching, waiting. Who is he calling?

He stops pacing and clears his throat when the call is answered. "Hey, yeah, yeah, I'm fine. Don't worry," he says quietly into the phone, his back to me. "I know it's late, but I need you to call someone for me. It's kind of an emergency." He listens, then sighs. "I just told you I'm fine. This isn't about me." He pauses and turns to me, holding his phone away from his ear. "What's your aunt's name again?"

"Sheri."

Blake angles away again and talks into the phone, his voice lowered but not quite enough. "Can you call Sheri Harding and tell her that her niece is locked out of their ranch? Yeah, her niece, so *his* daughter." A long pause. "I know, but you're the only one who's awake at this hour and can help." Another pause. "Okay. Thanks." He ends the call, puts his phone back in his pocket, then walks back over to me.

"Who was that?" I ask.

Both Blake's hands are now in his pockets and he rocks back and forth. He stares at the ground for a few seconds, then says, "My mom."

"Your mom?"

"She has a lot of connections. Also – small town, remember? Smaller than you'd think."

Okay, ominous, but I guess it doesn't matter *how* I get into the ranch just as long as I eventually do. I keep quiet and wrap my arms around me, not really sure what to do now besides wait it out.

At this time of night, the summer warmth has cooled down and there's a soft breeze blowing strands of my hair into my eyes. On the other side of the road, there's just sprawling, empty fields that fade into the dark. The moon is full tonight, and the stars dance high in the sky above us. Thanks to LA's chronic light pollution problem, I've never seen stars so vibrant before.

Blake and I stand together in the silence of the night, the only sound being that of a cricket's incessant chirping, and we don't say a word to each other. The more time that passes without either of us speaking, the more the pressure builds. I'm the one who cracks first.

"Thanks for staying with me," I say.

He leans back against his truck. "Pretty considerate for a jerk like me, huh?"

Any attempt at further civil discussion is disrupted by the startling shrill of the bell, signaling the opening of the gate. The gate slowly peels open and reveals Aunt Sheri on the other side, a fuzzy bathrobe wrapped tightly around her.

"Mila! Oh, sweetie, I'm so sorry!" she splutters. Her slippers scuff the ground as she rushes to me, pulling me into her arms as though I've been missing for five days. "Is this damn gate playing up again? Didn't the code work?"

"It's okay," I reassure her, awkwardly patting her on the back until she unravels me from the hug. I look into her guilty expression and offer up a playful grin to put her at ease. "I think I wrote it down wrong. Also, I really need to get your number."

"Oh, *of course*! I didn't even think … I just assumed you had it already …" Sheri's words trail off into nothing as her gaze shifts over my shoulder. "Hello, Blake."

"Evening, Miss Harding," Blake says, nodding his head as a polite greeting. Oh, so he *can* be nice if he wants to be?

Sheri gives me a strange look and says, "I thought you were going out with Savannah?"

"She was," Blake answers for me. "We were all in my truck. I'm just dropping Mila back off to you."

"Well, thank you, Blake. And thank your mother again

for me. I didn't know what to expect when I answered the call."

"Will do," he says, but there's a strained tension between the two of them that I don't understand. They never really meet each other's eyes. "I better head home now. Goodnight, Mila."

"Goodnight," I mumble, perplexed. So now he's all gracious and sweet?

Blake jumps back in his truck, waves, then drives off. His taillights shine bright in the distance until all at once they disappear, and he's gone.

7

My phone rings and I answer the call, half-asleep, to the sound of Ruben's enraged voice yelling down the line at me.

"Your father told me what happened last night. Totally, utterly one hundred percent unacceptable!"

"Good morning to you too, Ruben," I mumble, sitting up in bed and checking the time on my phone. Eight a.m. Sunlight is filtering into my room, but my eyes are too sensitive, so I clamp them shut and rub at my eyelids. "Isn't it only, like, six in LA? Why are you up so early?"

"Mila, darling, there's no rest for the wicked in this industry," he says dryly. "Your father was attending a very important dinner last night and you think that's a good time to have your little hometown buddy call him? Where precisely *were* you? It didn't sound like you were at the ranch as per my instructions."

"He isn't my *buddy*," I protest. My throat feels scratchy from dehydration, and I pull back my sheets and stick a bare leg over the side of my bed so that the AC hits my skin in just the right spot.

"Then what happened? Are you befriending the

Tennessee locals by offering personal phone calls with Everett Harding?"

How could I have forgotten how much of a pain in the ass Ruben is? He's kinda like an uncle to me, but one that I loathe for always being on my back about *everything*. "Of course not! I was at a—" Abruptly, I stop myself. Maybe I shouldn't be confessing to Ruben that I've broken his rules so soon.

"You were at a *what*, Mila?" he prompts.

"Okay, I went out with an old school friend to a tailgate party," I say in defeat, but I have to rescue this so that Sheri doesn't get in trouble too. "Sheri didn't know, but don't worry, she's set me straight now. No leaving the ranch. Got it."

"Mila," Ruben practically growls. "Not even twenty-four hours and you've created a shitshow. Must be a new record. You just couldn't stop yourself from mentioning your father, could you?"

"I didn't! Someone else did!"

He sighs. "Can I suggest that you bond with those relatives of yours, help muck out a horse stall or two, maybe read a couple romance novels? No leaving the ranch. No. More. Parties. Understood, Mila?"

I slowly peel open my eyes, adjusting to the light, and wake up enough to get defensive. "Ruben, that's impossible. How do you expect me to maintain a low profile in Dad's *hometown* where everyone knows exactly who we are? You should have packed me off to a different continent if you really want me to remain undetected."

"Don't be ridiculous!" he huffs. "Like I could trust you out in the world." Then his tone shifts. "To be honest, I don't care *where* you are. But I'm taking over your social media accounts as of now."

I squeeze my phone harder. "What?"

"I've changed all your passwords," he announces. "You only have to put out one tweet – *one* photo on Instagram – that even remotely hints at the fact that you're back at the old stomping grounds, and the paparazzi will start sniffing around."

"Ruben, has anyone ever told you that you're the most annoying person in the world?" I ask sweetly, wishing I could climb through the phone and strangle him.

"Yes, darling, plenty of times. But I'm the absolute best at what I do." I hear him blow me a kiss down the line. "Now behave, Mila sweetie, and keep yourself busy at that ranch. Don't have me call you a second time."

The call goes dead, and I throw my phone to the floor and slump back against my pillows, groaning into my sheets. I wish I could be a normal sixteen-year-old who doesn't have her father's manager controlling her every move, but as Mom always reminds me, I'm *not* normal. It's not easy on her, either. She's the wife of a goddamn movie star. The rumors that circle are insane, and the pressure to play the role of the perfect, gorgeous, supportive wife gets to her too. No wonder she focuses on her own life within the industry with so much passion. It lets her be her own person.

Hell, I wish I had my own identity.

With a tired yawn, I stretch out my arms and then slip out

of bed. It's an odd thing, waking up in a brand-new room. Back home, my bullet journal sits on my mirrored glass end table; my favorite body lotion and perfumes are aligned in perfect order along my dresser; my jewelry is arranged in dainty little boxes along the shelves on my walls. Here, everything is all over the place, spread out over the floor. I make a start on unpacking, but I feel even more exhausted by the time I sift through everything. I've piled my clothes into groups across the floor, lined up all of my self-care products, and set my teddy bear on my pillow. Then I give up on putting everything away and head downstairs instead.

The smell of freshly brewed coffee wafts from the kitchen, so I follow the scent. The house is so silent that I'm surprised when I find Popeye in the kitchen. He's fiddling with the hinges on a window, a wrench in hand, while gazing outside across the ranch he is so proud of. I look out at the fields with him. I think it was actually my great grandfather who built the Harding Estate up from nothing after the Second World War, then Popeye and my grandmother inherited it and raised their own family here. Dad would have been in line to take over if life had played out like generations before him might have expected, but his ambition threw a wrench in the works. That's why Sheri has been helping Popeye out with the ranch all these years, because I imagine one day it will belong to only her. The ranch used to be so much bigger when I was a kid – a few hundred acres larger – but Popeye sold off most of the land a few years ago right before the security walls went up so that it's much more manageable. I can't imagine Dad *ever* returning to live here, even if his career were to end at some point. It's so far from who he is today.

"Good morning," Popeye greets me, holding up the wrench. "Sheri is with the horses, but she said she'll cook you a hearty breakfast once she's back. I'm trying to fix this darn window that won't stop creaking."

"That's okay. I can grab something myself," I say. I pad across the wooden flooring and plant a kiss on his cheek. "Good morning, Popeye."

My hand is on his shoulder, and he squeezes his fingers around mine, his skin warm. He looks down into my eyes. "So, I hear you got stuck outside the gate last night."

I throw my arms around him from behind and bury my face into his shoulder blade, inhaling the scent of … Well, the scent of Popeye. Like someone who has lived his entire life on a ranch. "Yeah, I did. Let's not joke about it."

"It's been just Sheri and me around here for so long it's easy to forget we have someone else to consider for once," he says, though his tone is more downbeat than playful.

I'm painfully aware that we really haven't visited as much as we should have over the years, and an image of Sheri and Popeye sitting at the dining table, just the two of them, day after day, tugs at my heart. It's kind of like, when Dad packed up his life and moved to LA with stars in his eyes he forgot about the lives of those he left behind.

I unwrap my arms from around Popeye's shoulders and he sets his wrench down, then crosses the kitchen. He rifles through a drawer rammed full of papers and cables, then holds up a plastic device like a small TV remote. "This is for you," he says. "I'm going to call that technician and give him a piece of my mind if he doesn't show up and fix that gate soon, and when he does, you can use this electric remote to get in and out. But until then, please make a note of the *correct* code."

I move across the kitchen to take it from him, turning it over in the palm of my hand. "Thanks, Popeye."

Sheri appears at the back door to the kitchen, shaking her hair out of its ponytail. She's wearing an old shirt and tattered jeans caked in dirt, and she kicks off her grubby rubber boots by the welcome mat. Sheri is blessed with naturally gorgeous features, so even when covered in horsehair and muck, she still manages to look like a million dollars. Dad once told me that, in her early twenties, Sheri was set to marry a paramedic from the city, but he was tragically killed in a car accident out on the interstate. She has never gone on to marry anyone else or have kids of her own. It seems to suit her, though; she always seems cheerful and contented.

"Oh, good morning, Mila, you're awake!" Sheri says, crossing the kitchen. She lifts a strand of my hair behind my ear. "Did you sleep well?"

"Yeah, right up until Ruben woke me up. He wasn't too thrilled about last night."

"Last night?" Sheri repeats, stiffening. "Ruben knows you went out?"

"Yeah. About that..." I say sheepishly. "There was a little ... Incident. Someone took my phone and called my dad."

"Oh, Mila!" Sheri groans, turning for the sink. She lathers

80

up her hands with dish soap and rinses them beneath the faucet. "Now Ruben will call *me* and give me hell!"

"No, he won't," I say with a shy smile. Although I haven't had much of a chance to grow close with my family over the years, I do like Aunt Sheri, and I really appreciate that she's willing to take me in for the summer. The last thing I want to do is make life difficult for her. "I covered for you."

"Thank you, Mila. That's the kind of teamwork we need to have, okay?" she says with a relieved laugh, shaking the water from her hands. She might be my aunt, but I get the sense Sheri is still young at heart. "Oh, Dad! What are you doing with that wrench?"

Popeye gestures with the tool. "Fixing this darn window! That latch *you* broke last week. I don't want this place turning into a tumbledown shack. Not now, not fifty years from now, not ever," he grumbles.

"Okay, but perhaps this isn't the best time …" With a groan, Sheri turns back to me. "Mila, we have church at ten, so make sure you're ready to leave in an hour." Her eyes catch on my frayed jean shorts. "And our church's attire is semi-formal, so please wear a skirt."

"*Church?*" I repeat as though she's spoken a language I don't understand.

"It *is* Sunday," she says, brows pinching together as she scrutinizes my bewildered expression. It seems to dawn on her that I'm not confused about which day it is, but rather confused about the notion of attending church in the first place. There's a distinctive shift in her demeanor. "I assume Everett doesn't take you in LA?"

"No."

Popeye mumbles something unintelligible under his breath and walks out of the kitchen, banging the wrench down on the table with a clatter. Sheri lets out a disappointed sigh.

I fear upsetting her further, so in as positive a tone as I can muster, I tell her, "Skirt it is. I'll get ready."

I mean, how bad can church really be? It's clearly super important to Sheri and Popeye, so I guess that means it has to be important to me while I'm here in Fairview.

Sheri disappears off to check on Popeye and I toast myself some bread, taking it upstairs to my room with me. I should probably call Mom at some point rather than just text her, but honestly, Ruben has sucked all the energy out of my soul, and I've had enough of a reminder of my life back in Hollywood for one day.

I spend ten minutes doodling in my bullet journal instead, designing a new spread for this fresh chapter of my life here in Fairview. I create a section entitled "New Memories" which I plan to fill out with any memorable events that occur while I'm here, and I make a note with yesterday's date and the words "tailgate party". Hopefully, stuff will actually happen over the summer, because I'll feel super lame if the pages in my journal remain mostly blank.

Then, I shower and get dressed so I'll be on time. I keep my hair down in its natural waves and I put on a denim skirt, the most modest blouse I packed, and sandals. Part of me wonders if denim is even allowed, but it's the only skirt I brought with me.

When I head back downstairs an hour later, Popeye is sitting in the shade out on the porch and looks handsome in his brown slacks and white shirt. His silky white hair has been smoothly combed over and he even smells like cologne. He reaches for my hand again when I join him, and I realize that I'm the only grandchild he's ever had. No wonder he looks at me as though I'm something pure and special.

"I'm glad you're coming with us," he says. "Lots of young people attend, so it's not just us oldies."

"If church is important to you, Popeye, then I want to see what it's all about," I tell him, though it's not one hundred percent the truth. I'm not *thrilled* about going, but I know my words are ones he'll be happy to hear. And that's really all there is to it – you keep your grandfather happy, even if you have to lie a little.

8

The church Sheri and Popeye attend is on Fairview Boulevard. It's a large, red-bricked building with white awnings and lots of immaculate, bright flower baskets. It triggers a memory from five years ago. I've been here before. It's the church where my grandma's funeral was held. I was only eleven, but I remember when my parents and I flew home to Fairview to attend the service. Popeye restlessly paced the fields of the ranch back then, distraught, while Dad and Sheri had to put their own grief to one side and take care of the funeral arrangements. And then we all gathered here, in this church, and said goodbye to the grandmother I'd barely seen since we left for LA. That's why it became important to me to keep in touch with Popeye a lot more once I got a little older. I didn't want to forget about him too, because I'd already learned how distance does that to people.

This morning's service doesn't start for another fifteen minutes, but the parking lot is already pretty full, and people are chatting among themselves at the church doors, basking in the sunshine before heading inside.

I've only just slid out of Sheri's van when someone taps me on the shoulder. I spin around and Savannah greets me with a wide smile.

"I didn't know you were going to be here this morning!" she says cheerfully. "I should have guessed, though. I see your aunt and grandpa every week. Hi, neighbors!" She twists around me to give them a friendly wave, and both Sheri and Popeye return the favor.

Savannah focuses back on me, looping her arm through mine. "Do you want to sit with us?"

I glance at Sheri, checking for permission, and she nods. "Sure," I tell Savannah, glad of her easy friendship.

We head for the church doors and meet up with her parents and Myles, and I stick with Savannah and her brother while Sheri and Popeye chat with Patsy and her husband.

I follow behind Savannah as us Hardings and Bennetts head inside the church. The space is lined with rows and rows of pews and there's a raised wooden platform at the front with a podium, and everyone is speaking in chirpy tones while they wait for the service to begin.

It doesn't take long for the pews to fill up and I end up squished in between Savannah and Myles. Sheri is at the end of the row, with Popeye sitting by her side.

"So, this is what you guys do around here?" I whisper, in fear of raising my voice too loud. "Tailgate parties, then church in the morning?"

Myles wiggles his thick eyebrows at me, a dazzling grin taking up too much of his face. "Yeah, your life back in

LA must seem pretty uninspiring in comparison. Sorry."

I grin back at him and roll my eyes just as the chorus of voices dies out all at once. When I glance up at the stage, the preacher, or minister, or priest – or whatever the heck they call that guy – has taken up his role in front of the podium, adjusting the mic. And then what follows is the most mentally draining hour of my *life* where I have no idea what is going on.

Half the words the preacher says I've never even heard of and the other words I *do* understand, I can't comprehend the context in which he uses them. Bible verses are quoted, prayers are said, hymns are sung (which I lip-sync to). Everyone seems to be deeply invested in the proceedings and I appear to be the only one whose gaze continuously roams the church, staring at a clock on the wall, at the sunlight streaming in through a decorative window, at the wooden paneling on the ceiling.

And then, just as the service is showing signs of wrapping up, my eyes land on something I really didn't expect to see. *Blake.*

I haven't spotted him until now, mostly because there's been some tall guy's head in my line of sight all this time, but said tall guy has shifted over slightly in the pew, and now I can see it as clear as day – Blake's freaking head.

He's on the other side of the aisle and toward the front, diagonal from where I'm sitting. I can tell he's slouched back in the pew, with his head tilted to one side and his face resting flat against the palm of his hand. I can't tell who he's with – there's women on either side of him. His mom?

Grandma? Either way, it's a relief to see there's one other person here who seems as bored as I am.

The service ends and noise reverberates around the auditorium as voices rise and everyone stands, stretching their muscles and rubbing their lower backs. These wooden pews aren't all that comfortable, and I can feel a knot forming between my shoulder blades. Amid the commotion of bodies weaving around, I lose sight of Blake, though I don't know why I'm even bothering to look for him.

The throng of churchgoers – which includes me now, I guess – spills out of the front doors and into the sizzling hot air outside. I expect everyone to hop in their cars and head straight home, but I discover there *is* one thing even more dull in this life than a Sunday service – and that's the mingling and chit-chat that comes afterward.

An older gentleman with silver-like hair approaches us, shaking Popeye's hand and discussing what a wonderful sermon the preacher just gave. I stand awkwardly behind Popeye, trying not to draw attention to myself, while Sheri is twenty feet away talking with some women that include Patsy Bennett. I hear her laugh, which is nice.

"And who's this, Wesley?" the man asks, flashing me a smile.

Popeye looks sideways over his shoulder at me and I notice his movements seem a bit jerky this morning. "This is my granddaughter. Mila," he says proudly. "She's spending some time at the ranch with us over the summer."

"How wonderful!"

I return the stranger's smile and am saved by the sound of Sheri's voice calling my name.

"Mila," she beckons. "Come over here, please."

I leave Popeye behind and weave through the congregation of people, but it's only as I draw nearer and it's too late to pretend I didn't hear her call my name that I realize *why* she's called me over. The group she was talking to a second ago is gone now, replaced instead by a different woman who stands with Blake by her side.

I feel myself tense up. He's wearing black slacks and a plain white shirt, long-sleeved and buttoned tight around his chest. His hair isn't as wild as it was last night. It seems to actually have gel in it to tame the unruliness, so that it looks tousled on purpose rather than as if he'd just rolled out of bed.

"Mila, this is … LeAnne Avery," Sheri says politely, gesturing to the woman by Blake's side, but her words don't flow as easily and warmly as they usually do. It's as though she's struggling to be genuine. "I was just thanking her again for calling me last night, otherwise who knows how long you'd have been stuck outside."

So, this is Blake's mom. *Duh.* She's tall and slim, dressed smartly in a royal blue pencil skirt and a cream, ruffled blouse. I can see where Blake gets his features from. LeAnne Avery has brunette hair pin-straight against her shoulders and eyebrows so dark and prominent I wonder if they can possibly be natural. She smiles at me, and I see them – the dimples in her cheeks, exactly like Blake's.

"Hi, Mila," she says, clasping her hands together in front of her. She looks at me inquisitively for several long seconds while the corners of her mouth twitch as if she's battling to keep that smile in place. "I'm glad you got home safe."

"Hi. Thank you so much," I force out, feeling Blake's eyes locked on me.

"And how have *you* been doing, Wes?" LeAnne asks as Popeye approaches. I notice her accent isn't as pronounced as Blake's, or anyone's for that matter. Less of a twang, more neutral. She gets Popeye wrapped up in a conversation, and Sheri joins in.

Which leaves Blake and me standing around like two spare parts.

"So, you go to church," I say flatly.

"Clearly."

He nods to the side, gesturing to the edge of the parking lot by a row of shrubs, then walks off in that direction. What the hell? I steal a peek at Popeye, LeAnne and Sheri. None of them are paying attention to us, so I reluctantly drag my feet to catch up with Blake.

"So why are *you* here?" he asks.

"Because my aunt and my grandpa wanted me to be. So, I guess I'll be here every week, too."

Blake narrows his eyes as though he's trying to read me, but I give nothing away, keeping my expression calm and neutral. "How long are you sticking around in Fairview for, anyway?"

"For as long as I have to."

"For as long as you *have* to?" he repeats, raising a suspicious eyebrow. "That doesn't sound like someone who's here because they want to stay with family."

Crap. I'm caught off guard by his observation and I rack

my brain for a response that will clear up my mistake. But the longer I'm frozen in silence, the more Blake realizes he's hit the nail on the head.

"Anyway," he says, clearing his throat and saving me from having to speak, "I'm sorry about last night."

"You're ... I'm sorry – what?" Did he just apologize without any kind of prompt?

"I'm sorry about last night," he says again.

"Why?"

"Because you were right. I was being a jerk." He shrugs casually as though he doesn't want to make this a big deal, like he's sheepish about having to own up to his actions. "I knew I wasn't doing you any favors, and I'm sorry if I got you in hot water with your dad or anything."

"I wish you could tell that to Ruben," I say under my breath. I idly tug at the ends of my hair, absorbing Blake's sincere apology, and feel a bit ... Conflicted? He riled me up the entire evening last night, but now he seems almost – nice. Which is really, really confusing considering I didn't want to see his face ever again. But he *did* come to my aid last night, after all ... "Thanks for your help with the gate."

"Blake!" LeAnne calls, waving her son back over and breaking the moment of awkward silence between us.

Blake holds up two fingers to her, asking for two more minutes, then steps closer to me. "Give me your phone," he says.

"Absolutely not!" I protest indignantly. Does he think I'm that stupid after what happened last night? Protectively,

I increase the distance between us again. "No one is ever touching my phone again."

"Okay, then here's mine." He digs his phone out from his pocket and hands it over. When I don't immediately take it from him, he reaches for my hand and forces his phone into my palm. His fingertips are warm as they brush against my skin and I hate the unauthorized little jump my heart takes. "Add your number."

I eyeball his phone in my hand with uncertainty. "And why would I do that?"

"Didn't last night teach you anything? You need to save people's numbers so that you can call them in an emergency."

"No offense, but you're probably the last person I would ever call in an emergency," I remark, but Blake laughs as though we are merely bantering with each other.

"Just do it, Mila," he instructs, like he honestly expects me to do what he says.

It's not like I'm giving out Dad's private number or anything, but nonetheless I still hear Ruben's voice in my head, warning bells ringing. I have to be careful about whose hands my number gets into, because although it's not the end of the world if it ever got leaked online, I would be endlessly harassed by Dad's fans and the media trying to get gossip and information. And that is a headache I really don't want to deal with.

"Please don't pass it on to *anyone*," I say, fixing him with a threatening look as I add my number to his contact list. I hand him his phone back. "It's the least you owe me."

"Your precious digits are safe with me," he says somewhat

mockingly, hand on his heart. He checks out my number on his phone, then lifts his head and stares at me with an expectant gaze at the same time as my phone begins to vibrate. Before I can even attempt to reach for it, Blake hangs up. "There, now you have my number too. Just in case you get bored of hanging around with Savannah." He winks and then strolls back across the parking lot to meet his mom. She puts her hand on his shoulder and guides him over to speak with some of the other churchgoers.

I shake my head to wipe away the hint of a smile and then make my own way back to the crowd. I haven't seen Savannah and her family since everyone congregated outside, so I figure they've made a quick getaway. Luckily for me, Popeye and Sheri have decided to finally leave too. I find them back at the van.

"What were you and Blake talking about?" Sheri asks, a slight hesitation in her voice.

"Just stuff," I say, reaching for the door.

"Mayor Avery is so gracious, isn't she? Even now…" Popeye comments, and I jolt to a standstill.

"Excuse me? *Mayor* Avery?"

"That friend of yours," Popeye grins, motioning over my shoulder. "His mother is the mayor."

I stretch up on my tiptoes to peer at Sheri over the roof of the van. "Blake's mom is the Mayor of Fairview?"

"Oh, honey, no," Sheri says with an amused chuckle. "The Mayor of Nashville."

Holy crap! Blake's mom is the freaking Mayor of *Nashville*? That's huge.

I search the crowd for Blake. He's still with his mom and they're talking with the preacher now, though Blake seems disinterested. His mom, however, nods enthusiastically and wears an elegant smile that only a politician could pull off so smoothly. I register it all, the way she holds her head high and her careful, calculated movements. It seems kind of obvious now that there's a certain authority to her. She's part of the Nashville government, a leader. She has won a freaking election. *Of course* she carries herself with such grace and self-assurance.

Blake catches my stare. He taps his pocket where his phone is and mouths, *"Call me."*

Okay, mayor's son, I think, rolling my eyes.

Then I instantly feel guilty for thinking of him as the mayor's *son*, rather than as Blake Avery. I hate being known as Everett Harding's *daughter* instead of Mila Harding. So yeah, I'm a total hypocrite.

I glance back at him, but he has already looked away, and is now busy shaking the preacher's hand. I watch him for a moment, his courteous body language matching his mom's, and I realize something.

I think Blake Avery might be the only person around here who understands what it feels like to live in someone else's shadow.

9

I help Sheri around the ranch over the next few days because, honestly, I think she's glad of an extra pair of hands other than Popeye's. I've noticed that his pride doesn't really match his capabilities these days, which makes him tough to please and a bit of a difficult partner to work with. Sheri teaches me everything I could possibly need to know about the six horses they keep here, like what to feed them and when, and how to groom them without getting kicked in the face by a massive hoof. After some reluctance, I even help muck out the stables. We tidy up the porch too, and when Sheri returns from the hardware store with a van full of buckets of paint I jump at the chance to be the designated painter for the Harding Estate – it's due for its annual summer touch-up. Whenever we moved into a new home in LA, Mom and I played music on full blast and painted each room ourselves rather than hiring a decorator. Our splotchy paintwork in the bedrooms made our homes feel a little more normal and down to earth.

By Wednesday, I've painted all of the downstairs window frames around the outside of the house and have given up in the heat for one day. I'm padding through to my room from the shower just after five when I hear my phone buzzing on my nightstand. I grip my towel tighter around my body and dive across my room because I know Ruben hates it whenever I dare to let his calls go to voicemail, so I frantically grab my phone and shove it up to my ear before it rings off. I hope he hasn't been calling me the entire time I've been in the shower, because if so, he's going to be furious.

"Ruben, hey. I was in the shower," I splutter before he has the chance to say anything. "I'm sorry if you've been calling for a while."

"Who's Ruben and why does he need to know that you're showering?"

I rip my phone from my ear and stare at my screen, checking the caller ID. It's my new "friend", Blake Avery. Warily, I tune back into the call. "Oh, sorry. Hi, Blake. Ruben is my dad's manager. He calls a lot."

"Sounds like he's your manager too, then."

"Lovely as it is to hear from you …" I smile to myself and sit down on the edge of my bed. "Is there a reason you're calling me?"

"Do you remember that church you attended on Sunday? The one where that guy gave you his number and asked you to call him?" Blake asks sweetly. "Well, it's now Wednesday, and has my phone rung? No, not once, so I thought I would call and check you're still alive."

"I've been busy helping out around the ranch," I tell him, which is the God-honest truth. The idea of calling Blake has crossed my mind more often than I care to admit, but

I have repeatedly shut it down as it made me feel nauseous with nerves. So, I decided to play it cool and hang out with Sheri instead.

"And are you busy right now?"

"No …" I say hesitantly, unsure of what this may lead to.

"Great. How quickly can you get ready?"

"Huh?"

"There's this place I like in Nashville. Myles has bailed on me because Cindy Jamieson has a free house tonight and wow, how could he turn *that* down? But I still want to go," Blake explains. "And you said I owe you, right? So, I'm going to give you the chance to actually have a *real* Nashville experience. Can you be ready in thirty minutes?"

My gaze lands on my bullet journal on my nightstand and I think of the pages I made last weekend, the one for listing all of the memories that I make here in Tennessee. If nothing else, an evening in Nashville sounds like it could help fill up some of the blank space.

"Can I ask where we're going in Nashville?" I ask, trying not to let those pesky nerves creep into my voice.

"It's a surprise, Miss Mila," Blake says in a tone that makes it obvious he's grinning on the other end of the line. "I'll see you outside the gate."

The call ends and I sit in my towel for a few minutes, mulling over his words. So, we're going to Nashville – just the two of us, by the sound of it. It could be for anything, so I'm not sure how to dress. Also, I haven't even asked Sheri for permission. I debate checking with her first before I go through the effort of drying my hair, but then I remember our pact. Sheri made it clear I'm allowed freedom as long as I keep her in the loop.

In a mad rush, I scramble around my room to be ready on time, because the sheer thickness of my hair alone is a problem that takes twenty minutes to solve. I blow-dry it straight and then pull a flat iron through the ends while simultaneously searching through the disorganized mess that is my closet. I finally put everything away the other day, but in no order, which I deeply regret now. Eventually, I find my favorite pair of fitted jeans, a washed-out blue color and ripped at the knees, which Mom never hesitates to tell me looks awful, and pick out a cherry red cropped Bardot top. I don't wear red enough, despite how well it pops against my hair, so I line my lips with red lipstick too.

I'm applying a second coat of mascara when a text lights up my phone. It's from Blake. He's outside the gate, exactly thirty minutes after our phone call.

I grab a small shoulder purse, tossing my phone, perfume, lipstick, and wallet inside. I've still got the fifty dollars Sheri gave me over the weekend, so I hope that whatever Blake has in mind doesn't cost more than that.

It only sinks in that I'm actually going out alone with Blake when I'm heading downstairs. I've been so focused on getting ready at lightning speed that I haven't had time to really think about it. Honestly, I don't even know this guy, but his mom is the mayor, so I guess it's a safe bet that he isn't dangerous. Annoying, sure. But most likely safe. Plus, the Bennetts are his relatives and *they* seem pretty normal.

Sheri is fixing dinner – or *supper*, as she calls it – when I find her in the kitchen. I spot Popeye through the window, sitting outside on the porch in the early evening sun, sipping a glass of sweet tea.

"Hungry?" Sheri asks, hearing my arrival.

"About that …"

She turns to look at me and her eyes widen, obviously surprised to see me so glammed up after three days of borrowing her old tees and with splotches of dried paint adorning my hair and my cheeks. I position my purse in front of my stomach so that she doesn't notice my piercing.

"I'm going to Nashville with Blake," I say in a neutral tone, but for some reason my cheeks grow hot.

"Is this a date?" Sheri quizzes, her tone one of worry rather than tease. Pots are bubbling on the stove behind her. "With Blake *Avery?*"

"No!" I shout. "It's not a date," I add more calmly. Blake needs a sidekick for the night, and I need to make memories in order to survive out here. "He's just showing me around."

"And what exactly are you heading into the city for?"

"Well, I don't know, exactly …" My voice trails off. "But he's already outside. I have money and your number and – oh! The correct code for the gate this time," I say with a grin.

Finally, a trace of a smile appears on Sheri's face. "Okay, you can go, but only because you'll be bored spending the night here with us. Please, behave, be careful in the city and don't be late."

"I will and I won't!" I say, then skip outside onto the porch. "Hi, Popeye. I'm going out."

"With your friend from church?" Popeye wraps his hands

around his sweet tea and purses his lips at me. "Blake Avery?"

"How did you …?"

"Bless your heart, Mila," he says warmly, as he looks out over the field, the sun low in the sky. "Your grandmother only ever wore red lipstick like that when we went on our dates."

My heart feels weighted all of a sudden as I remember once more the grandma I never really knew. It's been a long time since she passed, but Popeye must still think about her and miss her every day.

"Goodnight, Popeye," I murmur, then squeeze my hand over his and kiss his cheek. I've lost out on too many years of affection.

Blake has been waiting outside for at least five minutes now, so I dash down the porch steps and head for the gate. I open it from the inside, revealing Blake's truck. The black paintwork shines under the hazy, golden sunlight.

Blake rolls down the passenger window and leans across the seat. "Get in, Hollywood, we have places to be!"

I pull open the door and climb in, my heart annoyingly racing a bit, which I totally believe is from rushing to the truck and not because I'm even remotely nervous.

"Hey," I say coolly, pulling on my seatbelt. I try not to fidget too much. After all, this is also the same guy who started the chain of events that ended with me almost in tears at the tailgate party, so I have a justified reason for being anxious about how tonight may go …But still, I don't want Blake to notice.

"Hi," Blake says. His brown eyes briefly run over me,

but only for a second or two, and I wonder if he's going to compliment me. He doesn't. "Are you ready for the greatest night of your life?"

"That's a pretty bold statement," I point out. "Where are we going?"

Blake starts the engine, his fingertips creeping over to the dials on the truck's entertainment system. He glances at me out of the corner of his eye, a charming grin edging onto his lips, and bumps the music up. Country rock blasts in my ears. "We, suga', are off to a honky tonk!"

My expression is blank. What the heck did he just say? Between the excessive volume of the music and the extra emphasis he added to his accent, it makes it even harder to understand those crazy words that left his mouth.

Blake registers my indifference and lowers the volume back down. "You're going to personally offend me if you open your mouth and tell me that you don't know what a honky tonk is."

I blush a little too hard. "What is a honky tonk?"

"Maaan!" he groans dramatically and bangs his hand a couple times against the rim of the steering wheel. "You clearly don't have a single drop of southern spirit running through your blood. You're from here! From Nashville! Music city! Only the *home* of honky tonks! And you don't know what they are?"

"Are you going to tell me?"

He shakes his head in disapproval. "Somewhere that plays live country music. *Obviously*."

"I should have guessed," I say with a roll of my eyes. Every time I've been in Blake's truck, he has played country music. Country pop, country acoustic, now country rock ... He is super stereotypical for a Tennessee kid.

"I'm taking you to my favorite," he continues. "Honky Tonk Central on lower Broadway. They serve good food there too. And don't even ..." He briefly squeezes his eyes shut and inhales. "Don't even *dare* tell me you don't know what a meat and three sides is."

"Hey!" I hold up my hands. "Of course I know."

Blake runs a hand up the nape of his neck, flashing me a smile. "Well, there's something."

We leave behind the country roads of the Fairview outskirts and head out of town on the highway. Blake's playlist keeps us company for most of the drive, though he constantly switches the volume from too-loud-to-think to just-low-enough-to-hear whenever one of us tries to speak. He tells me more about honky tonks while I try not to snicker whenever he says those words and we chat a little about Nashville, so the topics we cover are all safe. Safe because we don't talk about ourselves too much, and he doesn't mention my father, and I certainly don't mention his mother. So, we stick to random chat about music until half an hour later when he parks in downtown Nashville.

"Wait," Blake says when I release my seatbelt and reach for the door handle. I pause and raise an eyebrow. "Just a heads up. This isn't Hollywood, so it's not glamorous or anything. Don't expect too much."

My lips form a tight line. "Why do you need to justify it to me?"

Blake doesn't have an answer. He eyes bore into mine as he reads my expression, then he shrugs guiltily. "I don't, I guess. I just assumed you're used to places much … higher-class than the one I'm about to take you to."

"That doesn't mean I won't like it."

Do I come across as a spoiled brat to him or something? I've grown up with a lot more privilege than most kids, sure, but Mom always taught me to be humble. It's been embedded in me since a young age that I'm incredibly lucky and to appreciate the life I live, and Mom has always been a hell of a lot more frugal than Dad is. Dad churns his way through new cars every couple months, whereas Mom still uses the same handbag he bought her for her birthday six years ago even though the seams are fraying. My allowance has always been capped, too – once it's spent, that's it. No more for the rest of the month. If I *really* want something bad enough, I only need to bat my eyelashes at Dad, but I never do. In that respect I'm much more like Mom.

That's why Blake's assumption grates on me – it seems kind of judgmental.

"Okay," Blake says, exhaling. He climbs out of the truck and I follow suit.

The final remnants of sunshine that lingered on the way here are gone, the sky deepening with blue and streaks of pink above the streets of Nashville. The air is still hot and sticky, and it's *noisy*. Traffic and the purring of car engines; voices and the tinkle of music. I inhale the scent of sizzling meat and my mouth waters.

It's so nice to look up and see buildings leaning over

me, rather than staring out across the ranch and seeing *nothing*. Despite starting out in Fairview, I think I was always destined to be a city girl. I love the commotion, the sea of new faces, the endless opportunities that present themselves. Sometimes, my friends and I back home just head out without any plans in mind, ready to roll with the tide and see what LA has in store for us. The city is full of possibilities and that's what is so enchanting – you never know exactly where it will take you.

It's been a couple years since I visited Nashville, and although it's an entirely different world to LA, it still holds that promise of home to me. My passport states Nashville as my place of birth, so I guess I *am* a Tennessee kid after all.

My steps are perfectly in sync with Blake's as I follow him on autopilot while my head is on a swivel, eyes wide to take in my surroundings. We turn onto Broadway and are suddenly thrust into the heart of the city. The Bridgestone Arena stretches out in front of me and I glance down the street, pulled in by the quirky neon signs that illuminate the evening sky. There's an array of different musical genres blending together, emitting from rooftop patios, and I see the endless choice of grills and restaurants where that delicious smell of food wafts from. Groups of friends mingle on the sidewalks, their laughter the soundtrack of happy summer evenings. Downtown Nashville has a unique buzz, its own little bubble filled with good spirits (everyone is happy), good food (I assume), and good music (obviously – we're in *Nashville*).

"Huh," Blake says, and I snap out of my engrossed daze.

"What?"

He regards me with a faint smile, like he has been watching me for a while. "Nothing."

We keep moving, heading down Broadway, until I'm drawn to a sharp halt by a life-size Elvis Presley figure outside a souvenir store. It's the most Nashville-y thing *ever*, so I pull out my phone to snap a picture. I'm mentally preparing a witty caption and hashtag in my head when I remember that I have no access to my social media accounts anymore. And even if I did, it's not like I could post anything, anyway. Low profile, head down and all that. What a fun summer vacation, thanks to Ruben and, well … Dad, I guess. He did after all agree with Ruben that sending me here was the best decision. Not for me, but for his public image.

That thought runs through my head a little too intensely, stalling me. I don't really think that. I don't believe for a second that Dad really cares about his career more than he cares about me, but the tightness in my chest makes me wonder …

Wow, where did that thought come from?

"I think it's kind of unfair to count Elvis Presley as a country icon when his heart was mostly in rock and roll," Blake comments next to me. We are still standing by the figure, the photo I took displayed on my phone. I swallow and shove the device back into my purse. At least Blake is oblivious to my momentary standstill, and I welcome the distraction, even if it is only him babbling on about music again.

"You really love your country music, don't you?" I ask.

A flash of color rises in Blake's cheeks and he holds up his hands in surrender. "I'm a born and bred Nashville guy. What else do you expect?" He cracks a smile, then nods ahead. "There. On the corner. That's the promised land."

I follow the direction of his gaze and on the corner of the block Honky Tonk Central is bustling with revelers. The orange brick building is lined with balconies where people mingle in the fresh air, flashing lights flicker from inside, and I'm pretty sure a lot of the music I hear right now is coming from there. Groups spill through the front doors beneath the electric blue *Honky Tonk Central* signs. It's clearly the prime social hotspot, smack dab in the middle of Nashville's main street, but …

"It's a bar." I can't hide the deflated look on my face when I turn to Blake in confusion. Last time I checked, I was still only sixteen, and him seventeen.

"A *music* bar," Blake corrects as we walk down the block. "They serve food too, so we're allowed in. We just can't buy a beer."

I suddenly feel way out of my depth as we near the bustling building, so I stay behind Blake and follow his lead. After all, he says this place is his favorite and that he comes here often, so he must know the ropes around here.

When we reach the entrance, there's a bouncer manning the doors, which makes me panic that we'll instantly be turned away. I check Blake's demeanor, but his shoulders are broad, head held high, walk confident. What did his mother *feed* him when he was a kid? Protein shakes in a baby bottle? He looks way older than me, but still not old *enough*, because as we drift toward the door behind some middle-aged women, the bouncer sticks an arm out to block him.

"We start carding at eight, so make sure you kids are out of here within the next hour and a half," the bouncer says over the music. His hardened features transform into a cheeky grin as he drops his arm to let us through. "Don't make me come and find y'all!"

Blake gives the bouncer an affirmative, law-abiding nod and strides ahead into the bar like he owns the place. I wish he didn't move so fast, so swiftly, because he's dashing off across the room before I even get the chance to look around. On my left, there's a small stage where a woman belts her heart out to what I'm sure is a Carrie Underwood song. Her voice reverberates around the bar, booming from the speakers while people sing along and cheer. A huge wooden bar takes up most of the space, bodies packed all around it while beers flow freely, and groups of friends gobble down nachos at wooden bar tables by the windows. I've never been anywhere like this before. Everywhere I go with my parents is glitzy and formal. This is carefree, and fun, and homely. Relaxed. It's like an entirely different world. Even when we've spent time in Nashville before, Dad wouldn't be caught dead in a place as honest as this. He has developed a taste for the grander things in life, and places like these don't really match the A-list image.

Blake seems to remember I'm with him, because he stops and cranes his neck to look back at me. "Not this floor," he says, his voice muffled from the noise. He points upward. "We're going up."

We cross in front of the stage to a stairwell in the corner and head upstairs, the music from the floor above merging with the fading voice of the singer below. Others brush past us on their way down, all boozed up and cheerful, and I can't wipe the smile from my face. Dad would never, ever let me hang around in here, so I'm going to grab my chance to explore Nashville in all of its glory. And maybe even Fairview too, if there's anything there worth exploring.

There's three floors in this place, but Blake stops off on the second. We emerge from the stairwell into a floor that is a replica of the one beneath – a stage set up where a band in cowboy hats is jamming out to country rock, a packed bar at the opposite end of the room, and plenty of high tables spread out over the floor in between the bustle of dancers. I don't know what food I'm smelling, but whatever it is, the scent is drool-worthy.

We grab an empty table near the stage and my legs are so short I have to stretch up onto tiptoes to climb onto the cushioned bar stool. Blake watches, already seated, in amusement. It's easy for him – he must be, like, six feet tall.

"Welcome" – he spreads his hands wide and gestures around the heaving room – "to Honky Tonk Central."

"I like it," I say over the music, glancing over to the stage on my right. The band is young, but they're damn good. I'm not massively familiar with the genre, so I can't even tell if they're covering songs or singing their own. The guitar riffs vibrate from the speaker above my head and I'll be surprised if I leave this place with my eardrums intact.

"Wait until you try the quesadillas," Blake says. He flags down a waitress and orders some sort of appetizer platter to share without consulting with me first. He plays that natural-born leader role well, just like his mom.

I cross my arms on the table in front of me. "How do you know I don't have any allergies?" I ask when the waitress disappears to place the order.

He mimics my action, folding his arms and leaning toward me, brown eyes challenging. "*Do* you have allergies?"

"No."

"Then relax, Hollywood – I just want to show you the best that this place has to offer. We don't have much time here thanks to Myles dropping me at the last second, so let's enjoy this while we can."

He twists around in the bar stool to face the stage, one sculpted arm still propped up on the edge of the table, while I sigh at yet another of his little comments. He nods in sync with the beat of the drums and I notice the way his lips gently move as though he's murmuring the lyrics under his breath – I guess the band isn't playing original music – and the way the rest of his body moves. Shoulders swaying, fingertips tapping against the table, the neon spotlights flashing in his gaze. It's like the mere sound of a rocking country tune ignites something inside of him, because I think he forgets that he has company. He is enthralled, soaking up the atmosphere.

It's only when the food arrives that he snaps out of his

happy trance and that *I* realize I've paid more attention to him than I have to the band. My cheeks heat with embarrassment as though he has caught me in the act, but it seems that he's none the wiser.

The platter he ordered for us, I must admit, is delicious. It's a mixture of chips and salsa, mozzarella wedges, chicken quesadillas and buffalo wings. I try to eat as gracefully as I can to begin with, but soon I've spilled half a quesadilla down my shirt, much to Blake's amusement, and we both carelessly help ourselves until there's only one quesadilla left.

"Take it," Blake says, pushing the dish toward me.

I push it back. "No. You can have it."

"I won't argue."

He grabs the quesadilla and shoves half into his mouth with as much grace as a toddler eating spaghetti while I watch in repulsion. *Ew.*

"What?" Blake asks innocently as he swallows the food in his mouth.

"Do you have to eat it like that?"

"Like what? Like this?" There goes the remainder of the quesadilla rammed into his mouth and his chewing is exaggerated this time, all sloppy and loud while he looks me straight in the eye. He is definitely smirking in between all the chomping.

I can barely watch. "Gross, Blake." Even my cheeks hurt from how hard my face is scrunched up in disgust.

"Remind me never to take you out for ribs then," Blake says, rolling his eyes as he wipes a napkin over his lips. He scoots his bar stool in closer and rests his elbows on the table, hands interlocked in front of him as though he's ready to interview me. And, apparently, he is. "So, Miss Mila, what's the deal? Tell me one thing, because I can't figure it out. Are you happy to be here?"

I glance around the room and soak in the atmosphere all over again; the music that's full of energy, the smiles on everyone's faces, the free-and-easy laughter from those who are on their fourth beers, the rhythm of the dancers. I meet Blake's patient gaze. "I already told you I love it. It's different from what I'm used to, and the music isn't so bad—"

"No," he interrupts, shaking his head. "I mean are you happy to be *here*? In Tennessee. In Nashville. In Fairview." He pauses and the corner of his mouth twitches. "Home." The word carries a lot of weight and I wonder if it's so obvious that although Tennessee is where I was born, it doesn't feel like home.

"I … Of course I'm happy to be home," I start, though my voice wavers from the lack of a single ounce of confidence. "I missed my grandpa a lot, and my aunt too. I thought it would be cool to visit them for a while. And there's always something special about coming back to that place where you spent your childhood."

"Nicely played, Mila," Blake says, pressing his lips together. "But you're lying."

"Excuse me?" I blink at him, my tone sharpening with indignation.

"You're lying," he repeats. "You aren't here by choice. You said so at church."

Damn, I forgot about that. It was such a minor thing, simply saying I'm here for as long as I "have" to be, instead of "want" to be. I knew he'd picked up on my careless word choice at the time. I didn't realize it would have alerted him that there's more to my story, but clearly he's been waiting for the opportunity to dig deeper.

"Okay. So what if I'm not here because I want to be?" I snap back defensively. "What does it matter to you?"

Blake narrows his eyes at me, either surprised by my abrupt retaliation or the fact that I haven't bothered to deny his claim that I'm lying. He studies me with what I think is fascination, but I have no idea why he thinks I'm so interesting. "I think you're here for a very specific reason, and I'll hedge a bet that it isn't a particularly positive one."

"Hey, Sherlock. Stop sticking your nose into my business," I say, teeth gritted. I fold my arms and angle away from the table, locking my eyes on the band instead. My face is blazing and my heartbeat thumps in my ears; there's a pressure building up inside my head that's so intense the band goes out of focus.

But Blake keeps on pushing. Over the sound of the music, I hear him say, "You might think you're super important just because the world knows who your dad is, but trust me, no one around here actually cares that much. So how about you be normal and just tell me why you're really here."

"*Super important?*" I whip my head back around, stunned. "I don't think that!"

"Then why freak out when I told people who you are? Why be so secretive and defensive?"

He's waiting for an answer, fully aware that he's got me cornered. He presses his lips together and cocks a brow. I'm so furious I could smack him. How dare he push me on this? He doesn't know a single thing about me. Arms still crossed, my hands balled into fists, I glare at him across the table.

"Because I'm under a lot of pressure, okay?" I finally respond. "I'm trying to do the best I can in a bad situation, and *you* aren't making it easy."

"So, you admit you're in a bad situation?" Blake says smugly, knowing yet again he's got me tripping over my words.

"Okay, I'm done talking."

Suddenly, someone clears their throat next to us, but even that isn't enough to pull Blake and me out of our stare-off. Neither one of us wants to crack first. Blake's gaze is challenging, and I know mine is dark and threatening.

That someone clears their throat again. "It's after eight, folks," the voice of the bouncer says. "Can I see some ID?"

"Don't worry," I mutter churlishly, grabbing my purse and sliding off the bar stool. "We were just leaving."

Eye contact broken.

I want out of here, away from Blake and his nosy interrogation. I brush rudely past the bouncer and storm across the bar without even bothering to check over my shoulder if Blake is following or not.

Lesson learned: If a guy is such a jerk the first time you meet him that you end up in tears from his actions, never *ever* give him the chance to redeem himself. What was I even thinking, agreeing to come here with him in the first place?

I rush down the stairwell two steps at a time to the first floor. It's gotten busier since we arrived an hour ago and there's such a dense horde of people dancing in front of the stage that I have to barge my way through, but I finally make it outside into the night. The entrance is chaotic with people coming and going, so I disappear around the corner and find a quieter spot to steady myself. I press my hand to the wall of Honky Tonk Central, squeeze my eyes shut, and suck in a breath of warm, humid air.

"I'm guessing those great drama skills are in your genes?"

My eyes flash back open to find Blake standing a few feet in front of me, shoulder resting against the wall, hands in his pockets. The electric blue of the neon *Honky Tonk Central* sign shines in his glowering eyes.

"Because that was kind of dramatic to storm out like that," he finishes. "Not to mention damn rude."

"Rude? *I'm* rude?! Just leave me alone," I spit, barging my shoulder into his as I set off along Broadway. There's nowhere to go besides back to his truck and although getting in a car with him is the last thing I want to endure right now, I have no other choice. It's either get a ride home from Blake, or find a cab to take me back to Fairview since there isn't a direct bus service.

I hear Blake's footsteps behind me, his pace fast to keep up with my quick cadence. "Mila. Mila, c'mon," he tries. "Mila, *wait*."

Damn, that boy is persistent. I stop short and spin around,

and he's following so close that he collides straight into me. We both stumble, and he grasps my wrists, steadying us both. Aggressively, I snatch my hands from him, but don't turn away. I realize his body is mere inches from mine, our chests almost touching. Neither of us steps back, and I stare up into his eyes, giving him the chance to prove that it's worth waiting to hear what he's got to say.

"Hey, come on," he says, releasing all of the air in his lungs. "Don't be like that. I'm honestly not trying to upset you." Up close, his brown eyes are scattered with lighter flecks, almost like dots of caramel. "I'm just trying to figure you out." He gazes up for a moment, as if searching for words. "You know, because I'm probably the only person around here who might understand you."

I tilt my chin, drawing my face up even closer to his. "Why?" I demand, still fuming. "You think you understand a single thing about my life just because you're the mayor's dumbass son?"

Blake's eyes darken, and I almost flinch at the shift in his mood. He's the one who steps back first. "Exactly," he says flatly.

"You and me" – I motion between us, shaking my head, my voice rising as I storm on – "we are *not* the same. Our lives are completely different, so back off, *mayor's kid.*"

"Mayor's kid?" some passing guy echoes, coming to an unsteady halt. He jabs an angry finger out at Blake. "You're Mayor Avery's kid? Tell your mom to stop calling out for gun reform. The quicker she gets bounced from that office, the quicker ..." His slurred words trail off as the woman he's with drags him away, mouthing hasty apologies to us.

"Thanks for that," Blake says bitterly, turning his attention back to me. We are still standing on the sidewalk in the middle of Broadway while people weave all around us, but we both seem to have forgotten for a second that we aren't alone.

"You're welcome," I say, holding my head up high. "Just take me home. Please."

"Fine! But you deserve to be left here to take your chances with a cab." He pulls his truck keys out of his pocket and strides off, muttering, "*God.* I should've fucking invited Lacey."

I don't know who Lacey is, but I wish he'd invited her instead too, because this has turned into a disaster. We are both walking too fast, fueled by our aggravation at each other. Our mouths are set in rigid lines and anyone who sees us now must surely wonder what the hell is wrong with us. We don't fit in with the easygoing, energetic atmosphere. I'm energized all right, just in all the wrong ways.

"You can delete my number from your phone after this," I add hotly, unable to resist the pettiness.

"Now see? *That's* dramatic," Blake says with a sneer. "Get *over* yourself."

We turn the corner off Broadway and the parking garage is in sight. It's less busy here, and I cut in front of Blake and block him off from going any further.

"Look, Blake," I tell him, my tone dialed down a bit, "I don't trust you enough not to get me in trouble. So please just let this go and believe me when I say I'm here by choice, because I missed my grandpa, because I missed Fairview, and there's nothing else to it. Okay?"

"Even though I know you're lying?"

I swallow back the venom in my voice, and nod. "Even though you know I'm lying."

10

"He used to play in the cricks till the sun set, then come home for supper soaked through and covered in hives," Popeye says. "And one time when he must have been around thirteen, I had to get into Lake Van and drag him out by my bare hands. I could'a strangled that boy half the time."

It's late Friday morning and Popeye and I are relaxing together on the porch, drinking his favorite sweet tea while he shares stories of the past. The sun is exceptionally bright today, so I slump back in the canvas lawn chair with my legs crossed and sunglasses shading my eyes. Aunt Sheri is busy doing what Aunt Sheri does best – never quite sitting still, always keeping herself occupied with the maintenance and upkeep of the ranch. I can see her off in the distance, popping in and out of the stables.

"Did he always want to be an actor?" I ask Popeye.

"Not always," Popeye says, a slight tightness to his words. He's positioned in a shaded spot across the porch from me. It's so peaceful out here, breathing in the fresh air and basking in the warmth and the silence. "We thought it was a phase. Just a teenage hobby that he'd eventually grow out of. But oh no, he pursued it straight into college. It's beyond me that theater and drama is even a real degree."

I steal a cautious glance at him out of the corner of my sunglasses. Diving into the world of theater and drama *is* of course a real ambition to have, but Popeye seems disgruntled. "Are you disappointed?" I ask, treading carefully. "That Dad didn't stay here to help run the ranch with you?"

Popeye looks at me, and I quickly tilt my head in the opposite direction, so I don't have to meet his eyes. "Well, that was the dream," he says quietly. "I took over from my father and have been proud to carry on the family tradition, so of course I hoped for Everett to do the same. I would never stand in the way of what he wants, but I just wish he had a *real* job."

"Acting *is* a job, Popeye."

"Learning a script and fooling around on a film set?" Popeye scoffs, dismissively waving his hand as though he can't bear to even think of it. "That's an easy life … Sitting in a trailer getting his hair styled by three people at once – how can that count as *work*? I guess I'm a bit old-fashioned. All that hoo-ha for posing in front of a camera, I just don't get it," he grumbles.

"Learning a script like the back of your hand is actually really hard. Dad stays up all night sometimes, he's always walking around the house practicing his lines," I say defensively, Popeye's scornful tone making me feel uncomfortable. His son is a global superstar, his success recognized in every corner of the world … Surely Popeye can appreciate the hard work Dad put in to achieve such a status? Surely Popeye is proud of his son?

"Oh, Mila, of course I'm glad it all worked out. It would have been a real shame if his choice of career meant he wasn't able to provide for his family … It was a huge gamble," Popeye mumbles, thoughtfully rubbing his chin. "Still, even if the risk paid off, he should visit more often. Or even call. I haven't spoken to Everett since … Oh, since February."

"What?" I sit up and lift my sunglasses. "You guys haven't spoken in months?"

"No." Popeye's smile is cracked with hurt. "But don't you worry about that, Mila. I'm just glad that I get to speak to you."

I lower my sunglasses back over my eyes and stare off at the walls in the horizon, keeping us safe in our own private bubble. A million different thoughts race through my mind. I know Dad has been busy and he hasn't kept in touch with Popeye or Sheri as well as he maybe should have, but I didn't realize just how distant he really is. He hasn't called his own father since *February*? Visiting isn't always possible due to Dad's hectic schedule, I know that, but how difficult is it to pick up the phone every once in a while? And to think I felt guilty for only calling once or twice a month … But now it seems I'm the one who calls the most.

"Mila!" Aunt Sheri calls. She strides through the long grass, approaching from across the field. Her face is in shadow beneath a cowboy hat and she holds up the remote for the gate. "Your friends were outside. I've let them in. The technician did a good job for once – and the system is up and running again!"

Friends? I don't quite think I have any friends here yet, but I leap to my feet anyway and head toward the gate. It's fully open by the time I get there, and Savannah and Tori are taking apprehensive steps onto the property, their movements cautious as though the ranch is a minefield.

"Are we allowed in?" Tori asks. She spins around in a slow circle, taking in the ranch in all of its not-so-glory.

Ever since those walls were erected a few years ago, the ranch has been closed off to anyone who's passing by and that's probably left people wondering what exactly lies beyond them, but there's not really much to look at. People most likely imagine the ranch to be kept in pristine condition, with its own farmhands and pedigree horses and a newly built mansion home. *So* not true. The Harding Estate is nothing if not humble.

"Why wouldn't you guys be allowed in?" I ask with a laugh, gesturing for them to come forward and join me. Aunt Sheri must be watching from afar, because the gate begins to close behind them.

"Well, it's just..." Savannah starts, but then relaxes her shoulders and smiles brightly. "Never mind."

It takes me a second to figure out what she was about to say. *This is Everett Harding's former abode*, or something fan-girly along those lines. I shake the thought away and swiftly move on.

"So, what's up?"

"We thought we'd drop by and see how you are," Tori says.

The nose piercing she sported at the tailgate party isn't

there today and her look in general appears more conservative. I stare at her ankle boots, wondering how they don't make her feet swell in this heat. I'm wearing flip flops, which isn't exactly ranch attire, but at least they keep me cool.

"And my mom says Sheri still keeps horses," Savannah says with an excitement that really isn't all that subtle, her eyes roaming the fields over my shoulder in search of our stables.

Tori rolls her eyes and cups her hand over one side of her mouth as she whispers to me, "Yeah, she's one of those horse freaks."

I look at Savannah and smile. "So, you're here to saddle up?"

"Seriously?" Her blue eyes grow wide and she looks as though she may burst like a firework, childlike happiness radiating across her face.

"Sure," I say. "We all can."

"Wait, wait," Tori says, panicked. "Me? On a horse?"

"It'll be fine," I reassure her, even though my confidence is lacking just as much. I've helped Sheri out with the horses over the past week, sure, but grooming a horse – including brushing and braiding their mane – is a lot different than actually riding one. And I haven't done that yet; the whole galloping-around-the-fields thing. Sure, I trotted about on my pony, Misty, when I was six, but that feels like a lifetime ago. But I don't want Savannah and Tori to question my bloodline of ranch-owning relatives, so it's time to ramp up the courage.

We head down the dirt track road toward the house,

where Popeye gives us an enthusiastic wave from the porch, and then find Sheri walking through the field with a bucket in either hand. She seems skeptical and somewhat concerned when I ask if we can ride the horses, probably because she knows I have no real idea what I'm doing, but when Savannah assures her she has riding experience and will keep an eye on me and Tori, she loosens up a bit and agrees to let us take out the most calm and obedient horses she has. She leads us down to the stables and introduces us to our mounts, then she shows us (well, me and Tori) how to saddle up along with very detailed, specific instructions on how to ride.

"Do we *have* to do this?" Tori whines, securing the clip of her helmet. She stares doubtfully at the aptly named Domino, who stands placidly chewing on a piece of hay.

"You don't want to miss out on the gossip, do you?" Savannah says. She gives me a pointed look and the two of them exchange another one of those private, knowing smiles that only best friends have.

Gossip? What gossip?

"Fine," Tori huffs. "Let's go, cowgirls."

We guide the horses out of the stable and into the glorious sunshine. Every morning here is a gorgeous one, unlike the smoggy dawn skies of LA. My scalp feels hot already from this ugly helmet perched on my head, and I'm still wearing *flip flops*. I'm not fooling anyone – I am definitely not a country girl who rides her trusty steed off into the sunset, but at least Sheri seems highly amused as she watches us from afar.

Savannah effortlessly pulls herself up onto her horse, seated confidently while Tori and I struggle. Her French braids actually look nice under a helmet, whereas I must look ridiculous with strands of hair falling into my eyes and Tori looks just as silly attempting to climb onto a horse while wearing a skirt. My horse – Fredo – is patient, and I finally swing my leg over him while Savannah fights laughter. It takes Tori longer to get herself organized and by the time we're all ready to set off, there's a scowl etched onto her face.

"This is not what I consider fun," she grumbles.

We head off across the field at a slow walk, though I can't focus on anything besides trying not to fall out of this saddle. I wobble a lot, clinging onto the worn leather reins, praying that Fredo doesn't get spooked and gallop wildly off. Falling off a horse and ending up in the ER isn't the type of LA-detox I was sent here for.

"Mila, we have a confession," Savannah says after a while of peaceful strolling. For all we're complete amateurs at this, Tori and I do a good job of keeping in line on either side of her. We bounce along, our horses in a perfect row of three. I tear my eyes from Fredo's luxuriant mane and glance over at Savannah, who watches me with a teasing smirk on her face. "We're here because we want to talk to you about Blake."

Now *that* nearly knocks me out the saddle. His name instantly gets my back up. "Blake?" I say as nonchalantly as possible, staring straight ahead and trying not to let them see my triggered reaction at the mere sound of his name. "What about him?"

"You guys went on a date the other night," Savannah says matter-of-factly.

"Uh-huh," Tori says. She leans forward on her horse so she can see around Savannah, wiggling her eyebrows suggestively at me.

"What?" I splutter. How do they know about my night with Blake in Nashville? I didn't tell anyone. "We absolutely were *not* on a date. Did he ... Did Blake tell you that we were?"

"He didn't *specifically* use the word, but trust me, it was a date," Savannah says with a smug shrug of her freckled shoulders. "He took you to Honky Tonk Central! That's literally his favorite place on planet earth, and he wouldn't take just anyone there."

I blink down at my horse's ears, which twitch as if he's listening too, seemingly barely aware that I'm weaving my fingers through his mane. Savannah somehow knows all of the details, like where and when Blake and I hung out, and if *I* didn't tell her, then ... "Blake told you about Wednesday night?"

"Well, no," Savannah admits. "He told Myles, and Myles was kind enough to offer up the information to me."

Wednesday night was such a disaster and I cringe even thinking about it again. Blake and I fought in public, like two dumb kids who couldn't keep their attitudes in check, and ended up on such vile terms with one another that neither of us uttered a word the whole drive home. When we got back to the ranch, I jumped out of his truck, slammed the door shut, and never looked back.

Ugh.

And I thought about it a lot that night while trying (and failing) to fall asleep. It's not like I'm keeping some huge secret that will blow the world apart if anyone found out. In fact, I'm not really keeping a secret at all. I'm just trying to do what my dad and Ruben need me to, and that is to keep my head firmly down, be sensible, maintain a low profile, and don't do anything that will draw attention to myself. Because any attention drawn to me then inadvertently draws attention to Dad.

The worry isn't someone finding out the real reason I'm here, it's the wrong *person* finding out. It only takes one person with a malicious agenda or a desperation for some side cash to sell a flimsy story to the press about Everett Harding's daughter shacking up in Fairview for the summer alone. The tabloids would spin the story however they wanted – that I ran away, that there's a rift in the family; whatever they think will get more hits.

Which means that Blake ... Blake is definitely someone I have to keep at arm's length. No matter how hard he pushed, he wasn't ever getting the truth out of me on Wednesday night.

"Sooooo," Tori says. "Are you and Blake going to become a *thing*?"

I scoff, throwing my head back at how hilarious such an assumption is. Blake and me? A thing? The only *thing* Blake Avery is to me is a parasite that crawls under my skin.

"No way," I say, my words firm so that there's no chance of Savannah and Tori mistaking me for simply being coy.

"He told everyone at the tailgate who my dad is when it was obvious I didn't want anyone to know, and Wednesday night was … Well, it was truly bad."

"Really? What happened?" Savannah asks, surprise evident in her voice. Perhaps "bad" wasn't how she expected me to describe the evening, but it's one of the more pleasant descriptions I could have used. "All he told Myles was that you guys went to Honky Tonk Central and got food, and that he had a good night."

Now I'm the one who's surprised. "He didn't mention the fact that we blew up into an argument? And that we didn't talk the entire way home? And that I may have been *slightly* dramatic?" In hindsight, Blake was right – I was acting up, being a bit of a brat. Panic does that.

"Um, *no*," Savannah says with a stunned look. "Why were you guys arguing?"

"Ooo, angsty," Tori comments. "I'm pretty sure it's statistically proven that when two people keep clashing, it's because their fate is to end up together. So, Mila, sounds to me like Blake is your future husband. Count me in on bridesmaid duty."

Savannah ignores Tori's injections of deranged humor – which get nothing more than an eye roll in response from me – and asks again: "Why were you guys arguing?" She stares straight at me, but I can't hold her gaze long enough because I keep checking that Fredo isn't about to walk me into a row of trees.

"He kept questioning me about stuff I didn't want to talk about and being super rude," I admit quietly, deciding to trust these two at least. I hope Savannah and Tori don't take this as an opportunity to interrogate me too. "And I don't know what his deal is. It's like he gets a kick out of watching me squirm."

"Hmm." Savannah goes quiet for a while as we continue through the field, listening to the soft sound of hooves cutting through the grass and the occasional whinny from the horses, like they're chatting to each other too. Eventually, when she sits up straight again, her expression seems brighter. "I could be totally wrong here, but I wonder if he's just trying to shift the attention to someone else. It worked at the tailgate – everyone was talking about *you*, Mila. Don't kids who were bullied in grade school usually turn out to be bullies in high school or whatever?" She holds up a hand to stop me from interrupting, even though I had no intention to. "And no, I'm not saying Blake is bullying you. But the psychology is kind of similar. What do you think, Tori?"

"Since when were you this clever?" Tori asks, staring at Savannah in amazement as though she's never heard her best friend offer such a reasonable explanation. "But you could be on to something here."

Am I missing a piece of the jigsaw here? This is the worst part about being the new face in town. You don't understand people's backstories and the years of social foundations being formed, re-formed and carefully balanced.

"What are you guys even talking about?"

"*Well*," Tori says, taking over, "maybe you know this already … but Blake's mom is the mayor. The Mayor of Nashville. Which is, like, a super big deal."

"Oh, yeah, my grandpa told me. But that does remind me …" I say, narrowing my eyes at Savannah. "When were you going to mention that your *aunt* is the *mayor?*"

"I guessed Sheri might tell you." Savannah blushes sheepishly and adds, "It's not really something you slip into casual chat."

"ANYWAY," Tori continues. She moves her hands a lot as she talks, waving the reins around in the air. All of her attention is focused on me, because I'm the one who's out of the loop. "Fairview is a small town, and everyone knows the Averys. Kind of like how everyone knows the Hardings." She smiles. "So, Blake tends to get a lot of grief over the whole *my-mom-is-the-freaking-mayor* thing. Not in a mean way or anything, but his friends get on his back about it a lot. They're always messing with him."

"It's nothing major," Savannah adds. "Just remarks here and there, but I can tell it's getting old to him. Plus, random people he doesn't know sometimes give him a hard time over his mom's politics and stuff." I flinch at the memory of that anti-gun-reform guy in Nashville. "But now *you're* here. And no offense to my aunt or anything, but an A-list movie star kind of blows the whole city mayor thing out of the water. Which takes the attention off Blake for once." She taps her chin thoughtfully, gazing up at the blue summer sky. "And I wonder if he's relieved to be the one who can give someone hassle, rather than always being on the receiving end."

"That's one option, Oprah," Tori says. "The other is that he simply hates you and we're just overthinking this." She flashes me a grin.

I mull over Savannah's words in my head, willing them to make sense so that I at least have some explanation as to why Blake treated me the way he did. I get it – having a parent who's a public figure isn't the easiest thing in the world. There's a lot of pressure that no one else can really understand, and there's also a *lot* of rules. That's why I'm here in the first place, because living a normal teenage existence where my mistakes are simply a learning curve is *not* allowed in the world of keeping up appearances.

If there's one thing I've learned growing up, it's that Dad's job affects us all. He isn't the only one who has to stay in line – at least in the eyes of the public – his family does too. Mistakes aren't allowed. And I bet it works the same way in Blake's world.

I pull abruptly on Fredo's reins and am surprised when he actually comes to a stop.

"What?" Savannah says, pulling her horse around.

"Guys. Wait. Hold up," Tori calls over her shoulder as her horse continues to stroll peaceably off on its own. "Guys! How do I get him to stop?"

Right now, helping Tori out with her horsemanship is not the biggest priority. Savannah and I stare back at one another, our dialogue shifting to become only between us two.

"You really think that could be what this is all about?" I ask.

"I *am* his flesh and blood, aren't I?" she says. "That's why I also know he doesn't usually take random girls out. Maybe he's just showing his interest in the least expected ways."

She winks and then nudges her foot into her horse's ribs, taking off at a canter that builds to full speed across the field. She hunches forward, effortlessly holding on as the horse gallops through the grass, and the last I see of her face is a dazzling grin. I think she's been waiting for this moment all along, like a firework that has finally exploded.

"Savannah!" Tori screeches as her horse accelerates off in pursuit of Savannah's. Uh-oh. The horse is moving fast, throwing her body around in the saddle, as she clings on with all her might.

Fredo, meanwhile, stays put. Under the hot sun, I remain calmly seated and watch my new friends in amusement. Tori is wailing so loud the birds spook up out from the trees, but she clings on as her horse finally slows down to a more reasonable pace. Savannah, though, is pounding confidently around the field's perimeter with breezy laughter and no sign of launching a rescue mission.

I pat my horse along his graceful neck. "Fredo," I tell him. "I sure am glad I picked you."

11

"So, what I *really* miss is the pool. Like, it's so hot *all the time* but yet we don't have a pool here? Where's the logic? I'm dreaming of just diving in and cooling off."

"Ranches don't necessarily have pools," Mom points out. "And I don't think it's much of a priority for Sheri and your grandfather."

"Yeah, I guess … Maybe I'll have to do like the locals and try out the lake." I roll over in bed and prop my phone up against the lamp on my nightstand because my arm is growing tired from holding it up. I've been on this video call with Mom for a while now, filling her in on how life has been at the opposite end of the country. "Hey, you know what else I miss? My Twitter account. My Instagram feed. Do you think you can convince Ruben to give me back my social media accounts? Because he's being a hard-ass and it blows."

Mom frowns sympathetically, her face pixelated for a second. She's sitting, talking to me via her laptop, at our dining table, the same one where she held me close and reassured me that everything was going to be just fine a week ago. Of course, she's looking as glamorous as ever and the sight of her makes me miss the scent of her perfume. "I'm sorry, honey. You know it's out of my hands. I've tried to talk Ruben into an arrangement that works for both you *and* your dad, but he's getting really sick of me bringing the subject up."

"But how can he expect me to lie to my friends and act like I'm here for a vacation that I was desperate to take, when he won't even let me share anything about it online?" I give her a stern look, hoping for backup. "That's weird, Mom. If this was legit, I'd be posting on Instagram about how much fun I'm having. It would make this whole charade believable. But the fact that I've just completely disappeared off the radar? That hardly gives the impression I'm enjoying my *vacation*."

"Mila, I'm sorry," Mom apologizes again, even though none of this is her fault. She has as much power in the PR dynamics of Dad's career as I do, which is *zilch*. We are both under Ruben's thumb. "My own schedule is pretty packed, otherwise I would have disappeared off the radar with you! We could have gone to Europe together. A mother-daughter getaway to Cannes, Nice, Monte Carlo! Oh, imagine!"

"And miss all of Dad's events? You know what the gossip columns would say about that." I heave a sigh. If Mom and I ever dared to take off on our own adventures without Dad, the tabloids would have a field day.

Mom gasps, her tone mocking. "*Marnie Harding… Sunning herself on the Cote d'Azur – without Everett… Is there trouble in paradise?!*"

It's always nice to have someone else who understands,

even more than I do, just how difficult it is to live in Dad's shadow. It makes me feel less alone whenever Mom reminds me of her own pressure. She has things a million times worse, and if she can manage to cling on to her sanity, then I have no excuse.

"Do you guys know yet when I'll be able to come home?" I ask.

"The theatrical release is in three weeks," Mom says, resting her chin against her fist and staring off at something over to the side. "And I imagine for the first two weeks of screenings, at least, that the production company won't risk *any* bad press." Mom pulls a face. She is part of the industry, but still she knows it can all be a bit extreme sometimes. For most of us, there are bigger issues in the world than a fractionally underperforming movie.

I sit up and stretch my legs over the side of my bed, playing with my fingers in my lap. I stare at the floor, noticing the patterns in the wood. "Am I really considered such bad publicity for Dad?"

"Oh, of course not! But the tabloids . . ." Mom lets out a weary sigh. "You know what they are like when they smell blood, and those headlines last week weren't ideal, I must admit. It isn't fair on your father, and it isn't fair on you. But this is the life we live." She stretches for something, disappearing out of the frame, and then returns with a glass of white wine in her hand. She takes a sip and then sets the glass down with a clink. "Trust me, I'm on my best behavior for the foreseeable future too. You know the kind of thing . . . No unflattering facial expressions in public."

A figure drifts past her in the background, so quickly I almost miss it.

"Was that Dad?" I ask, picking my phone up from the nightstand so I can get a better look at my screen.

Apparently, it *is* Dad, and he must hear my question because he pops back into the frame behind Mom's shoulder. He has a phone pressed to his ear, nodding solemnly along to whatever the caller is saying. A pair of sunglasses rests atop his head as always, like they're permanently bolted there. I guess he's afraid of stepping outside without them. It's easier not to forget them if he never takes them off in the first place. He gives me a brisk wave and then disappears again.

"That's Ruben on the line," Mom says in a lowered voice. Her eyes drift around the room, following Dad I presume, and he must leave the kitchen because she raises her voice again. "Your dad's stress levels are through the roof right now, and Ruben is *not* helping."

"So that's why he's barely talking to me then?" I say flatly. "*High stress levels?*"

"Mila," Mom says sternly, defending Dad against my scornful remarks. She pouts her lips, immaculately painted a bold red. "You know how things are when there's an upcoming release. Life gets a little crazy. I've barely seen him lately either."

"That doesn't mean he can just forget about me." I can't help being petulant now. "Out of sight, out of mind, I guess."

"You know that's not true," she says, and she's right. I just don't like feeling as though I'm not any kind of priority for him, even if it *is* only temporary. "I'll check his schedule and specifically pencil in some time for him to call you, okay?"

So now I have to be *timetabled* into Dad's life? "Okay," I say, disgruntled but too fed up to point out how twisted this is.

"Now listen," she says, pointing her finger into the camera at me. "If you and Sheri are going to break Ruben's rules, *please* don't let him catch you. He gives me enough headaches as it is and I can't cope with him ranting."

"Can you try once more to convince him?" I plead, crossing my fingers.

"Mila, if I bring this up with Ruben *one* more time, I think he might burst a blood vessel. You know that vein in his forehead? The one that bulges when he's angry?" Mom can't hide her own laughter, so she takes another sip of wine to smother it. "Well, it's been *really* popping lately."

"Can you ask Dad to talk to him?" I try again. I don't laugh with her, because an angry Ruben is never a nice Ruben. His stress levels must be even higher than Dad's right now.

"That's if I can catch him in between phone calls..." Mom tuts, shaking her head in frustration. "But until then, just keep being super careful whenever you leave the ranch, okay?"

"I promise," I sigh, holding up my pinky, Savannah-style.

Mom laughs and I see her shoulders relax. "Now then, tell me what you're up to. Any plans?"

"Well, I've decided to conduct some research," I say.

"And what exactly are you researching?"

My gaze wanders to the window where the sunset is a bold orange on the evening horizon. I smile as I tell her ...

"A boy."

12

The next morning at church, I spend half of the service blinking at the clock and the other half burning a hole in the back of Blake Avery's head. We slipped in late, so we're squashed in at the very back of the hall. It's the prime position for staring Blake down. I've already decided that I'm going to corner him as soon as everyone spills outside into the sunshine.

And I know – I shouldn't be sitting in church paying more attention to a boy's neckline than listening to the preacher, but hey, I can't help it.

Blake is sitting up on the second pew with his mom, his shoulders broad and straight. They were slouched ten minutes ago, but I noticed the subtle nudge she gave him. Being visibly bored at church is clearly not the done thing.

When the preacher dismisses his flock, I scramble to my feet and guide Sheri and Popeye outside so that I can claim a good vantage point for spotting Blake on his way out. We're one of the first few people outside, so I claim a spot by some shrubs to the left of the church doors.

"Are you waiting for someone?" Sheri asks, shooting me

a funny look. She probably thought I was rushing to get home, so now she's wondering why we've stopped.

"Don't you … Doesn't everyone hang around to catch up after the service?"

"Not always. Lunch is already cooking, so we need to get going," she says, reaching for Popeye's elbow to stop him from sneaking off and turning him toward her van instead.

"Hold on!" I say.

"So, you *are* waiting for someone," Sheri says with a teasing smile. The churchgoers are slowly gathering outside, but I haven't spotted Blake yet. "Look, feel free to hang around and mingle. I'm sure the Bennetts will happily give you a ride on their way home."

Popeye gives me a cheery wave goodbye, and they disappear across the parking lot.

I remain in my spot by the doors, stretching up on my tiptoes for a better view, until finally I spot Blake and his mother emerging. I don't hesitate for a moment longer, mostly because I don't want to allow my nerves the chance to kick in, and set off toward them. They're drifting through the crowd, LeAnne's movements careful and elegant, and I abruptly step in their path.

Blake scowls at the sight of me; obviously he didn't expect me to come looking for him. I shoot him a wry smirk before turning to his mother with a pleasant smile.

"Mayor Avery," I say politely with a nod. How are you supposed to greet the mayor? Am I supposed to shake her hand, even though we met last week? Do I even call her "Mayor Avery"? If not … Well, too late.

"Oh, hi …" she says with a hint of confusion in her tone. Maybe teenagers don't tend to randomly approach her; either way, she doesn't seem that thrilled by the interruption. "Mila, isn't it? I hope you didn't get locked out of that ranch again."

"Luckily, no!" I fake a laugh. "I was hoping I could borrow Blake for a second. Blake?" I angle my body toward his and fix him with a sharp look, one that dares him to defy me.

"Sure," he says. "I'll be back in a sec, Mom."

Just like last week, we split off from the throng to gain some privacy, only this time I'm doing the leading and Blake is doing the following. I turn around to face him, fold my arms across my chest, and stare him down in my most dramatic way.

"Are you here to throw a sucker punch my way?" Blake mocks with an easy smile. He steps back and lifts his fists like a boxer shielding his face. "'Cause you sure do look like you wanna hit me, but just remember where we are. Church."

"Oh, stop it, Blake," I snap dismissively. "You're right, though, I'm not your biggest fan after what happened in Nashville. I'm okay with the idea of ignoring your existence around here for the summer, but there's something I need to ask you first."

Curiosity seeps into his gaze. "Shoot."

"And answer me truthfully, please. You owe me. Again."

The smirk falters and he nods seriously, pushing his hair back. Now is the wrong time to notice his arm flexed taut under the white sleeve of his shirt.

"At the tailgate party, you made sure everyone found out

who my dad is. And at Honky Tonk Central, you were asking me questions you *knew* I didn't want to answer," I start, arms still crossed. "So, tell me – are you just an asshole or, mayor's son, are you trying to put the attention on someone other than yourself for once?"

"Don't curse outside church," he says with a disapproving shake of his head.

"Blake," I say sternly. I'm not in the mood for games.

He surveys the assortment of waiting vehicles over my shoulder. "Where's your family?"

"They left. I'm going to ask Savannah for a ride home," I say flatly. His distraction techniques aren't the most advanced. "Just answer my—"

"Do you trust me?" he cuts in, dropping his hand from tugging agitatedly at the back of his hair.

"No."

He smiles knowingly, as though he didn't expect anything less of my reply.

"Let me take you home instead," he says. "But later. After you come back to my place."

"What?" I blink at him, completely taken aback. Go back to his place? Did he totally miss me telling him off right now? I'm not trying to hang out. I'm trying to get a straight answer – to understand what game he's playing. "I'm going home. Sheri has lunch on the stove, and also – oh, yeah – why would I ever go anywhere with you again?"

"Because let's not have this discussion here," he says. "No funny business, I swear. Just lunch, and then I'll answer your question *truthfully*."

I study his expression, trying to gauge the sincerity in his eyes. He doesn't look away, only lets his gaze bore back into mine, letting me scrutinize him. However much I hate to admit it to myself, he seems genuine. Like the same easygoing Blake who grossly chewed that quesadilla at the honky tonk.

"*Fine*," I say with a disgruntled huff, trying to ignore that little voice in the back of my mind telling me that this is a stupid idea. Wasn't Wednesday night already Blake's second chance? Am I technically giving him a third right now?

"Let's go," Blake says with that annoying dimpled grin.

I hesitate slightly – but if the only way he will give me an honest answer is to go back to his place, then so be it. I just pray this doesn't blow up in my face … again.

"Are you sure your mom won't object?" I ask. In the back of my mind, I wonder if Sheri will be okay with this. I didn't bring my phone along to the service with me, but she *did* say it was fine for me to catch a ride home later. Even if later means missing lunch at the ranch.

"Let's find out," Blake says.

We weave back through the mingling churchgoers toward Mayor Avery. She's engaged in chit-chat with one of the church elders, enthusiastically nodding while the gracious smile on her face never fades. Something about it makes me suspect it's forced.

I spot Savannah for the first time, expression blank as her parents talk to others. She catches my eye and gives me a friendly wave, but her hand suspends mid-air when she realizes I'm with her cousin. Her pleasant smile transforms into a suggestive smirk, and when she winks, I have to look away before I blush. Do she and Tori really think Blake and I have something going on? Because no, no, *no*. No way.

But then why exactly am I following him over to Mayor Avery to check if it's okay if I gatecrash their Sunday lunch?

My palms feel clammy as we reach LeAnne, but Blake knows better than to interrupt when she's mid-conversation, so we wait patiently alongside her; me staring at the scalding concrete and Blake staring at me. I pretend not to notice.

LeAnne says goodbye to the church elder with lots of pleasantries, then turns to her son, seemingly surprised to find him back by her side already. "That was quick," she comments. "I'm done here. Let's make a move."

"Can Mila come back with us?" Blake asks, sounding like a five-year-old, the words falling from his lips in a quick jumble. He seems a bit nervous, though I wouldn't have pegged Blake as someone to get anxious around his mother, even if she is the mayor.

LeAnne seems caught off guard by the on-the-spot question. She regards me carefully as though she is determining whether or not I am worthy of entering their home. "Of course," she says, but her tone comes across with a degree of caution. "There's plenty food because Blake here tends to guzzle down the contents of the fridge as though he's been starved for years." She squeezes Blake's shoulder and smiles at him in a way that never really reaches her eyes.

Blake doesn't return the smile, just shakes her hand off his shoulder. "I'm parked over here, Mila," he says.

As the three of us head over to Blake's truck, I can't help

but keep glancing at LeAnne out of the corner of my eye. Her stride is confident and purposeful, the same as Blake's.

We climb into his truck – me in the backseat, of course – and he blasts the AC as his Spotify library comes to life. We get going, pulling away from the church and onto Fairview Boulevard.

In the privacy of the truck, LeAnne kicks off her heels and says, "Wow, Mr. Jameson is truly the most annoying person I ever interact with on Sundays. Blake, remind me next week to avoid him."

I fiddle with my hands in my lap, trying to ignore that pressing feeling of being intrusive simply by being present. I'm, at best, a stranger to the Averys, but LeAnne clearly has no issue with letting her facade slip in front of me. I stare out of the window, pretending I'm not listening. Maybe she's forgotten that I'm in the backseat.

Only, she hasn't.

She cranes her neck to look at me, inquisitive. "So, you're Everett's daughter," she says. It isn't a question. Everyone knows.

Blake draws in a breath. "Careful, Mom," he warns. He catches my eye in the rearview mirror, the same way he had the first night I met him. "Mila doesn't like to talk about her dad."

"Oh," LeAnne says, her perfectly painted lips forming a literal "O". "I'm sorry, Mila. I didn't realize there were issues there."

"No, no," I say quickly, sitting up straight. The last thing I want is for the mayor to get ideas in her head about the

Harding family being a broken one, so I quickly correct her. "Blake just means I don't like bringing up the subject of my dad around people. I don't want everyone to … I don't want to draw attention to who he is."

Something like understanding flashes across LeAnne's face. She settles back into her seat and gets comfortable, watching the road unravel before us. "That makes sense," she says, then gives her son a sidelong glance. "Blake denies I exist half the time. Don't you, Blakey?" She pats his leg and he irritably swats her away.

"I don't deny anything."

She rolls her eyes as though this is a topic they often clash over, then to Blake's evident fury she turns off his music and switches over to radio. "Enough of those soppy lyrics, don't you think, Mila? Time for a change of tune …"

Blake looks at me in the rearview again. His jaw is clenched, his expression hard, and his eyes carry an apology. For what, I don't know. Sorry for inviting me? Sorry for his mom's not-so-perfect-mayor behavior?

We listen in silence to a talk show for the rest of the journey. It crosses my mind at one point that I have no idea where Blake lives – is he a ranch kid like his cousins? – and I spend most of the fifteen-minute ride surveying the surroundings and wondering what kind of house the Mayor of Nashville would live in. A mansion? A cute little bungalow? A ranch on the outskirts of town with security gates just like the Hardings?

"I would have thought you lived in the city," I try by way of conversation.

"I do," LeAnne says, but doesn't offer anything more than that.

"Mom has an apartment in Nashville," Blake explains. "But our family home is here."

I don't recognize the area of Fairview that we're in, but it's definitely not the north side of town where the Harding Estate is, and it isn't downtown, either. We're somewhere on the outskirts, maybe on the south side, passing a wide street of large houses, all of them spaced generously apart from each other. The truck slows and pulls into one of the driveways, coming to a stop behind a sparkling new Tesla.

So, the Mayor of Nashville lives in … a relatively normal home. Which is exactly what Savannah and Tori probably thought when they walked through our gates and saw the old ranch that Everett Harding once lived in.

I peer out of the window. The house may not be some exclusive mansion, but it's big and well-maintained. The grass around the property is freshly mowed and colorful flowers spring up from the soil. There's an American flag on a pole in the corner of the front lawn, swaying in the soft breeze.

"I'll start preparing lunch," LeAnne says as she slips her heels back on and steps out of the truck. Before she closes the door behind her, she leans back in and asks, "Mila, you aren't on any of those Hollywood plant-based diets, are you? You're good with meat?"

"Meat is fine," I say. "Thank you," I hastily add, letting her remark slide, even though I'm growing sick of people around here assuming that everything about me is *Hollywood*. Sure, I live in a seven-bedroom house within the gated community of Thousand Oaks, and *sure*, my dad is a movie star, but that doesn't mean I'll turn my nose up at honky tonks, or that I'm automatically on some strict celebrity diet (I absolutely refuse to be part of Mom and Dad's ridiculous protein-only one), or that I'm anything more than just Mila Harding.

Blake rests his hands on the top of the steering wheel, his eyes following his mom as she struts toward the house, waving cheerfully to the neighbor across the street, then lets herself in the front door. I'm not sure why we aren't going with her. Blake and I remain in the truck together, quiet and still.

"So … are we getting out?" I ask, releasing my seatbelt and placing a hand on the door.

"Holy crap," Blake mutters. "She *really* pisses me off." His eyes are still locked on the front door of his home, where his mom has just disappeared out of sight, and I notice he's gripping the steering wheel so tightly his knuckles are white.

Oh, so he wants to talk about his mom. I scoot over into the middle seat so that I can lean forward to get a better look of him. "Yeah, I kind of picked up on that. I'm sorry she insulted your music taste."

Blake laughs, but there's no humor in the sound. "In more ways than one."

"I get that she's the mayor and that means having a public face and a private face, but I didn't think she would be so – relaxed? – in front of me," I admit. After all, she doesn't even know me, so how can she trust me?

"Yeah, sorry, I didn't think so either," Blake says with a sigh. He lets go of the wheel, flexes out his fingers, then releases his seatbelt. He turns to look at me in the eye. "But I guess she sees you the same way I do."

"What – like someone you can taunt?" I half-joke.

Blake's expression falters. He presses his lips together, trying not to smile. "Like someone who understands how it feels to be under a microscope." He pushes open the car door. "*Now* we can get out."

We climb out of the truck and into the humid air. Blake heads up the driveway and I follow, but we don't make for the front door. Instead, he leads me around the back of the house and into a huge yard. It's fenced off and private from the neighboring properties. Wooden decking curves around the house where big bi-folding doors lead inside, and wicker furniture decorates most of the space. For some reason, I can't really imagine Mayor Avery sunbathing out here with a margarita in her manicured hand.

At the foot of the yard, there's a cabin. It's natural-looking, rustic wood, complete with windows and a big set of glass doors.

Blake strides ahead, already at the door of the cabin. "Welcome to my bachelor pad," he says with a grin, and I think how it's the first real smile he's given me today. He pulls a set of keys from his pocket. "You're okay with dogs, right?"

"Dogs?"

Too late.

The cabin door swings open and a bundle of golden fur

pounces from inside, hurtling across the grass toward me. Two heavy paws land on my stomach with so much force that I'm knocked completely off balance. I land on the grass, hard, and the beast jumps all over me, sniffing at my ears and licking my face.

Blake's apologetic laughter rings out as he grabs hold of the dog's collar and hauls it off me. I stare up at him, collapsed on my elbows on the warm grass while I catch my breath. Blake is holding back a bouncy Golden Retriever, its tongue hanging excitedly from its mouth as its curious black eyes remain fixated on me. Blake kneels down by its side, still holding tight onto the collar.

"Mila, this is Bailey," he tells me. He scratches under Bailey's chin, then leans in close to one of his furry ears. "And Bailey, this is Mila, okay? *Miss* Mila. Be nice to her."

"You have a ... a puppy?"

"Yup. My baby." He stretches over to grab a fallen stick from the grass and then hurls it across the yard, releasing his grip on his dog's collar. Bailey takes off after it. "Sorry, I should have warned you better. We're still trying to nail the training," Blake apologizes. He walks over and offers his hand to me.

"You're in luck," I say. "I *love* dogs."

I slip my hand into Blake's and he pulls me up, but with a little too much effort. I nearly fall straight into him. We stand in front of one another, barely a foot between us, our hands still interlocked. His skin is warm, his fingertips gently calloused. We mirror each other's stare and there's something in his eyes I don't recognize, something sparky and vibrant... Something that sets free butterflies in my stomach.

Bailey comes pounding back over, stick between his teeth, and I pull my hand free from Blake's.

"Hi, Bailey!" I say, kneeling down. I weave my hands through his soft, thick fur and then play a little round of tug of war with the stick.

My parents won't let me get a dog back home, despite me begging every birthday and every Christmas, because they believe it would be unfair to bring a pet into such a hectic lifestyle. I get their point, but it sucks. There's a lot of things we don't have time for these days.

"He likes it best like this," Blake says, playfully nudging me out of the way. He gets down on his haunches and grabs hold of the stick with both hands, wrestling to free it from Bailey's death grip. Bailey growls and snarls, as viciously as a ridiculously cute puppy possibly can, until finally Blake wrestles the stick free and throws it across the yard again.

It's hard not to watch, entranced. There's something rather adorable about watching a guy play rough with his dog under the summer sun while still in his slacks and a dress shirt, fresh out of church.

"Enough, Bailey," Blake says, breaking the spell. "Come on, Mila, let me show you inside."

Straightening up, we walk over to the cabin, where he holds the door open and gestures for me to go on in. He looks a little nervous as I step past him and into the cabin, which is essentially a man cave.

There's a TV mounted onto the wall in front of a couch

that's covered in blankets, a foosball table, and home gym kit that takes up most of the space in here, complete with a squat rack and one-hundred-pound weights. The walls are decorated with posters of musicians, and in the very center of the room, directly in front of me, is an acoustic guitar perched in a stand.

"I don't live out here or anything," Blake says as he closes the door behind us. Bailey has padded inside too and flops down into the dog bed beneath the TV, gnawing on his new favorite stick. "This is just where I relax."

I sit down on the edge of the couch and play with the hem of one of the blankets. My eyes circle the cabin one more time, the sunlight streaming in through the windows and lighting up every item. "This is cool," I say with an impressed nod.

"Yeah, I like it." Blake sits down on the edge of the foosball table. Anxious now, he stares at the ground and swings his legs gently back and forth. "So, I believe you're still waiting for an answer."

Oh, yeah. That's the reason I'm here in the first place, right? To get an answer out of Blake. Or at least *mostly* the reason...

I fold my hands together in my lap and straighten my shoulders, trying my best to look like I mean business so that he takes me seriously. I'm not in the mood for him to give me any joke answers.

"So, Blake Avery," I start formally, clearing my throat as though I'm an attorney, ready to deliver my closing argument. "You are so, *so* confusing. One minute, you're telling me you like my piercing and introducing me to honky tonks and shoving food down your throat in front of me – which, for the record, is gross – but is all still pretty normal."

Blake listens attentively, eyes glistening in the sunlight.

"But then out of nowhere," I continue, unfazed, "you put all this pressure on me, like you *enjoy* making me uncomfortable. So, Blake – are you a jerk, or are you just glad there's finally someone else who can take the attention off of yourself?"

"Did you rehearse that?" Blake says.

My expression hardens. "Answer me." (And yes, I did.)

"I'm not a jerk," he says seriously, his intense eye contact unnerving. "And I'm sorry if I ever made you uncomfortable, because I didn't mean to." Blake sighs and slips off the edge of the table. "You're right – usually the attention is on me. *Blake, does the mayor know you're drinking on school property? Blake, you better keep the music down before the mayor shows up.*" He moves closer, his expression earnest and his eyes only on me. "And then you show up out of nowhere, and I think: *Great, everyone will have something else to talk about for once.*"

"Convenient," I mumble.

His mouth twitches, fighting a smile. "Right. Convenient is *exactly* what you were."

"Oh. So, you do want everyone to talk about *me* rather than *you*," I say, my shoulders sinking. This is what I didn't want – a stir. Ruben's words echo in my head, all that crap about maintaining a low profile … But how is that possible in a town as small as Fairview? Nothing exciting ever happens – and then Everett freaking Harding's kid pitches up?

"Well, yeah," Blake says. He steps in front of the couch and props his arm on top of a rack of vinyls. "Most of Fairview High are wondering if Everett himself is about to show up too."

My heart sinks. I should have never gone to that tailgate party. And honestly, I should have never even befriended Savannah again. I should have stayed within the ranch boundaries, painted flaky woodwork, listened to Popeye's stories from the Vietnam War, and learned to take care of the horses with Sheri. I should have done what Ruben and my father expected of me – to remain silent, poised, and obedient, a perfect pixel in the Everett Harding picture, with no wriggle room in which to simply be Mila Harding.

"Mila?" Blake says with concern.

I look up at him, my heart thumping hard in my chest. "Did you not think –" I try, but my throat has gone dry "– that there was a *reason* I didn't want anyone to know who my dad was?"

The crack in my voice reveals my panic, and Blake moves suddenly to sit down on the couch next to me. He hunches forward, hands on his knees, searching my face for a hint of what exactly this *reason* may be.

"You don't sound pissed at me anymore. Should I be concerned?"

Bailey shuffles over and jumps up, paws on the edge of the couch, furry head nestling into Blake's lap. His tail wags enthusiastically, but Blake pushes him off.

"Not now, Bails," he whispers. He points firmly to the dog bed and Bailey skulks off to the other side of the cabin. "Good boy." Blake fixes his attention back on me, his expression intense. When I don't respond, he takes a stab at guessing. "You don't want anyone to know Everett Harding is your dad because you don't want everyone in Fairview kissing your ass? You want to make real friends and not fake ones? You're bored of talking about him?"

I shake my head. "I didn't want anyone to focus on who my dad is," I say, my voice flat, "because no one was supposed to know I was even here in the first place."

Blake furrows his eyebrows. "Huh?"

I turn to look at him sharply. "C'mon, Blake. You've already figured out that I'm not here because I *want* to be."

If he feels smug about being right, he doesn't show it. Instead, he relaxes back against the couch and stares ahead for a few seconds, pensive. "When I pushed you so hard in Nashville, it wasn't just for fun, Mila. I was giving you a chance to get something off your chest. Anything at all." He sits forward again, edging in slightly closer to me this time. His knee bumps mine. "So. Anything?"

I glance down at his knee by mine and instinctively pull my leg away.

I'm probably the only person around here who can understand you . . .

Those words of Blake's from our argument in Nashville circle inside my head, on a constant loop. I told him our lives were totally different, but when I steal a peek out of the cabin doors at the pristine house, I think of LeAnne. The

Mayor of Nashville, with her son under strict instructions to keep his act in order so that there isn't even the possibility of a single blemish on her record. A familiar feeling for Everett Harding's daughter.

I tilt my chin up and my eyes meet Blake's.

Maybe he *is* the only person around here who could possibly ever begin to understand me, to understand life as the kid of someone in the spotlight with an image to maintain. I bet there are a lot of people out there wishing to ruin the mayor's reputation, and Blake must surely be under pressure to act a certain way.

So, I take a deep breath and start talking.

"The *Flash Point* movies," I say. "The latest one hits theaters next month."

"Yeah, I know. The trailer plays during every damn commercial break on TV."

I give Blake the side-eye, and he holds up his hands apologetically and then mimics zipping his lips shut.

"The production company is convinced that if there's bad press about any cast members then the movie won't make as many millions at the box office. And the whole no-bad-press rule extends to family members, too. Like me."

"So, you're bad publicity?" Blake asks, intrigued.

"Only by *accident*," I groan. I sink my head into my hands and rub at my temples. Even now, I can still taste the sweet fizz of that champagne from the press conference. The final straw in the very, very short list of Mila Harding's mistakes. "The past few months I've done a couple of things that would be minuscule if I were anyone else, but in Dad's world they've been escalated into totally end-of-the-world stuff."

"Like?"

"Like being photographed giving the finger to the paparazzi. And TMZ have a video of me throwing up at one of Dad's events." I drop my hands from my face and raise my head, my cheeks blazing red. "If you've not seen it already, then please, please don't google it or anything."

"I promise I won't google the video of you throwing up," he says with a smile, his hand clasped over his heart. His knee touches mine again, but this time I don't shift my leg away.

"There's a lot riding on this new movie and Dad's every move is being scrutinized while they roll out the publicity campaign, so—"

"So, it'll be easier if you're not there to mess things up for him?"

Ouch. It's the truth, but still it sounds harsh hearing it from someone else.

I look up at Blake and his frown has both pity and empathy in it. Maybe he *does* know exactly how I feel. Guilt rises in my throat; I know my mouth should be sealed shut. Ruben would have me for dead if he knew I was about to spill this reality to Blake, but I can't stop myself. Knowing that someone else gets how it feels to have so much pressure hanging over your head – well, it feels … comforting. Comforting to know that someone else can't afford to make any so-called mistakes either.

"I'm too much of a risk," I murmur. "They don't trust me

not to stir up anything vaguely resembling bad publicity again. And the movie comes first."

"So, you're here until it's released?" Blake finishes. He evidently knows how these things work. He knows the lengths to which someone in the public eye will go to preserve their reputation. It's not just A-listers. The Mayor of Nashville can live without dramatic headlines, too.

"Probably longer. It needs to earn however many millions of dollars at the box office first. Dad's manager thinks I shouldn't even leave the ranch. I think he expects me to be totally incognito, invisible, but my aunt lets me *live*, obviously. So, yeah. No one was really supposed to know that I was here, I don't think. But now everyone does."

Now that I'm saying this out loud, I realize how ridiculous it is. I'm trapped in Fairview so that I don't potentially create bad press for a movie that I'm not even *involved* in. If only I'd not been hungover and humiliated that morning after the press conference, I could have fought my corner harder. I could have held my nerve and told Ruben that no, I wasn't going anywhere. And I should have dared to ask my father where his loyalties really lie.

"Don't you think it's hilarious how everyone assumes life is *great* when your parent is some kind of star?" Blake scoffs. Then his expression grows gloomy. "They don't know the half of it. Do you have any siblings?"

My throat feels so restricted now, I can barely speak. I angle my body into his, and our knees press closer still. "No. Do you?"

"No," he says, then rolls his eyes. "*So* great, right? No one else to share the burden with. All focus is solely on you. I *love* being an only child," he adds dryly.

"Yeah, it sucks. You don't *want* the focus to be on you."

"And I took it upon myself to keep putting you on the spot in front of everyone at the tailgate party," Blake says after a moment. Looking troubled, he remorsefully touches my knee. "Fuck, Mila. I'm sorry – I know you were so upset that night."

Transfixed by Blake's hand on my leg, I can't reply. I look at his fingers, the way his grip tightens as though he's unaware he's touching me. He follows my gaze down to his hand then pulls it back with a jolt. Pink flushes across his neck.

"I wasn't *upset*," I protest. "I was mad. There's a difference."

Suddenly, there's a loud rap at the glass doors of the cabin. Blake and I both start at the same time, yanked out of our bubble as I twist around. Bailey lunges from his bed and barks madly at the door, making my heart beat even faster. LeAnne stands outside the cabin, her hands pressed to her hips, peering through the glass.

"Lunch is served."

Her features are tight, and she does little to hide her disdain as she glances between Blake and me for a long while. Eventually, she turns on her heels and stalks back to the house, leaving me wondering if I imagined the disapproval in her look.

13

Inside, the Averys' home is exactly how I would expect the home of the Mayor of Nashville to be: elegant and pristine, slightly soulless, but with a half-empty box of election flyers in the corner of the kitchen.

It may be an old manor house, but the interior has clearly been recently renovated. The kitchen seems brand spanking new, with fitted gloss counters and an oven that looks barely used. Even the floor is covered in shiny, sparkling white tiles. And no one would ever know that a meal has just been cooked – already the dishes are washed and packed away, the stovetop wiped clean and the scent of disinfectant in the air.

"This way," LeAnne says. Still dressed in her pencil skirt and blouse, she plucks out a bottle of wine from a rack on the wall, grabs a corkscrew from a drawer, then crosses the kitchen into the adjoining dining room.

Blake and I follow her to a vast glossy table. The chairs are padded with silver crushed velvet, so luxurious that I hesitate to sit down, almost terrified in case I so much as leave a crease.

"You can sit here," Blake says, pulling out a chair.

There's music playing softly from a speaker somewhere and the scent of roast beef and all its trimmings fills the room, making my stomach lurch with hunger. Awkwardly, I sit down where instructed and toy with my hands in my lap.

Blake sits down directly opposite me; LeAnne takes the head of the table. There's three other empty chairs, but I get the feeling they aren't used much. As LeAnne sets the bottle of wine down on the table with a thud, I surreptitiously search her hand for a wedding ring. There isn't one.

The atmosphere, despite the luscious food and the poppy chart music, isn't all that comfortable. Maybe it's because Blake seems quieter than his usual self or maybe it's because of the look LeAnne gave me outside. Did she see Blake's hand on my knee? Maybe she's super protective of her son.

Blake clears his throat and pulls his chair in close to the table, distractedly piling potatoes onto his plate. "This looks great, Mom," he says, breaking the silence. "Thanks."

LeAnne gives him a weak smile and then pops the cork of her bottle of wine, pouring herself a glass.

"Mila," LeAnne says, turning her focus to me, "please feel free to start."

If there's anything more awkward about eating dinner with a guy and his mom, it's being expected to just help myself to the food. Like, how much beef do I actually give myself? How many carrots am I allowed? It's like those first few nights with Sheri and Popeye all over again, when I was tiptoeing around, trying my best to relax and be comfortable, but without overstepping in a home that isn't mine.

"Thank you for letting me come over," I say politely, joining Blake in serving up some of the dishes. "This all looks amazing."

"You're welcome, but you can thank Blake," LeAnne says with a pointed glance in his direction. Her tone is nondescript, blank. She raises her glass to her lips.

Blake glowers at her for a fleeting moment and they exchange a tense look, one that I can't read. All I know is that suddenly I feel very unwelcome here. But why?

"So, Mila," LeAnne says, swishing the wine around in her glass, "are your parents going to be joining you here in Fairview?"

Blake coughs. "I'll grab us drinks," he says quickly, rising from the table.

"Oh. Thanks."

I cast my eyes down to my lap as he disappears into the kitchen, leaving me alone with his mom. I lift my head again. "No, not this time. They're busy."

"I can imagine," LeAnne says. She sets her wine down and begins to plate up some food for herself too, forking up some beef and continuing, "You must live a crazy life out there. What with all those fans and paparazzi. How does your dad even begin to keep up with it all?"

I swallow the small nibble of carrot in my mouth. This is the last conversation I want to be having right now. Talking about Dad with a virtual stranger? Why can't she ask me if I'm enjoying Fairview? Or if it's nice to spend time with my grandfather again? Why does everything have to be about Dad and never about me?

"Yeah, it gets pretty wild sometimes, but I suppose you just get used to it." My voice is distant, disinterested. Hopefully, LeAnne will get the hint that I'd rather not go there right now, but just in case she doesn't I turn the focus on her instead. "But I'm sure you understand how it is. After all, you're the mayor."

Blake returns, caution written all over his face, and sets down a can of soda in front of me. He sinks back into his chair and studies me, then his mom. There's something really, really weird about the way he's acting, but I can't put my finger on why. Surely he isn't *this* nervous about having a girl stay for dinner? Especially when there's nothing going on between us, anyway.

"Yes, I am indeed the mayor," LeAnne says lightly, rolling her eyes. "But I tend to attract protests and hate mail, even the occasional confrontation at Whole Foods, while your father must have nothing besides hordes of adoring fans."

I squint at her and wonder if she is always this patronizing. "Actually, he has his fair share of haters," I retort coolly against my better judgment. "Someone once jumped a barrier and sucker punched him square on the nose. It's not all that glamorous."

LeAnne's face lights up. "Is that so? What a pity. Your poor father." She takes another sip of wine, the glee in her eyes unmistakable.

Blake abruptly sets his silverware down with a clatter. "Mom," he hisses.

She casts a dismissive glance his way, ignoring whatever

point it is that he wants to make. "So why have you decided to come to Tennessee on your own?" she asks me.

"My parents have hectic work schedules at the moment, so I thought I'd clear out of their way and come visit my grandpa and aunt for the summer," I say nonchalantly, never meeting her eyes, as I lie through my teeth. "It's great to be back."

LeAnne purses her lips in a show of sympathy and clasps a hand to her chest. "How *is* your aunt Sheri doing? I feel awfully sorry for her stuck across town on that ranch. Bless her heart."

"She's fine," I say defensively, my tone growing sharper. If LeAnne doesn't quit sounding so condescending, I'm going to find it impossible to warm to her. "She has Popeye – sorry, my grandpa. He keeps her company, along with the horses."

"Of course. But still, it's a shame her brother took off for Hollywood and left her to support your grandfather and that big old ranch all on her own." She shakes her head, as if in pity at the thought.

"*Mom*," Blake hisses again. "Can you please stop interviewing Mila?"

LeAnne stares him down. Clearly, she isn't happy about being scolded by her own son. I watch the two of them for a few seconds, unspoken warnings flashing in their eyes, the music still playing quietly in the background. I even hear a clock ticking from somewhere in the kitchen.

Blake is the first to quit their staring match. He pulls his shoulders into line and stabs his fork into the meat on his plate. "Mila, I haven't told you about my music yet," he says breezily, forcing us onto a different topic, saving me from his mother. But also – music? *His* music?

"Oh, no," LeAnne mutters. She pushes her chair back with a screech and stands. "I'm not listening to you talk about *music* again. I'll leave you two to it and finish my meal upstairs." With her plate of food in one hand and her glass of wine in the other, she strides out of the dining room and we both listen to her footsteps fading as she moves toward the central staircase.

I look at Blake, my mouth hanging ajar.

Mortified, Blake props his elbows up on the table and buries his head in his hands, groaning. At least I'm not the only one here who thinks the Mayor of Nashville is a bit weird. What *is* her problem?

"I shouldn't have asked you to come back here," Blake admits, dropping his hands from his face. "My mom can be … difficult."

"I don't think she likes me much," I mumble. We've both stopped eating and have set our silverware down, staring at the empty chair LeAnne has left behind. I don't think I'm imagining her disdain. The hardness of her gaze and the patronizing tone of her voice made her dislike unmistakable. "Did I do something wrong?"

I think back to the small – *very* small – handful of interactions I've had with LeAnne Avery. She became aware of my existence when I was locked out of the Harding Estate, and Sheri introduced me at church the next morning. I'm certain I was polite when we met. And today, the only thing I can imagine possibly doing wrong is either being a little too abrupt when I asked to speak to Blake back at church, or invading their meal together, or having Blake's hand on my knee. None of those things seems like reason enough to be spoken to with such blatant scorn.

"No, no, no," Blake says, shaking his head. "Trust me, the problem isn't you. The problem is my mom being bitter."

"Bitter?" I raise an eyebrow, intrigued. "About what?"

Blake momentarily freezes, appearing almost regretful. He swallows and bows his head, returning to his food. "Ah, nothing. Just forget it. We can finish up here and I'll take you home."

Silenced, I say nothing more. This is totally in the running for the most uncomfortable Sunday lunch ever.

I keep my head down and pick at my food, no longer hungry. Blake doesn't say anything else, either. He sighs every once in a while over the sound of the music that's still playing. Somehow, the buzz of chart hits doesn't quite fit the mood at this table. What *is* going on?

"Well," I try. "Are you at least going to tell me about your music?"

The strain in Blake's features fades, replaced instead by a warm shyness. "Another time. I promise," he says.

So I don't push it; he doesn't seem to be in such a friendly mood anymore.

We return to eating in silence. There's a lot of food still leftover by the time we've cleared our plates.

"Bailey can get it," Blake finally says, his voice lighter than before. He gathers up the empty plates, dumps them through in the kitchen, then grabs the dish of beef. "C'mon."

We're back to acting casual again, as though there's not just been this huge tension?

"Bails!" Blake yells.

He sits down on the edge of the decking, dish on his lap. I join him, but with a gap between us this time, and try to keep the confusion from showing on my face. There's definitely no leg brushing this time.

Bailey bounds across the yard toward us, tongue lolling as the smell of freshly cooked meat in the air catches his attention. This time he slides to a stop in front of Blake, obediently sitting and awaiting a command. Again, his long tongue hangs from his mouth. It kind of looks like Bailey is smiling – and I want to smile too.

"Paw," Blake instructs. He holds out his hand and shakes the paw Bailey holds up. "Other paw. Lie down. Good boy." He flicks a slice of beef into the air and Bailey snatches it between his teeth, slobbering all over the grass. Blake catches my eye. "Your turn?"

Well, how can I possibly say no?

"Bailey," I say in a high-pitched voice that's nothing like my own. I repeat the same instructions Blake gave him and a real smile spreads across my face as Bailey sits, lies down, and shakes my hand. Then I toss him another slice of meat.

Blake seizes this safe opportunity. "Things got a little heated back inside. I—"

His words die in his mouth when there's a loud rumble from behind us. LeAnne bangs hard against the kitchen window, enraged. "I was going to make sandwiches with that tomorrow! You think that wretched dog deserves prime cut meat?"

"Oh please," Blake growls under his breath. "*Fuck off.*" But, of course, it isn't quite quiet enough.

LeAnne storms to the doors and flings them open. Her hands are on her hips, her stance challenging. "Repeat that," she orders. "Right now."

Blake looks at her over his shoulder. "Nothing," he says in defeat. I can see how badly he *does* want to repeat exactly what he said, but he must know better than to insult his mom that much.

"That's what I thought," LeAnne says. She bangs the doors shut behind her as she disappears, but I become hyperaware that she may still be watching us from the windows again.

I scoot a *little* bit further away from Blake.

"I'll drive you home now – it's best that you don't see me losing it with her," he says quietly. He dumps the dish of food on the grass and gives Bailey free rein to dive in, then fishes out the keys to his truck as he stands. "Because she's really, really pushing it today."

14

There's a definite tension in the air during the drive back to the Harding Estate, but for once that tension isn't palpitating between Blake and me. No, it's only Blake who is on edge.

The entire, uneventful drive across Fairview, his teeth have been clenched and his attention focused fully on the road ahead, barely blinking. Of course, music plays from the speakers, but the volume is low, and he doesn't hum along like he usually does. It's clear his anger is fueled by the peculiar interactions with his mom back at his house, though I'm nowhere near putting my finger on what exactly is wrong. Is he angry at his mom for her questions over dinner? Do they simply not get along? There was no way I'd anticipated that level of strain in their relationship.

When we pull up outside the huge Harding gate, I know I have approximately five seconds to say something other than goodbye. So, I sit forward and ask, "Are you okay?"

The truck comes to a stop and Blake kills the engine, his movements lethargic. "Yeah." He plays with the keys dangling from the ignition. "I just know I have to go back and face her."

If Blake can coerce me into telling him the truth about my dad, then I don't believe I'm crossing any boundaries by pressing the matter further. "Face her about what?"

"About the comments she made over lunch." Blake frowns and props his elbow up against the window, angrily weaving his fingers into his hair. "You'd think a woman in her position wouldn't be so damn childish."

"Childish?" I arch a brow. Sure, LeAnne's questions were invasive and her responses patronizing, but I assumed that was just her true personality shining through.

"Making those comments about your family," Blake mumbles. He sounds irritated all over again, but I can't get a good look of his face. He's still staring out of the window, staring off across the empty fields. "It's pathetic. All because . . ."

"What did I do?" I cut in.

"It's not about you." Blake snaps his head around to look at me. "It's about your dad."

"My dad?" I blink, because his words make zero sense to me. "But she doesn't know him."

Blake looks at me as though I'm naive for not understanding what the hell he's talking about. All he says is, "Fairview is a small town, Mila."

I still don't get it, but there's no time to ask Blake for a dumbed-down version of the point he's trying to make. The buzzing of the gate rings out across the empty road and a figure comes bounding out from the inside.

"Where have you been?" Sheri yells into my face as she yanks the truck door open. "Your grandpa and I have been worried sick, Mila! You never showed up after church! I called Patsy to check if you were over at their ranch, only to be told you never even asked them for a ride!"

Before I can respond, Blake clears his throat and leans over the center console. "Miss Harding, my apologies. But I invited Mila back to my place for lunch. It's my fault. It was spur of the moment and we lost track of time." He gives a conciliatory smile.

Sheri doesn't reciprocate. In fact, this is the first I've ever seen her so angry. There are deep lines of frustration in her brow. "You couldn't answer your phone? You couldn't send a simple text?" she asks me.

"I'm sorry, Sheri. I didn't take my phone to church . . . You said phones weren't allowed." I've definitely overstepped the line by disappearing for two hours. The worry in Sheri's eyes stirs up guilt within me, because, after all, she's doing me a favor taking me in. And she obviously cares about me. The least I could do is make her aware of my whereabouts like we agreed. "I'm really sorry," I apologize again.

Sheri heaves an exasperated sigh and steps back from the door, gesturing for me to get out. She waits silently as I step out of the truck, but it's clear she has more to say. Just not here.

"Thanks for the ride," I tell Blake, looking back into the truck at him. I have more to talk about with him too, but it'll have to wait.

He salutes me goodbye with a small smile and the truck pulls away.

Sheri clamps a hand around my shoulder and steers me

toward the gate. I can feel her worry radiating through her fingertips. We head onto the estate together as the sound of Blake's truck dies in the distance. He's going home to face LeAnne Avery; I'm about to face Sheri Harding. And I'm thinking that I have no idea what it means to face Sheri.

Her hand still on my shoulder, we walk slowly up the dirt track to the house, the sun blazing overhead. I keep my head down and wait for her to speak, but she stays silent. When we reach the porch, she steps in front of me and folds her arms across her chest, her expression more panic-stricken than stern.

"I really didn't mean to scare you," I say quickly. "I got talking with Blake after church and –"

Sheri shakes her head to silence me. "Mila, while you're here, you're my responsibility, and we *agreed* that you would tell me where you are at all times. When you didn't return from church and the Bennetts had no clue where you were either, I thought I would have to call Everett, or that dreadful manager of his, and tell them that I had no idea where you were. I thought I would have to tell them I've been letting you go off by yourself."

I lunge forward and wrap my arms around my aunt, holding her close. Sheri's chest heaves against me and I feel her starting to relax.

"I'm sorry, Sheri," I say thickly, feeling genuine guilt. Sheri is a few inches taller than me, but nonetheless I soothingly rub her back as though our roles of parental care have been reversed.

Sheri straightens up and runs her hand over her weary face. "Mila, sweetie, let's take this inside."

Together we advance up the porch steps where I spot Popeye peering through the window, one hand cupped over his brow to squint through the blinding sunlight. As we near the front door, he hurries to meet us.

"Is everything okay?" he asks, his face lined with concern. He stretches out a hand.

"Yes, Dad, everything is okay," mumbles Sheri, slipping her hand into Popeye's and giving it a reassuring squeeze. "Mila forgot her phone. She was at the Averys'. For lunch."

"Oh, he won't like that." Popeye tenses. "Lunch with –"

"Who won't like what?" I question.

Sheri casts a cautious look at her father.

"Who?" I repeat, harder. "Who won't like it?"

Sheri chews her cheek again, a telltale sign that she's mulling over whether or not to spill information to me. "Everett – your dad . . ."

". . . does not like LeAnne Avery," Popeye finishes.

"Why? Because of her policies or something?" I say, confused. "Why would he care about the mayor when we don't even live here?"

"Oh Mila," Popeye murmurs, his real eye now twinkling at me. "So blissfully unaware."

"*What?*" I push.

Sheri walks to the kitchen and pulls out a chair at the dining table. I hadn't noticed the scent of food lingering in the air until now, but a fresh pang of guilt hits me when I spot some foil-covered dishes over on the counter

– presumably leftovers that would have been my share of the meal.

There's the *tap tap tap* of Sheri's fingertips against the oak table, a hum of contemplation in the air. "It really isn't my place to bring it up," she says after a moment. "You should talk to your parents."

"I should talk to my parents about Mayor Avery?" I say, nonplussed. I mean, why would my parents even know who the Mayor of Nashville is?

"Yes, because your grandpa is right. Everett and Marnie would not be thrilled to discover that you've been visiting LeAnne's home," Sheri says, her mouth twitchy. Then, as an afterthought, she adds in a low voice, "Or that you seem to be getting cozy with her son."

"Blake? No – no, there is definitely no coziness between us."

Sheri shoots me a knowing smile. With her foot, she kicks out the chair next to her and gestures for me to join. "Dad, do you mind giving us a minute? Mila and I need to finish our conversation."

Popeye grunts. "I may as well just be a piece of furniture these days," he grumbles. He spins around and advances across the living room, but before he heads out onto the porch, he says, "Y'all be nice to one another."

Sheri waits until the creaking in the floorboards fades away, then fixes me with a penetrating stare. "I'm sorry if I raised my voice at you before. I was just . . . I thought – well, if you didn't show up, I thought Ruben would personally hop on a jet over here to throttle me with his bare hands."

Still nervy, I snicker at the image. I don't think Sheri and Ruben have ever met, but it says a lot about Ruben's intense management regime that people are terrified of him just from the way he treats them over a phone line.

"It's not funny, Mila," Sheri says sternly, looking down her nose at me. For a second, I fear she may get cross again. "They don't want you out of my sight."

"*They?*" I repeat, holding my breath.

Sympathy flits across Sheri's gaze. "These go-nowhere, see-no-one orders of Ruben's? They were your father's idea," she says.

I exhale sharply. It feels like a punch to the gut. It's *Dad* who wants me to remain locked in this ranch for the summer, with no freedom and no life of my own?

All – for – a – fucking – *movie*?

I know to expect these things from Ruben; it's his job to manage Dad's career and that means Ruben ultimately has the final say if he truly believes his decisions are for the best. It made sense until now that this was all Ruben's idea. I could survive knowing this was just Ruben being Ruben, with his bizarre stunts and overreactive measures, but to hear that Ruben, for once, is following Dad's orders . . . Wow, that hurts.

Dad wanted this. He wanted me here, thousands of miles away from Mom and him, locked up and silenced in the old family ranch. He *chose* this as a summer for me.

The feeling of being second best to Dad's work is one I've always told myself I've imagined. I have shaken off the endless, rolling tides of resentment and jealousy and convinced myself that sometimes, like when Dad's latest project is due for release, it's normal for his career to be at the forefront of his mind. It's okay that he doesn't have time to have breakfast together in the mornings before school, it's okay that there's a conflict in his schedule that prevents him going out for dinner with Mom and me, because he's *busy*. Once the initial rush of excitement from the movie's release is over, he'll turn his focus to me again . . . Except, he never quite does.

And now . . . Now I know, as clear as the blue skies outside, that it's true.

Dad's career *does* come first. Otherwise, he would never have removed me from his picture-perfect life simply because I dared to smudge the frame without even meaning to. If I were of the utmost importance to him, he would have told the production executives to shove it. He would have told Ruben to lay off me. He would have kept me at home where I belong, no matter how many more times I messed up. But now there is no denying that I'm not his priority.

Tears scorch my eyes and I blink fast to keep them at bay.

But then a kind hand squeezes my thigh.

"I didn't want to let you know that," Sheri says regretfully, scooting her chair in closer. "But I need you to know how serious this arrangement is. Your dad will not be happy if he finds out I'm giving you freedom, and you're old enough to notice that we don't have the best relationship as it is."

I fasten my damp eyes on her. "I'm sorry," I apologize once more. "I really do appreciate what you're doing for me, and the last thing I want is to make life difficult for you. I promise this won't happen again."

"Thank you, Mila," she says with genuine relief, and then her eyes crinkle at the corners with a knowing warmth. "Next time you're out with a certain *boy* named Blake Avery, you make sure you give me the heads-up. Promise?"

15

On Friday afternoon, I trek the mile or so to the Willowbank ranch with a box of apple stack cake positioned carefully in my arms. Sheri exhausted herself over this so-called Tennessee favorite – *Mila, how can you not know what Tennessee Mountain Cake is?* – for hours in the kitchen yesterday morning while the scent of spiced apple lingered all through the house. And now the dessert has set overnight and is ready to be delivered to those it was baked especially for – the Bennetts. In Sheri's words, this masterpiece is an apology for frightening Patsy last weekend over the whole "Didn't you give Mila a ride home from church?" episode. I have been given the pleasure of acting as messenger, because it gives me a suitable excuse to leave the ranch.

Over the past few days, Sheri and I have kept to our agreement perfectly with no slip-ups this time. She lets me go beyond the Harding Estate gates whenever I so desire, as long as she knows where I'm off to and I'm back by the curfew she specifies, which is never all that strict. But I've been reasonable, and haven't taken advantage. I'm well aware now of the risk she's taking. Savannah and Myles picked me up one evening and we drove by McDonald's for sundaes, and I walked three miles to the nearest store and back to buy two big bags of Cheetos. However, I've quickly realized that, when residing at a ranch in the middle of nowhere and with only a learner's permit to my name, there aren't that many options available to me. That's why Fredo and I are becoming such great friends – I saddle him up every morning and take him out into the fields for a gentle trot. Nothing more, because I'm still too afraid to pick up any speed in case I end up breaking my spine.

But today, I have the purpose of delivering a cake, and I walk with a spring in my step and a Dodgers cap shading my face from another day of blazing heat. My face is so weather-beaten from being outdoors that if I sprout any more freckles across my nose and cheeks I may just become unrecognizable to my friends by the time I return home.

The Bennetts' three-story farmhouse looms before me as I near Willowbank ranch and a dismal feeling settles in the pit of my stomach. When Savannah looks out of her bedroom window, she can see for miles across the rolling countryside, off into the cluster of trees beyond. When Sheri and Popeye look out of their windows, their view is partially blocked by the walls in the distance. It's another reminder of the impact Dad's demands have on people around him.

Dad, who I keep trying to push to the back of my mind. His disregard for what will keep me happy still hurts and I'm not ready to process it. I haven't even raised it with Mom yet because it's obvious she too believes this is all Ruben's doing, so I've stayed clear of the topic and instead emphasized how *boooooring* the Harding Estate is in hopes that she'll pass this information on to Dad. If I want to continue enjoying some freedom, he and Ruben need to believe I don't have any at all.

"Mila!"

The sound of Savannah's voice snaps me back to reality. It's a welcome distraction from the confused, negative thoughts that swell and churn inside my head.

"Hey! Is your mom around?"

Savannah jogs over to greet me, her expression seeming pleasantly surprised by my unexpected visit. She's wearing jean shorts and a bikini top, with a huge straw cowboy hat atop her head. Dangling from her ears today are two plastic, neon ice-cream cones. Cute. "Yeah, she's somewhere out in the field checking a water mains with Dad. What's that you've got there?"

"Aunt Sheri's famous Tennessee Mountain Cake," I announce with gusto, holding the cardboard box up and tantalizingly flipping open the lid. "Made fresh yesterday morning and delivered, obviously, by yours truly."

"Ohhh, I *love* stack cake!" Savannah says as she peers hungrily into the box. "Let's go put it in the kitchen."

I shut the lid and follow Savannah toward the house. The strong odor of sunscreen tickles my nose as we start up the porch steps. "Have you been sunbathing?"

"Well, of course," she says. "I don't like water – you know I nearly drowned in a lake during a family trip to Kentucky once when I was eight? Oh, it was *awful*. My life flashed before my eyes that day and ever since I don't go near water.

177

Honestly, in my eyes our pool is nothing but a death trap, so I prefer to stick to the daybed."

Precariously balancing the cake box in one arm, I reach out and grasp Savannah's wrist, mostly to silence her irrelevant babbling. "Savannah, my weight has dropped by five pounds from sweat alone because of the sheer humidity here, and you didn't think to mention that you have a pool?" I deadpan.

"Oh! I'm sorry," she says, flushed. She hits her forehead with the palm of her hand. "Yes, we have a pool! It's behind the house. But I think it's rather stupid for the entire pool to be one depth – no one thought my idea of having a shallow end was worth any consideration – so even if I *did* trust the water, I wouldn't even be able to touch the floor anyway."

"I'll trade you the Harding horses for the Willowbank pool," I blurt, cutting her off. This is a matter of desperation. "You can come over to our place and ride Sheri's horses whenever you like, if you please, please, *please* let me use your pool sometimes. You have no idea how much I've been dying to dive into one on days like these."

Savannah lifts the brim of her hat and the shadow over her eyes disappears, the sunshine glowing against her skin. "Um – *ab-so-freaking-lutely*!"

My grin mirrors hers, but before we can continue up into the house, a bark tears through the peaceful ranch.

At the foot of the porch steps, I twirl around to search for the source of the noise – is Savannah Bennett lucky enough to have a pool *and* a dog? – but am surprised to find a familiar Golden Retriever puppy pounding across the grass. He's hurtling toward us at a great speed, tongue lolling, tail wagging. My grin widens, but as he grows nearer, I realize Bailey shows no signs of slowing down, and my joy quickly transforms into alarm.

I clasp my arms tightly around the box of Sheri's cake and hug it to my chest, but I haven't secured it quickly enough. With another bark, Bailey lunges toward me. An involuntary gasp leaves me as I fall back against the porch's wooden handrail under the impact of the determined dog and the box is knocked out of my hands. Bailey presses his paws against my chest and licks my face.

"Oh, Bailey, *no!*" Savannah groans, reaching for his collar and tugging hard. "Down! Down!"

With a mighty shove, I push Bailey off me, but as he drops back down to the ground, his front paws promptly land heavily on top of the cake box. The crushing of cardboard and the squash of Sheri's apple stack cake makes me cry out in horror.

"Uh-oh," Savannah says. "Oops."

Bailey shoves his nose inside the damaged box and immediately chomps down on the cake. I exchange a panicked look with Savannah, who sheepishly bites her lip, before attempting to haul the dog away from the box.

"No, Bailey, STOP!" a voice yells. "What is he eating?"

Both Savannah and I look over. Blake runs toward us from the same direction that Bailey emerged from thirty seconds ago. If I wasn't so shocked, I would remember that this is the first I've seen him since the latest of our awkward encounters on Sunday.

"Blake! Will you control your dog!" I holler, marching a few steps forward and pointing at Bailey, whose nose is covered in sponge cake and spiced apples. "He just ... HE JUST RUINED SHERI'S CAKE!"

Blake arrives at the scene of destruction and drops to his haunches, hooking his arms around Bailey and dragging him back from the mangled box. Bailey happily licks the remaining cake from around his snout, and Blake holds him firmly between his legs. He pushes his sunglasses up into his ruffled hair and tilts his head up to meet my furious glare.

"She spent hours making that cake! I was supposed to deliver it!" I fume. "INTACT!"

"Mila, I'm s–sorry," Blake tries, but he can't get the words out. There is no attempt to suppress it – his full, hearty laughter fills the air.

"What's going on?" Myles asks, joining the three of us. He's dripping wet, barefoot and only wearing soaked swim trunks. He peers over Blake's crouched figure as if he's wondering what the chewed cardboard and mushed food used to represent two minutes ago.

"Bailey destroyed my aunt's cake," I say sullenly.

Blake howls with another bout of laughter. Myles joins in and then the two of them are snickering together, their guffaws growing louder and louder. The hilarity gets to Savannah as well, though she is at least trying to stifle her giggles. It's infectious and I break out into laughter too.

"What am I supposed to tell Sheri?" I ask through our symphony of chuckles. I glimpse at the destroyed cake again and clutch my sides as I laugh even harder.

"Tell her we loved the cake," Savannah says, stepping down from the porch steps. "It was so delicious we demolished it in seconds." She can hardly stop giggling at her own joke, but then splutters, "I'll get rid of this before Mom sees."

Blake drags a happy-looking Bailey back around the house with Myles, still guffawing, and I stay with Savannah to clean up. We scoop up whatever is left of the splattered cake and box with a dustpan and dump it straight into the outdoor trash so that Savannah's parents don't find out about the delicious baked goods they've missed out on. With a pinky promise, Savannah and I declare that Sheri will never know quite how enthusiastically her friendly culinary offering was received.

"Would you like to stay for a while?" Savannah asks. "We're hanging by the pool. It's just me and those two idiots. And let me just remind you that those two idiots are my brother and *Blake*." She smirks as she emphasizes his name.

"There's nothing going on with Blake!"

"Oh, c'mon!" she says with a sigh and an eye roll. She takes my elbow and brings me with her.

We head deeper into the field and around the back of the farmhouse, where my chest expands with a wave of happiness at the sight of *water*. The Bennetts' pool is larger than I dared hope it might be, circular and full of plastic soccer balls that bob along the water's surface, and along its edge there's a few scattered loungers.

"Are you joining us?" Myles calls from the opposite end of the pool. When I nod, he gives a playful wolf howl and dives headfirst into the water. A tidal wave splashes over the loungers, much to Savannah's annoyance.

She tuts and groans as she stalks over and angrily drags them further back from the pool. Myles screws up his face and sneers at her as he emerges from the water, and she hurls one of the plastic balls at him. He ducks back into the water before it can bounce off his head.

"Please sit next to me," Savannah says, beckoning me over. "I like to think he wouldn't be rude enough to try and soak a guest."

I join her, perching myself on the lounger next to hers. Heat radiates from the material and I gaze longingly at the vibrant blue, rippled water, craving more than ever to dive straight in. Savannah, who has already announced her fear of the water, has flattened herself against the lounger and returned to reading a worse-for-wear copy of a book about a certain famous bespectacled wizard.

"I love those movies!" I say avidly. "We actually went to the New York premiere of the final movie like ten years ago. It was the first premiere we ever went to." A wistful smile spreads across my face. I was too young at the time to take much in, but somehow I possess the deeply ingrained memory of Dad exchanging hellos with Daniel Radcliffe.

Slowly, Savannah lowers the book and gapes at me. "*Seriously?*"

The fascination and pure disbelief in her blue eyes bring me instantly back down to earth and I regret saying anything. I wipe the smile from my face and ruefully draw my shoulders inward.

"Sorry – that – that sounded like I was bragging, didn't it?" I mumble. Coming across to others, especially others whose everyday world is so different from mine, as a spoiled Hollywood kid is the last thing I ever intend to do.

"No! No! Tell me more!" Savannah urges, jolting upright and throwing the book off to the side. "I don't think you're bragging. You're just talking about your life, and you just happen to live a super cool one. Did you meet the cast?"

"I can't really – well, I was seven. It's kind of a blur," I say quickly. No matter what Savannah says, I would still rather change the subject to something other than how out-of-the-ordinary I am.

My gaze drifts over her shoulder, searching for an out, and I find Blake. He's by a water hose, firing the water erratically into Bailey's mouth. For the first time, I spot his truck parked on a sloped patch of grass. I wonder what I would have done if it'd been at the front of the house when I arrived with the cake – would I have made a quick getaway if I'd known he was here?

"Do you mind if I sit by the pool?" I ask Savannah hopefully. I note how childlike I sound, like a kid asking their mom with plead in their eyes if they can dash on ahead to the candy store.

Savannah retrieves her book and lays down. "*Fiiiiine*," she jokingly huffs, then dismisses me with a flick of her hand.

I make my move toward the pool and kick off my Nikes, stuff my socks inside them, then sit down by the water's edge and dip my legs in. The water is warm, but yet so blissfully refreshing and I throw my head back to the sky, closing my eyes and resisting the urge to slide my entire body into the pool. I send Sheri a quick text to let her know I'm staying at the Willowbank ranch for a while, and then, for a few minutes, I listen in peace to the sound of birds overheard and Myles splashing around in the other half of the pool.

"You aren't coming in?"

I start at the sound. I glance up beneath the shadow of my cap and squint.

Blake towers over me, beaming me an encouraging smile. He's wearing a pair of bright red shorts – correction, swim trunks – and a black T-shirt that clings to his chest. Now that I'm not blowing steam over Sheri's ruined cake, my head swirls with thoughts that aren't exactly appropriate.

"I'm not what you'd call pool-ready," I say, gesturing down at my jean shorts and tank top.

"Just strip off," Blake says nonchalantly, then, at my disapproving look, adds, "*Kidding*, Mila."

He kicks his slide sandals off to the side and then, with a gulp, I watch as he tears his T-shirt over his head. I knew before now that Blake is impressively muscular and toned, but the view without clothes is one I can't wrench my eyes away from. His stomach is just as defined as his chest and arms, but in a more modest way. The vague outline of a set of abs is definitely prominent, but only when he tenses, which he does now as he sits down next to me and slides into the water.

I lick my lips, aware of how dry my mouth is. *Even his quads are sculpted . . .*

Blake travels smoothly beneath the water's surface, all the

way to the opposite edge of the pool, where he emerges right next to his cousin, much to Myles's surprise, and shoves a wave of water into his face. Myles grabs Blake's head and dunks him back into the water for what slowly becomes an uncomfortably long time, until Blake erupts for air, and they both chortle with mischievous banter.

Savannah, over the top of her tattered book, scathingly shakes her head.

I paddle my legs back and forth through the warm water and inhale the scent of chlorine, watching Blake and Myles continue their war in amusement, enjoying how nice it feels to sit in the summer sun by the pool with a clear mind . . . Until Blake glides across the pool toward me. My stomach somersaults more than once and those inappropriate thoughts return.

Blake reaches me and rests his arms on the pool's edge, his breathing shallow. He flicks his wet hair and droplets of water splatter over me. Luckily, the water level rises to his chest, otherwise the sight of his bare body again would have me stammering my words. Blushing over the mere sight of hot guys is one thing . . . But hot guys that are wet and shirtless is another.

I try to look *anywhere* else. Bailey is collapsed in a heap under the shade of an old oak tree. "Is he okay?"

Blake follows my gaze to Bailey. "Yeah, just bloated probably, but that's what he deserves for being a scrounging cake thief."

As Blake rubs at his chlorine-irritated eyes, it dawns on me that this is the first time he has ever seen me without so much as a single stroke of mascara, and my hand flies up to pull my cap further over my face.

Blake's playful expression falters. "What – you're not looking at me now? Are we still being awkward about what happened on Sunday?"

"No – it's just ..." I say shyly, my voice low. "I'm not wearing any makeup."

It sounds ridiculous when I say it out loud, but I've always been rather self-conscious of my bare face. It's one of the effects of Hollywood, that relentless pressure to be picture-perfect. Whenever Dad has an event that Mom and I are to attend, she plonks me in her artist's chair and spends forever contouring my cheeks and nose, darkening my brows, applying a fresh set of lashes, before repeating the whole process all over again on herself. Then she'll breathe a definite sigh of relief when Ruben gives an approving nod to confirm that we have met his high standards.

These days, I don't even go to school without products clogging up my pores, and the only reason I have ditched the makeup most of the time while here in Fairview is because there is no one here who will clock my lack of cheekbone definition. Plus, the humidity makes it pretty uncomfortable. However, until now, I have always worn makeup around Blake.

With a snort of disbelief – boys will *never* understand such an issue – Blake plucks my Dodgers cap straight off my head to reveal my face in the sunlight. "Miss Mila, why have you been covering up those freckles?"

Protectively, I draw my chin in toward my chest as though

it's second nature to shield myself from prying eyes. Blake sets my cap backward onto his damp ruffled hair.

"It's only me. I don't care," he says seriously, noticing the color on my cheeks. "I've got this huge pimple right here. Look."

I lift my head and a smile creeps onto my face as Blake points out the blemish on his forehead. I place my hands behind me and lean back, relaxing my posture so that I'm not so closed off to him. The terrifying concept of being bare faced around him suddenly no longer seems to matter. Did he mean that my sun-kissed freckled cheeks are cute?

I purse my lips at him. "Did I give you the right to steal my hat?"

"What are you going to do about it?" he challenges, a glint in his dark eyes.

There go the somersaults again . . . I swiftly plough on, because I can't muster up a witty, cool reply fast enough, and leave my cap still on his head. "How are things with your mom?" I ask, back to treading carefully.

After Sheri seized me from his truck on Sunday, he sent a text to check up on me that evening. I reassured him that everything was okay on my end, though he was marginally less convincing about things being fine back at the Avery house.

Blake stops smirking. He shrugs and folds his arms over the pool's edge. "Why do you think I'm hanging out here? To get away from her."

I frown, watching Myles perform a series of underwater handstands. Over on the lounger, Savannah has ditched reading for snoozing – her straw hat is placed directly over her face, shielding her from the sun and, unbeknown to her, blocking out her chances of spying on Blake and me. If she saw the two of us chatting by the side of the pool like this, Blake already wearing an item of my clothing, but not much else, she would be shooting me teasing winks and suggestive grins.

"My aunt said my parents wouldn't want me to hang around with you. I don't know why. I haven't asked them yet," I say in a flat tone, dropping my gaze back to Blake. "But *you* know."

He looks up at me beneath thick, damp eyelashes. "It's ancient history. I told you, my mom is just a resentful person who clings to the past. I've been trying to talk sense into her this week, but it's not going great. I stayed here last night," he says in a sullen tone. "She doesn't want me to hang around with you either."

My stomach dips. What *exactly* happened between my parents and LeAnne Avery?

"And yet . . ." I trail off.

"And yet here we are," he finishes. The corner of his mouth twitches, concealing a smile. "My mom can be controlling, but I always do what I want in the end. And when will I ever come across another girl who knows how that feels?"

"I never said my dad was controlling."

"You didn't have to. It's part of the deal, isn't it?"

I think again of Dad being the one who conspired to have Aunt Sheri hold me captive at the Harding Estate for the summer, and my chest knots with a sickening feeling. My frown deepens.

Blake drifts a few inches closer to me, his damp shoulder touching my knee. Then, he takes me entirely by surprise and rests his temple against the side of my thigh. He gazes innocently up at me, surely unaware that my heart is now hammering in my chest. His deep brown eyes, framed by those wet lashes, are intoxicating. They draw me in, our gazes transfixed, until all the air seeps out of my lungs.

"I'm going to give myself sunburn," I splutter, plucking my hat from his damp hair and nestling it back onto my head. I don't even mind the sogginess – I'm just relieved to focus on anything other than the intensity of Blake's smoldering eyes and the feeling of his resting head against my thigh. But yet I don't shake him off.

My eyes roam the Willowbank ranch, flitting across the extensive fields much like those of the Harding Estate, until they land back on Savannah. She has lifted her hat an inch from her face and now peers out from beneath the brim with great interest. When she realizes I've noticed her attention, she drops it back over her face and pretends again to be asleep.

Blake's gaze continues to bore into me, unnervingly relentless.

Ignoring the throbbing of my heartbeat, I swallow and look back down at him with forced indifference, as though cute boys resting their head practically in my lap isn't a rarity. My fingers twitch with the overwhelming urge to touch his wet hair.

Blake's easy smile deepens into a grin.

"What?"

He lifts his head from my thigh and says, "You're nervous."

"Nervous? Why would I – why would I be nervous?" I say breezily with a strained laugh, but the hitch in my voice shreds any hope of being convincing. My hand finds my cap again, anxiously pulling the bill down over my eyes. A dead giveaway that I instantly regret.

"Because . . . you hold your breath when I do this," Blake says in a hushed, flirtatious undertone.

He rests his cheek against the side of my thigh once more, his eyes locked on mine. My breath catches in my throat again when, beneath the cool water, he skims his fingertips over my skin. Seductively and so slowly it's torturous, he runs his hand all the way up my bare leg.

"Do I make you nervous, Mila?" he whispers.

Electricity fizzes through my veins. It's a current of sizzling, rapid heat that radiates all through my body, working its way outward from the point of Blake's touch. He clasps his hand around my leg, just beneath my knee, and I momentarily freeze. My heartbeat is erratic and out of sync. I part my lips to speak, but words rise in my throat only to fade into nothing.

"Do I make you hold your breath?" Blake murmurs with a teasing glint in his eye. He lifts his head from my thigh again, but his hand remains on my leg. He edges in closer and presses his hard, broad chest against me. "I love that I do."

I can't tear my eyes away from him – he's so close now –

"Hello sweet, sweet Mila!"

Both Blake and I start at the sound of another voice, an abrupt reminder that we aren't alone. Blake quickly drifts away, his touch disappearing from my body, and innocently shakes the water out of his hair. I finally tear my attention from him and twist around to find Patsy working her way toward us.

"I didn't know you were here!" she says cheerfully, stopping at the pool's edge.

"I was – um – I was dropping off a cake," I blurt. "But Bailey ate it." I grimace over at the greedy pup who's still lying in the shade beneath the tree, overfed and snoozing, then look apologetically up at Patsy. "Sheri made it for you guys, so can you maybe . . . Can you maybe tell her that you loved it? It was an apple stack cake."

Patsy places her hands on her hips in sync with the rolling of her eyes. "Well, first, how about you tell Sheri to drag her butt out of that ranch and join me for coffee sometime? It's been too long!"

"*Mom*," Savannah nearly growls from the loungers. Miraculously, she's now awake again, sitting bolt upright and waving her hat in the air like an SOS sign. "Can you bring us some popsicles?"

"Treated like a butler around here, I am!" Patsy huffs, but nonetheless turns on her heels to fulfill Savannah's request.

I fire Savannah a suspicious look. She winks, lays down, and flips her cowboy hat back over her face and resumes "sleeping" while no doubt eavesdropping on every word that is exchanged between Blake and me.

"Where's your phone?" Blake asks, drawing my attention back to only him.

I can't decide if I'm relieved or disappointed that the heated moment between us is gone.

"Here." I touch my phone on the ground next to me. "Why?

"Myles! Come over here for a second!" he yells with a wild wave of his arm.

Myles, who I, quite honestly, have forgotten is in the pool, bursts from the water and runs his hands through his glistening strawberry blond hair. Curiosity draws his eyebrows together and he swims over to join us.

"Yeah?"

"Don't you think it's a little lonely in this pool?" Blake asks.

Myles's face flashes with understanding, and the two of them turn to look at me. There is no time to register their rogue, wicked smirks.

Blake dives beneath the water and hooks his arms around my legs the same time as Myles seizes my waist.

"NO!" I gasp, but it's too late.

The two of them pull me with all their strength, wrestling against my feeble attempts to fight them off. I kick my legs hard and try to shake off Blake's grip, and I push at Myles's shoulders, but my efforts are wasted. My screams blend with their laughter and, eventually, my own. They haul me into the water with a great splash.

My jean shorts suddenly weigh a hundred pounds and I rise quickly to the surface, gulping for air. Luckily, I am slightly taller than Savannah, so I can touch the pool's floor with my tiptoes. I run my hands back through my hair, pushing it out of my face. My baseball cap floats in the water.

A second later, Blake and Myles pop up next to me, choking because they can't contain their fit of laughter. They're howling even louder than they did when Bailey destroyed Sheri's cake.

"You – kicked me – in – the face!" Blake stammers breathlessly. He presses a hand to the edge of his jaw.

I place my hands on his chest and shove him hard. "You deserve it!"

Myles, as though fearing I may seek punishment on him too, dives under the water and glides back to his side of the pool, leaving Blake and me alone, wiping water from our eyes and breaking out into more laughter whenever we look at one another.

"*Boys!*" Savannah snaps, sounding like a scolding mother as she storms to the pool's edge and glares sternly at her brother and Blake. "Why would you do that to her? Those clothes probably cost hundreds! They're probably Gucci or something!"

"Because it's hilarious!" Myles says.

"It's okay, Savannah," I say, feeling at my clothes as I tread water. This is going to be a wet, squidgy walk back to the ranch. "These shorts are from the clearance rack at Forever 21."

"Oh," Savannah says, lowering her head in embarrassment. "Still. Blake? Why would you drag her in like that?"

Blake looks at me out of the corner of his eye and his gaze sends another shock of fizzling energy down my spine. As he opens his mouth to reply, he doesn't look at Savannah – he keeps his smolder trained only on me. "I thought," he says slowly, "that Mila looked hot."

The innuendo does not go unnoticed by me or Savannah. She looks at me for a long moment and I tilt my head down in embarrassment because I know exactly what she must be thinking – Blake has just given her positive affirmation that maybe there *is* something going on between him and me.

"In *that* case," Savannah says, "enjoy cooling off, Mila!"

16

There's a photograph inside a dusty frame on a shelf in the laundry room that catches my eye every time I'm shoveling clothes into the washing machine.

I focus on it now, absentmindedly moving a damp pile of my clothes over to the dryer, my gaze never leaving the easygoing, million-dollar smile on my dad's young face. Only back then it was more like a two-dollar smile, because his name hadn't yet created ripples in the movie industry.

It's a Harding family portrait from years ago – sometime in the '90s, by the look of those hairstyles. Dad and Sheri are just teenagers, and Popeye and my grandmother – *Mamaw*, which was my name for her – stand behind them, hands on their children's shoulders, beaming proudly. They're all suited and booted as though for church.

It's nice to see Mamaw in the photographs all around the house, because my limited memories of her are slowly fading as I get older. At least now her warm smile and lively mane of brown hair is ingrained in my mind again.

Staring at the photograph, I'm lost in thought as my phone begins vibrating in my pocket. I slide it out, expecting the call to be from Mom, but mentally crossing my fingers that maybe it's actually Blake calling instead. I haven't had the chance to see him again since the scorching day by the pool last week.

When I glance down at my screen, my stomach knots.

It's an incoming video call – from Dad.

So, Mom has found time in Everett Harding's schedule to pencil me in for the rare privilege of talking to him. I stare at my ringing phone in my hand, contemplating rejecting the call. The only time Dad has spoken to me since I left LA was the night of the tailgate party, and that was to yell at me. If he was worried about how I'm coping exiled out here in Fairview, he would have called long before now.

I move my thumb to reject him, but then I stop. There's something I still need to ask, and for that reason, and that reason alone, I accept the call.

Dad comes into focus on my screen. Shockingly, for the first time in forever, he isn't wearing his signature sunglasses, so his dark brown eyes shine back at me.

"At long last she answers!" he says with a smile, resting his elbows on the desk and leaning in closer to the screen.

He's calling from the computer in his study. On the walls behind him, there are shelves stacked with awards he has won during the past decade. Last year's Oscar for "Best Actor" takes prime position at the forefront, sparkling beneath the glow of tiny spotlights.

"Yeah, sorry," I say, leaning back against the dryer. "I forgot you probably only have a maximum of four minutes to dedicate to me. Do I only have three left now?"

"Don't be ridiculous," Dad says, exasperated now as he draws his arm over his chest. "I wanted to call and check in. How are things at the ranch?"

"Boring," I say, sticking to my deal with Sheri. Dad isn't to know that I've gone beyond the gates again since the night of the tailgate party. "Sheri won't let me go anywhere ever since I snuck out the night I arrived," I lie. And I know I'm my father's daughter, because I can muster up a good performance when I need to. I sigh heavily and even kick the dryer behind me for good measure. "I've just been sunbathing and helping with the horses."

"I think that's for the best," Dad says. "There isn't much to see in Fairview, anyway. You aren't missing out on anything."

The realization that Dad is lying straight back at me and has no intention at all of *admitting* that he got Ruben to send Sheri orders behind my back sends a tidal wave of rage ripping through me. However, I maintain a calm coolness – thanks again to my hereditary acting ability. If only I could utilize my skills around Blake when he's wearing nothing but wet swim trunks . . .

"The movie is out next weekend, right?" I ask politely, as though I'm not internally seething. "The eighteenth?"

Dad nods and stretches out his other arm now. "Your mom and I have the premiere next Thursday. I wish you could be there too."

And then, before I can stop myself, I mutter, "Why? I would probably *embarrass* you."

"Mila." Dad stops stretching and tilts his head to the side. "You don't embarrass me."

I stare at the wall rather than my screen, grinding my teeth together. "No, I just ruin your publicity campaigns."

I hear a sigh from Dad's end of the call, but it doesn't belong to him. It's lighter, feminine. I look back at my phone.

"Is Mom there?" I ask, glaring at Dad. "Is she supervising this? Making sure you actually talk to me?"

Mom, as suspected, is indeed in the study. She slips into the frame behind Dad and places a hand on his shoulder, leaning over him. The surprised look she rearranges her features into is so painfully fake. "Mila! I've just popped in to say hi, honey."

"Dad, have you been giving Mom acting classes?" I snap.

This is – seriously – ridiculous. Not only did Mom have to specifically schedule time for Dad to talk to me, she also has to watch over him while he does. I have never felt less important than I do in this exact moment. An inconvenience – *that's* what I am.

"Oh, Mila," Mom says, frowning. "I'm sorry. I'm just here to make sure your dad doesn't accept any phone calls right now. This is a no-work-allowed hour."

"Your mom thinks I'm totally trapped under Ruben's thumb," Dad scoffs, rolling his eyes in an attempt to inject some humor into the supremely tense atmosphere that stretches all the thousands of miles from Fairview to Thousand Oaks.

"You are," I say, unblinking. "But he's also under yours, apparently."

"Mila," Mom says sharply. "Your dad wants to talk with you. Can the two of you not discuss work right now?"

"Yes, Mila – how is Popeye doing?" Dad asks, but I'm really not in the mood for strained chit-chat.

"Popeye wonders why his son doesn't call him," I snap as I push myself off the dryer and pace the small laundry room, suddenly nauseous from the overwhelming scent of lavender. Before I end this video call, I need to ask the question that's been playing on my mind ever since Sheri planted the seed last week. "But you know that already." I stop pacing and brace myself. "Do you know the Mayor of Nashville?" I fire at them, moving my phone even closer to my face to scrutinize my parents. "Her name is LeAnne Avery. Ring any bells?"

Straight away, Mom and Dad both stiffen. There is a long silence as though they are holding their breaths, and then slowly they look at one another, obviously having a silent dialogue that I can't decipher. But what I do know is that LeAnne Avery's name has made them both uncomfortable.

"Mila, why are you – why are you asking us that?" Mom asks faintly.

"Has Sheri been running her mouth?" Dad questions. I watch as he grabs his computer and scrapes the monitor closer to him, amplifying the discomfort in his and Mom's eyes. "What exactly has she told you, Mila?"

"Nothing," I say. "She wouldn't answer my questions. She told me to ask you instead."

"But why are you asking anyone questions about LeAnne Avery in the first place?" Mom asks. She has gone a shade paler and I notice the way she keeps nervously squeezing

Dad's shoulder. I have hit a nerve, which only makes me all the more desperate to get an answer.

"We – um – bumped into her at church," I say, because I can't mention that I've been hanging out with her son. Besides, I *did* meet Mayor Avery for the first time at church. "Are you going to tell me how *you* know her?"

"You've been going to church?" Dad says, eyes widening. "You aren't supposed to—"

"Leave the ranch?" I finish, raising a challenging eyebrow. "Yeah, I know. Thanks for ruining my summer, Dad. Now what's the deal with the Mayor of Nashville?" I demand into my phone, riled up with frustration and determined to be heard. Right now, I don't even care about hearing Dad stammer out apologies and excuses for his military-style orders to ensure I keep out of trouble, all I want is a straight answer. How do they know LeAnne Avery, and why is that relationship on such terrible terms?

Dad clenches his jaw and sets his dark eyes on me. The look he fixes me with makes me relieved to be two thousand miles away. Visibly rattled, he slides back in his chair, straightens up, and without another word, slams the laptop screen shut.

17

By now, I have made it a habit to always wait outside the Harding Estate whenever someone picks me up.

It's just after nine and the sky is a deep, darkening blue, enough for the twinkle of the stars to be noticeable, and the air is balmy but tolerable for once. I sit beneath one of the spotlights mounted to the ranch walls, perched on a large rock, and running my fingertips along the dirt, creating lines in the earth. Goosebumps spread all over my arms, the way they always do whenever I wait out here at night; there's an eeriness to the silence of the country roads and the empty fields beyond.

A car sounds in the distance and I look up, staring down the long, dark road. Headlights flicker around a bend, and a few seconds later Blake's truck barrels toward me.

I jump to my feet and wipe my hands on my thighs. The LED headlights nearly blind me, so I cup my hand over my eyes as the truck draws nearer. I skip toward it and clamp my hand around the door handle before Blake has even come to a complete stop.

"Hey!" I say as I swing open the door and climb into the backseat.

The melodies of country music and the smell of musky cologne sweep over me. Savannah is already in the backseat, Myles rides shotgun, and Blake is, of course, driving. I think of the night only a few weeks ago when he picked me up for the tailgate party and of the way his brown eyes had met mine in the rearview mirror for the first time. A sharpness had flickered in his gaze then, but as I meet his eyes now they are irresistibly inviting.

"Hi, Mila," he says. The corners of his eyes crinkle with a hint of a smile. "This is the part where you tell us you don't know what a bonfire is, right?"

I roll my eyes and softly punch the headrest of his seat. "I've been to a bonfire before," I say defensively. "Malibu beach. Last summer. My hair reeked of smoke for the next two days."

"Well," says Myles. "Get ready to stink again."

We set off through the darkness, tracing the now-familiar route down the country roads toward civilization. I have no idea where the bonfire is being held, but as Savannah talks my ear off, I manage to steal peeks out of the window every now and again. Eventually, when we pass the church I've found myself attending each Sunday, I notice we're in downtown Fairview. Moments later, Blake turns off the main street and we pass a sign for Bowie Nature Park.

"Is it really a good idea to have a bonfire in a park? With trees?" I wonder aloud as the truck rolls toward the looming park ahead, with tall, thick trees clustered together in the darkness. "And right next to the fire station?"

"We're keeping it by the lake and nowhere near any trees," Myles says, casting a glance over his shoulder at me. "Don't worry. We wouldn't do anything stupid."

"Back in the fall, we tried it in my back yard," Blake says with a reminiscent chuckle. "Neighbors reported us for clogging the street with smoke."

"But not to the police!" Savannah says dramatically, then shudders. "To Aunt LeAnne, who came hurtling home from the city, guns blazing. Metaphorically, of course."

"Yeah . . ." Blake says quietly. He isn't laughing anymore. "That was a bad night."

Now apprehensive about the technicalities of this bonfire extravaganza, I bite at my lower lip. "So now you're throwing a bonfire in a public park instead? Don't you need a permit or something?"

"Don't question my actions, Mila," Blake says with a flippant wave of his hand. His eyes flicker back to the rearview mirror to look at me and they sharpen teasingly. "You should have figured out by now that they aren't always wise."

We pass through some wooden gates and crunch our way down a narrow path beneath a canopy of trees until we emerge into a parking lot. It's late and I don't suppose many people are interested in trekking through dark trails at this hour, so there's only a few other cars here. The headlights are all still on the brights and the cars are filled with occupants who are, seemingly, waiting for Blake to arrive.

"Grab everything you can carry from the back," Blake

orders, killing his engine after pulling into a parking spot. He whips off his seatbelt and points out of his windshield at a spot further ahead. I see the glisten of the moonlight against water, and I realize he's gesturing to a lake. "Carry it down there."

The four of us climb out of his truck and head around the back, where Blake lowers the tailgate. The truck bed is crammed full of what appears to be a random concoction of items, from folding chairs to a crate full of Dr Peppers to thick timber wood logs to old newspapers. I'm relieved to see that there's even some fire extinguishers. Sensible.

Savannah and Myles start grabbing items as more cars pull into the lot. All around us, people are emerging from trucks with their own supplies of chairs, drinks, and snacks.

"Just carry everything down to the water!" Blake calls out over the parking lot, waving a hand at the edge of the lake. "I marked out a spot for us the other night. Huge rock. Y'all can't miss it!"

There's an excited buzz of voices in the air as everyone treks off down the sloping ground toward the water. Myles darts off with an armful of logs and newspapers, and Savannah drags a couple chairs along the concrete, leaving Blake and me behind at the truck.

"Are you the dedicated events organizer for the teenage population of Fairview?" I ask playfully, giving him a side-long glance.

Blake looks back at me with a neutral expression and shrugs, stretching into the truck bed to grab the remaining items. "It's either lead or be led," he says, heaving the crate of soda into my arms. "And when your mom wins the mayoral campaign in your freshman year, you want to be one step ahead." The corner of his mouth curves into a smile but he looks anything but happy.

Blake continues to fill my arms with an assortment of items from the truck, stacking everything on top of the crate of soda until the pile is so high that my chin rests on a bag of Doritos. My shoulders slump from the weight of it all and I sway dangerously next to him as he wedges another folding chair under his arm, then reaches for the final object at the very back of the truck bed.

"Is that a guitar?"

Blake hoists the strap of the guitar case over his shoulder and fires me a funny look. "What else could it possibly be?"

"Is it *your* guitar?"

Now Blake laughs. He turns to face me, his hand around the strap over his shoulder. "C'mon, Mila. Country is the only music I ever listen to. I love honky tonks. Isn't it obvious?"

Uh-huh, yeah. It's pretty obvious. Hell, there was even a guitar on a stand in the cabin in his back yard. "*Of course* you play guitar."

Blake grins modestly, his dimples deepening, and a pink hue spreads over his cheeks in a cute flash. "I play guitar and I" – he pauses shyly – "sing."

"You can sing?" I echo. "Like, *actually* sing?"

He stares deadpan back at me. "What other kind of singing is there other than *actual* singing?"

"But I've never heard you sing!" I exclaim, nearly

dismantling the tower of haphazardly stacked objects in my arms.

"Well," says Blake, "the quicker I get this bonfire started, the quicker you'll get to hear me sing."

Guitar case balanced on his shoulder and a chair under his other arm, he reaches out to close the tailgate of his truck, but the sound of someone calling his name stops him. He cranes his neck at the same time as I peer over the bag of Doritos for a better look, and my heart skips with a beat of panic as a familiar face approaches.

"Howdy, Barney!" Blake says.

Barney beams back at him as he rests his arm over the back of the truck. "Lacey got back from vacation yesterday, so she's here, and I may or may not have just overheard her say that if you're actually nice to her for once you might just get lucky tonight." With a salacious howl, he digs a teasing elbow into Blake's ribs, then meets my reproachful stare. "Oh, Everett Harding's kid! You're still around."

"Her name," Blake says in a hard voice, slamming the tailgate shut, "is Mila."

Blake strides off and his truck beeps as he locks it behind him, leaving Barney and me staring at each other in surprise. I am hyperaware that my phone is sticking out of the back pocket of my jean shorts and that my hands are tied up carrying all this stuff in my arms, so I quickly shrug and then dash off after Blake before Barney can even *think* about stealing my property again.

I catch up with Blake and fall into step alongside him, power-walking to match his long strides. We're advancing past the parked trucks, down onto the rocky beach that surrounds the lake, and a crowd has already gathered at an open clearing up ahead, laying out their chairs and the same coolers they all brought along to the tailgate party last month. Only tonight, I notice, the group of partygoers is slightly larger.

We pass under some trees and emerge along the water's edge; it looks murky and uninviting in the dark.

"I thought my name was *Miss* Mila," I tease Blake while we still have a few moments alone.

"It is," Blake says, then lowers his voice and purposely brushes his arm against mine. "But only to me."

Despite nearly buckling under the weight of all this campfire stuff, I skip ahead a few steps so he can't see how painfully shy I get whenever he whispers one of his easy flirtatious remarks. I don't quite know why he gets under my skin so much, because it's not like I've never had a boyfriend before. I'm not a complete novice when it comes to boys.

There was Jack Cruz back in the fall who has been my lab partner for the entirety of sophomore year – we went out a couple times, shared our first kiss together on the beach, and even got a little handsy in his car one night. However, Dad wouldn't let me bring him home, not because he didn't approve – Jack Cruz's mom is a very affluent fashion designer – but because Dad, as I have learned growing up, is immensely paranoid with a whole mountain range of trust issues. He *especially* doesn't like strangers entering our home. I suspect Dad fears they'll see Everett Harding for who he really is when he isn't the handsome, Oscar-winning actor with the swagger to match. Jack Cruz thought my family was crazy – "Who do you guys think you *are*?" – and, thanks to Dad's all-around weirdness, Jack and I returned to being nothing more than lab partners.

But those two months I spent dating Jack feel awfully bland now in hindsight. I blushed around him too, and I found myself often lost for words whenever he whispered something sweet and flirty, but I never felt... I never felt *electricity*. I never felt that surge of energy in my veins or the flip-flopping of my stomach or heart palpitations so intense they hurt.

I never felt any of the things I have felt recently with Blake.

We reach the others by the lake and the ground is made uneven by rocks and dirt. The wide clearing Blake has chosen to host tonight's bonfire is, thankfully, a safe distance away from the nearest trees. Above, the sky is filled with twinkling, mesmerizing stars.

I dump the crate of soda cans and everything else piled on top of it down on the pebbles next to where Savannah and Tori are unfolding the chairs. Myles has already scampered off to get touchy-feely with Cindy. Everyone else has formed a wide circle with all the chairs, cracking open sodas, and protectively stashing their snacks between their feet as though a bear will emerge from the trees and loot the lot.

"I'll get the fire started," Blake says, setting down the last of his chairs. Carefully, he slides his guitar case off his shoulder and holds it out to me with a hint of trepidation flickering across his eyes. "Mila, I trust you to keep my guitar safe."

Savannah steps forward indignantly, flapping her arms around in protest. "You trust Mila and not me, your cousin? Your own *bloodline*?"

"Savannah, I stopped trusting you when you lost my favorite Hot Wheels car ten years ago," Blake deadpans, then thrusts the case into my hands. He smirks as he walks away, playfully shoving his shoulder into Savannah's and dodging the whack she tries to give him in return.

"If you break that guitar," Savannah says in between tutting, "you'll break his heart."

The fire takes a while to get going – Blake, Barney and a handful of other guys spend a long time systematically arranging all of the logs, newspapers and tinder into a circular pit marked out with pebbles. It takes even longer for them to light it, frustratedly passing the lighter around the group until, finally, a spark emits, and an orange glow can be seen catching and gently growing from deep inside. Satisfied, Barney and the others saunter back to their chairs, but Blake remains crouched by the fire. He pokes at the burning wood with a stick and occasionally tosses in more tinder as the fire begins to rage brighter and brighter.

"She's staring at him, isn't she?" Savannah says.

"*Mmhmm*," agrees Tori.

Their voices drift straight over me at first, but then I repeat their words in my head and realize they're talking about me. I blink through the dryness of my contact lenses and tear my gaze from the blazing fire, glancing between the two of them with a perplexed look.

"What?"

Savannah and Tori roll their eyes in perfect unison.

"I'm not staring at Blake," I say without a single ounce of conviction.

"*Right,*" says Savannah. She crosses one leg over the other and stretches back in her chair, and for the first time tonight I squint for a better look at her choice of earrings for the evening – two dangling flames. "Tori, you should have seen the two of them together in my pool! Blake couldn't keep his hands off her."

I narrow my eyes. "You were supposed to be napping!"

"You like each other!" she shoots back with triumph ringing in her voice. She jolts upright again and points a finger out at me, her face beaming. "Admit it!"

"Blake couldn't keep his hands off you?" Tori repeats, tapping her index finger against her lips as she stares down at Blake by the fire. "Damn. Lucky. I dared him to kiss me in eighth grade once and he chose the forfeit instead." With the drama of a Hollywood actress – I would know – Tori feigns heartbreak, clasping a hand over her chest and throwing her head back with a whimpering sigh.

Savannah casts her a glance of disapproval. "Tori, please let go of your childhood crush on him already. This is about Mila."

"No, this is *not* about Mila," I say. My face grows hot, but I convince myself it's from the spreading warmth of the fire that slowly radiates around the clearing. "Barney said something about – um – Lacey? Who is that?"

"Lacey?" Tori says curiously, taking a sip of her soda. "That's her over there; the one with the red streaks in her hair. And, for the record," she grumbles, "I started the colored hair trend around here."

As Tori shakes out her exuberant pink hair around her shoulders, I stare off in the direction she indicated. On the opposite side of the bonfire, there's a trio of girls standing around sipping from bottles of beer, giggling and chatting loudly. One of the girls, I remember, was at the tailgate party and had been thoroughly excited that Everett Harding is my dad, but I focus on the brunette with the red streaks in her hair that shine in the firelight.

Through the growing flames, she catches my stare. With a flash of recognition in her face, she turns to one of her friends and murmurs something in her ear.

"What did Barney say about her?" Savannah asks.

I scuff my chair against the uneven rock and angle more toward Savannah so that I'm not directly facing the fire or Lacey and her friends anymore. I cross my legs together on my chair and fiddle with the bracelet around my wrist. "That if Blake is nice to her, he might get lucky."

"Mila, you're not. . . *jealous*?" Savannah gasps and covers her mouth with her hand. "Did you know jealousy often means you *like* someone?"

I fix her with a heavy look. How can I be jealous when Blake and I aren't anything serious? But then why do I feel . . . weird? Why do I feel hostility toward a girl whose name I only just learned?

"Ignore Savannah being her usual annoying self," Tori says, glowering at Savannah in an attempt to silence her incessant teasing. Tori sits forward, clears her throat, then locks eyes with me. "Lacey Dixon is about to be a senior, which means she has had the joy of sharing classes with Blake for her entire life. She also has eyeballs, which means, like the rest of us – except for Savannah, because that would be incestuous – she thinks Blake is *fiiiine*. Also, her parents are close friends with Blake's mom."

Savannah laughs and grabs herself a soda, listening.

"However," Tori continues, "*unlike* the rest of us, Lacey believes Blake possesses the ability to care about anything other than his music. They spent all of last year going in circles with each other, mostly because Blake *clearly* isn't that interested in her, but dear Lacey still thinks he'll write her a love song one day. Bless her heart. God loves a trier!"

Tori suddenly goes mute and retreats into her chair again, and when I check over my shoulder I realize why story time is over – Blake is on his way over here.

"How's that fire looking?" he asks, giving the bonfire a clipped nod to show off his hard work. "Mom forcing me to go to Boy Scouts when I was a kid has paid off at last. These fires of mine get better each time."

"*Okay*, ego-head," Tori says with a scoff.

Blake flicks her shoulder with his finger. "*Okay, DJ.* Shouldn't you be on music duty? I don't hear any music. Do y'all?" He looks at Savannah, then at me. He doesn't look away again.

With a sigh of acceptance, Tori stands, but before she leaves she pulls out her phone. "Wait. Cute picture time! With Blake's crappy Boy Scout fire in the background."

"Oh, c'mon, Tori!" he groans, then laughs as he reaches for my elbow and pulls me to my feet.

"Wait," I say, panicking as Savannah rises too and the three of them crowd in around me, our heads pressed together, and Tori's phone held out before us, the fire behind. "You aren't going to post this anywhere, right?"

"It's just for memories! It'll end up in my scrapbook," Tori reassures me, then with cheery enthusiasm she urges us to "SMIIIIILE!"

I'm not quite sure if I manage to pull my face into a smile in time, but Tori doesn't bother to check. She puts her phone away and traverses the cluster of chairs before disappearing completely beyond the bonfire to get some music up and running.

Blake falls back into the vacant chair she's left behind, reaches for a soda, then admires his burning fire from afar. "A nice height, huh?"

There's a strangled cough from Savannah. "I'll – um – be over there if you need me," she says, waving a hand at nothing in particular, then dashes off in the same direction as Tori.

"I bet ten bucks she's off to hit on Nathan Hunt," says Blake.

Or she's giving the two of us some privacy . . .

"Yeah," I say, but nerves slowly seep through me, spreading all over my body as I lower myself back down into the chair next to Blake.

We haven't spoken just the two of us since that afternoon at the pool, and being alone with Blake, I've realized, is exhilarating. That rush of wondering what exactly will happen next . . .

"So, about this guitar . . ." I say, nodding to the guitar case positioned between our chairs. "You're a musician?"

Blake shifts his gaze from the fire to me, but embers of orange still flicker in his eyes. "No," he says, "but I'm trying to be."

He wedges his half-finished drink into the ground between the rocks, then swings his guitar case onto his lap. I watch in silence as he releases the latches, and with a glance out of the corner of his eye he lifts the lid to reveal an acoustic guitar.

With great care, Blake strokes his fingers over the mahogany wood of the neck. There's a few tiny scuffs in the body of the guitar, a sign it has been well-loved, but the honey-colored wood still shines under the firelight. He runs his hand along the fretboard and all the way up to the headstock that reads *GIBSON*.

"The original Gibson Hummingbird," Blake says with a shyness in his voice that I have never once heard before, his twang more pronounced than usual. He lightly brushes his thumb over the taut strings. "It was my dad's. He loved music too, but he lost his ambition, so he threw in the towel and passed his guitar over to me instead."

My lips part to form an "O", because this is the first time Blake has ever mentioned his father. It's not like I haven't noticed he doesn't seem to be around, but it's not the kind of thing you ask, especially if they're . . .

"Oh, he's not dead or anything," Blake says with a laugh

when he notices my expression. "Just an alcoholic who took off for Memphis to shack up with his side chick."

"Oh." That's not what I expected. "But you kept his guitar?"

"Well, yeah. It's a *Gibson freaking Hummingbird*, Mila." He tilts his head to the side and studies me, fascinated by my lack of knowledge. "I'll play this guitar until the day it has no life left in it."

"And is this what you want to do with your life?" I ask, edging in a little closer. I gaze curiously at the guitar again, then smile up at Blake. "Music?"

"Hey, it's in my blood," he says with a sheepish shrug and a grin to match. "I'm hoping to study at Vanderbilt next fall, and I've been begging Marty to let me play sometime."

"Marty?"

"He owns Honky Tonk Central. Says I'm too young to be playing in his bar. Won't even give me an afternoon slot when it's family-friendly!" Blake explains with an indignant scowl. "He thinks Mom will find some reason to shut him down if she were to find out that he ever let me perform there."

At the mention of his mom, I'm reminded of the way she abruptly walked out on dinner last Sunday when Blake dared to even mention the word "music".

"So, your mom isn't a huge fan of your guitar playing, is she?" I ask carefully.

Blake's lips falter into a smaller, saddened smile. "No. She doesn't think music is a viable career choice. She wants me to study business or something equally as draining. Like, you know, *politics*." A frustrated sigh escapes him, and he stares longingly at his guitar again, as if dreaming of a future that includes it. "Every time I try to discuss it with her, she shuts me down. Doesn't even like hearing me play. It reminds her too much of my dad."

I grimace in sympathy. "I'm sorry, Blake."

In the moments I spend absorbing the hurt in Blake's eyes over his mom's disregard for his passion, I realize that I have never really given much thought to what kind of a life I can have beyond being Everett Harding's daughter. Of course, I have fantasized about turning eighteen, taking off for college and being free of the confinements of Dad's world, but yet I have never really thought about what that means. Never worked out the finer details, never figured out what path I want to pursue, never took the time to discover who I am and who I want to be.

Blake may not have his mother's support, but he at least has ambition, and passion. He has a dream of his own. Blake has every intention of carving out his own path in life.

He's still gazing at his guitar, one hand over the fretboard, the other resting on the body. The bonfire continues to blaze, and its warmth grows stronger, casting heat and an orange glow over our faces. With a deep breath, I reach over and place my hand atop Blake's.

"So," I whisper. "Can I hear you play?"

Blake stares at my hand on his, our skin warm, but my heart sinks as he pulls his hand out from beneath mine. Then, a second later, he places his over mine instead, interlocks our fingers together, and squeezes. Our eyes meet and we share a tentative smile. He nods.

Letting go of my hand, he gets up. There's something incredibly charming about the way he throws the guitar strap over his head, nestles it on his shoulder, then ruffles his hair as if getting ready for his audience.

He leaves the empty case on the chair next to me, then trudges down to the bonfire. He stands as close to the fire as he can without getting burned, and spends a minute tuning his guitar, his lower lip between his teeth. During this time, the crowd has realized they're about to get a performance, and chat begins to dwindle. The music playing in the background from a speaker lowers.

Blake looks up at the sea of expectant faces and clears his throat. "Hey, everyone. I hope you like the new location, but remember that fire station we all drove by? Yeah, don't do anything stupid. Stay clear of the trees. Take all your trash home with you at the end of the night. Drinkers, don't drive. And please no one drown in the lake."

"Okay, Mayor Avery!" someone yells, but although their tone is playful and void of any malice, I know it must drive Blake insane.

Blake, his eyes searching for the culprit, forces a laugh. "Okay, well, in our usual bonfire fashion, the floor is open to anyone who wants to entertain us. And because none of you ever have the balls to go first, I guess it's up to me again."

"An original?" another voice emerges.

"Not yet," says Blake. "This is a cover of a song from one of my favorite artists right now. This is 'Chance Worth Taking' by Mitchell Tenpenny."

He clears his throat again, nervously this time, and fishes out a pick beneath the strings at the neck of his guitar. He bows his head over his guitar, positions his fingers on the fretboard, and begins to sing in a rich, melodious tone, with an opening strum that sends goosebumps rocketing over every inch of my skin.

With each word he sings, the soft southern lilt in Blake's voice reverberates around the silent clearing. His voice deepens, thick with passion for the lyrics. He sings with his head held high, but his eyes closed, his fingers gliding effortlessly along the fretboard, the strum of each string perfectly aligned. The song he's chosen to cover is slow, and the lyrics are nothing short of captivating.

No one breathes a word. We all watch in awe as Blake loses himself in his performance, like there's no one else here but him, singing to the darkness with the heat of the fire on the back of his neck. It's so truly mesmerizing that when his voice trails off on the final word I don't even realize it's all over until his peers hoot with applause.

Right now, he is so far from being the mayor's son. He's Blake Avery, the guy who loves music, who has a talent that makes a crowd of his friends fall silent in genuine admiration.

I wish I knew what truly being Mila Harding might be – someone with dreams and passions of her own.

Barney rushes over, pounding Blake hard on the back with a celebratory thump, and a couple others come over to join with fist bumps and handshakes. One of those people, I notice with a sickening lurch of jealousy, has red-streaked hair.

Lacey nudges Barney out of her way and throws her arms around Blake, drawing him in for a hug while she bounces enthusiastically on the balls of her feet. My jaw clenches.

But whatever that murky feeling is, it lasts a mere two seconds until I notice Blake hastily unwrap himself from her. He excuses himself from the group and turns ... straight toward me.

My heartbeat picks up all over again as he approaches, guitar swung behind him, and his hand clasping the strap over his chest. Over his shoulder, I notice a younger girl stepping in front of the fire with her own guitar balancing in her anxious hands, ready to follow in Blake's footsteps.

"So," he says breathlessly, wiping a film of sweat from his temple, "what's the verdict, Miss Mila?"

I part my lips, searching for the right words that will do his performance justice, but I'm still so stunned by how *amazing* he really is that I'm close to speechless. "It was ..." I try, but I shake my head, gaping at him as I struggle to sum up exactly how his voice made me feel. Finally, I swallow and say, "You're born to be a musician."

Blake's expression lights up. The apprehension in his eyes transforms into relief, and the tentative smile on his face widens into a grin so joyful that his dimples are the deepest – and cutest – I've ever seen them.

"Seriously," I say, jumping up, proper speech now thankfully returning. "That was – amazing. Your playing, your singing. Everything. You are amazing."

Blake's cheeks burn red at my compliments, and he grabs

his guitar case and gently slots his guitar back inside, nestling it into the soft velvet contours. As he clicks the latches shut, a new voice begins to sing behind him.

"That's Kelsey," Blake says, sinking down into a chair and placing his guitar case on the ground beneath him. "Loves Keith Urban. Always performs in local open-mic nights."

I sit back down next to him, and although his gaze is locked on Kelsey as her husky tone fills the air around the fire, mine is fixated solely on him. "No open-mic nights for you, I guess?"

"Please," Blake retorts. "The mayor's kid busking at some Fairview coffee shop? That's way too humble." He rolls his eyes. "Mom would rather I ran for student body president and spent my time protesting for better democracy within Fairview High, but that's Lacey Dixon's job."

The girl with the red streaks in her hair . . .

"Well, small-town bonfires are probably a bit too normal for a Harding," I joke. I slump back in my chair and glance around the circle of people around the growing fire. The glow of firelight flickers across faces, there's nods of appreciation as Kelsey builds into chorus, and friends huddle in close to one another with smiles and friendly laughter. "But I really like it."

"So, you like honky tonks and bonfires," Blake says, settling his gaze on me, "but maybe not tailgate parties."

I laugh, but I'm instantly silenced when Blake reaches over to take my hand in his. He interlocks his fingers with mine and, our palms pressed close together, he rests our hands on the armrest of my chair. I stare silently at our hands in surprise, but the warmth of his skin sets off those pesky butterflies in my stomach *again*.

"Am I not allowed to hold your hand?" Blake asks in response to my stunned expression.

"No. I mean, yes. You can. I'm just—"

"Nervous," he finishes with a teasing wink.

We sit together, hands entwined, and listen in appreciation to a few more people perform. Savannah and Tori never return, and no one bothers us, but I do wonder if anyone has glanced over and noticed that Blake and I are a little too cozy. After a while, Blake swings his case over his shoulder and stands. He settles his gaze on me.

"Come back to the truck with me," he says in a low voice. He begins to walk, pulling me with him.

My mind races with thoughts of Blake and me alone together, and the butterflies somersault in my stomach as we walk away from the bonfire and the party, heading back to his truck . . .

He leads me across the rocky, uneven ground back up toward the parking lot. There are more cars here now, but their occupants are all by the lake enjoying the bonfire and the girl guitarist's sweet voice. I look over my shoulder and can still see the fire and the bodies huddled around it, spread out over the mass of chairs. Although slightly distant, we can also still hear the crackle of the fire and the musing of voices and the folksy sound of a Taylor Swift cover. But here, in the parking lot, we are entirely alone.

When we reach Blake's truck, he lets go of my hand. He

lowers the tailgate and slides his guitar case onto the truck bed.

"Sit with me," he says.

He perches himself on the edge of the tailgate with ease, but I have to heave myself up to join him. My legs dangle over the edge and we sit side-by-side in silence for a minute, watching the flames flicker down by the lake. Two girls are singing a duet now, their entwined voices dancing through the trees.

The silence between us is comfortable, yet we both must be aware of the heightened tension. Blake and me . . . alone . . . sitting close in the back of his truck . . .

"I'm jealous of you," I say, breaking the silence. I keep my eyes trained on the dark water of the lake, my hands gripping the edge of the tailgate. "You know what you want to do. You are so much more than the mayor's son. You have goals, whereas for me . . . Well, I guess I kinda fear that I'll never be anything more than Everett Harding's daughter." My chest tightens when I say the words out loud, and I lower my head, blinking fast at the concrete beneath our dangling feet.

"You're not *just* Everett Harding's daughter," Blake says, angling to look at me. My gaze remains locked on the ground beneath us. "You're *Mila Harding*. Your own name. Your own person."

"But I don't have . . . a *thing*," I mumble, my voice laced with frustration. "Your thing is music. Savannah's thing is horses. I don't have anything I'm passionate about. I don't really have any hobbies except hanging out with my friends at the beach and taking the occasional dance class. I have nothing that defines who I am except for who my father is."

Blake lifts his hand, cupping my chin between his thumb and forefinger. He tilts my head up so I'm forced to look him in the eye. "You still have time to figure out what your *thing* is," he says. "You don't need a hobby to define who you are. The things you do and the things you say are what really matter. And you know what I think?"

I stare back at the caramel flecks in his eyes. "What?"

"I think you're the girl who cares so much about disappointing her father that you cried in the back of my truck," he says with a comforting smile. "You're the girl at church who helps her grandfather. You're the girl who laughed when she spilled her quesadilla down herself."

"But I'm always going to be living in my dad's shadow."

"Mila," Blake murmurs, bringing his face close to mine, "you absolutely should not be hidden in any shadows."

Brushing the pad of his thumb softly over my skin, he delicately lifts my chin a little higher. His gaze drifts to my mouth and my breath hitches in my throat, my entire body frozen in place. We meet each other's eyes again and his are burning with the same intensity as they did that day by the pool. They crinkle at their corners as he smiles, right before his lips meet mine.

The kiss is tender and caring, just Blake's mouth against mine while his hand rests beneath my chin. I don't want him to pull away. I want more than this, I want to really, really kiss him. My eyes are closed, and I can sense the pounding of both our heartbeats.

Parting my lips, I press harder into Blake, letting him

know that this is okay. My body eases out of its paralysis and my hands find their way to him, placing one on the edge of his jaw while I weave my fingers into his hair with the other. He takes the hint, kissing me more, and soon his free hand is on the small of my back, pulling me even closer.

And on the edge of this tailgate, with my hands on him and his hands on me, I am thinking: *Holy crap, I am kissing Blake Avery.*

And it is undeniably perfect.

That is, until Blake pulls away.

My eyes fire open in alarm, wondering if I've done something wrong, but Blake's looking over his shoulder now, eyes wide. His hand remains resting along my jawline.

"Sorry – I thought – I thought I heard a car," he whispers.

A car door slams shut somewhere nearby.

Blake instantly lets go of me and slides off the tailgate. He heads around the truck to investigate, leaving me alone and breathless. A second later, I hear the distinct groan of Blake muttering, "*Fuck!*"

He appears back in front of me wearing an expression of complete dread, and before I realize it his hands are on my waist and he's lifting me off the tailgate and setting me back on my feet without so much as straining a muscle.

"Is it the police?" I ask quietly. Panic begins to seep through me at the thought of the cops showing up here, because I really doubt it's legal to start your own bonfire in a public park during the summer season, and what if . . . What if Dad or Ruben got wind that I was involved in an altercation with the police?

Oh, I'm dead. I'm so dead.

Blake slams the tailgate shut, then runs his hand through his hair. "No. Worse," he says.

Right then, a voice hisses, "*Blake!*"

I recognize the voice instantly – it belongs to the real LeAnne Avery, the voice she uses behind closed doors when she isn't keeping up appearances.

The clicking of heels on concrete draws nearer and LeAnne steps into view around Blake's truck, her face like thunder and her arms furiously crossed over her chest. For once, she doesn't look as though she's just wrapped up a press conference. She's wearing jeans and a buttoned-up cardigan, and her hair is gathered in a high, pin-straight ponytail that swishes around her shoulders with each step she takes. She may not look like the mayor right now, but she still has the authoritative stance of one.

"I thought you were staying in the city tonight," Blake says, taking a protective step in front of me as though to shield me from the wrath of his mom.

"I changed my mind," LeAnne says coolly, but her fury is evident. She squeezes the car keys in her hand as though they're a stress ball. "You weren't at the house when I got back. I got worried."

"How did you know –"

LeAnne pulls her phone from her purse and holds it up. "Maybe if you don't want your mother checking your location, you should block me in the future," she says, her voice dripping with sarcasm. She puts her phone away and turns her back on us, studying the scene by the lake. Music is still playing, and everyone is happily mulling around, oblivious to the fact that Mayor Avery has shown up. "A bonfire?" she hisses through tight lips, twisting back around. "In a *park*? This was your idea, no doubt? You *idiot*, Blake!"

"We aren't harming anyone!" Blake argues, raising his voice in self-defense. "There's no trees near the fire. We aren't being too loud. We're just—"

"Singing around the fire?" LeAnne sharply cuts in, nodding to the guitar case on the truck bed behind us. She raises an eyebrow as though challenging Blake to deny it. "All this trouble just so you get the chance to play in front of an *audience*, huh?"

Blake remains silent, but, standing next to him, I sense the tremor of fury that ripples through him. In a seething voice, he growls, "You aren't the goddamn Mayor of Fairview. You don't control us here."

LeAnne, terrifyingly calm, closes the few steps that separate Blake and her. She draws her face to his, then puts her hand flat on his chest so that he's forced to look straight back at her. "Shut it down," she orders venomously. "Right now."

"Okay!" Blake barks in defeat, moving free of her. He brushes down his shirt and, nostrils flaring, cuts his eyes to me. "Mila, get in the truck."

"No," LeAnne retorts.

Blake's expression twists as he looks back to his mother. "*No?*"

"You are staying here, Blake," she declares. "You are sending all of those kids home. You are cleaning up every single item that was brought here tonight. You are putting that fire out and you aren't leaving here until you ensure the remaining ash has completely cooled down. I don't care if that means you're out here all night."

"I can do all that," Blake mutters. "But I gave Mila a ride," he insists, his voice stronger. "And Myles and Savannah. How are they going to get home?"

LeAnne doesn't say anything at first, but she sets her fierce eyes on me and I know I don't want to hear her answer. I shrink further into myself, drawing my shoulders in tight, wishing I could hide out of sight.

"I'll take them home," says LeAnne at last. She continues to glower at me with nothing short of contempt, as though I personally organized this little campfire singalong myself. "Mila, go to my car. Blake, go and get your cousins."

"But—"

"*Now.*"

Blake reluctantly sets off, stopping after a few yards to turn back with a weary, torn expression. "*I'm sorry,*" he mouths. Then he continues toward the bonfire to shut down the night.

"Mila," LeAnne says.

"What?" I bite back more aggressively than I mean to. How can she talk to her son like that? How can she always look at me as though I'm filth she's just discovered trodden into on her shoe?

"This way," she says, and begins to walk.

At first, I don't want to follow her. Just moments ago, Blake's lips were against mine and I was sinking happily into the scent of firewood and cologne and the sensation of his fingers brushing my skin. It all ended so quickly that I can't help but question if it ever really happened. There's still the soft taste of him on my lips, but it's vanishing like campfire smoke in the night air.

How can I go from kissing Blake in the back of his truck to now being ordered around by his mom?

But it looks like Mayor Avery isn't someone whose orders you ignore.

So, I follow her.

18

"Aunt LeAnne, this is *unfair*," Myles grumbles. "You believe in fairness, don't you? Your policies are all about being *fair*, aren't they?"

"Myles, you're cruising for a bruising," LeAnne says. "Be quiet."

"You have officially been relegated to my least favorite relative," he replies, fearless. "You're now behind Uncle Ricky, and *no one* likes Uncle Ricky."

LeAnne pointedly ignores him. Her eyes are set fiercely on the darkness ahead as she weaves her luxurious Tesla down the narrow country roads. The radio isn't on, so the deafening silence is only heightening the tense atmosphere in this car right now. Myles has spent the past ten minutes complaining in outrage, not only about the bonfire being shut down so soon after it began, but also about the embarrassment of having his aunt deliver him home to the Willowbank ranch, which makes me wonder if perhaps Patsy isn't exactly aware of what it was that her kids were getting up to this evening.

Savannah, on the other hand, hasn't said a single word. Neither have I.

Unfortunately for me, I am riding shotgun. I sit stock-rigid with my knees together, my shoulders drawn tight, and my hands under my thighs to stop myself from playing nervously with my fingers. I can't bring myself to even glimpse at LeAnne, so my eyes are fastened to the blur of trees outside the window. It's too awkward, not because I was kissing her son not so long ago, but because it's so painfully clear that LeAnne really does not like me.

The road we're traveling down becomes slowly recognizable in the dark. The Harding Estate can't be much further, except . . . We're coming at it from the wrong direction. We're going to reach the Willowbank ranch first. *No, no, no.*

A familiar sense of dread chokes itself around me. It's the same feeling that took over the night of the tailgate party, when I was already uncomfortable around Blake and ended up alone in his truck with him while he dropped me off. But this . . . This is far *far* worse. LeAnne is a million times more intimidating than Blake will ever be. Plus, I get the feeling she has significantly more power than her son to make my life a misery.

"Home safe and sound with no citations," LeAnne says as the Tesla quietly rolls to a stop. She twists her neck to glower at her niece and nephew in the backseat. "Now go on. Inside."

Myles throws open the car door and climbs out at lightning speed. "Thanks for being a buzzkill, Mayor Avery! If I ever move to the city, please be assured that you do *not* have my vote!" He slams the door and strides off through the field toward the Bennett farmhouse.

Savannah is much more civilized. "Thanks for the ride," she mumbles to her aunt. The sympathetic frown she offers me as she gets out of the car only intensifies my anxiety, but there's nothing she can do to help me right now. She disappears out of sight, following in Myles's footsteps.

The car begins to move again. LeAnne drives with both hands together on top of the steering wheel, her body bolt upright and slightly hunched forward. Any normal person, regardless of their opinion on the kid in their car, would surely force themselves to be civil and communicate to avoid an atmosphere as palpable as this one. It's terrifying that LeAnne remains perfectly quiet, like she *wants* me to feel uncomfortable.

The two minutes it takes to reach the Harding Estate feel like the longest two minutes of my entire life. By the time LeAnne pulls up outside the now-familiar gates, I have never been more relieved to see them. I grab my shoulder bag from the floor and root around inside it for the gate remote.

"I knew this ranch before it required any of these security measures."

My hands freeze and I look up. "What?"

LeAnne exhales a long, heavy breath. She slumps back against her seat, staring straight ahead into the darkness, unblinking. "Would I be right to assume that Blake hasn't told you?"

"Told me what?"

"Oh, he's a nice boy – Blake. Of course, he knows it's not his place to tell you," she says quietly. She rests her hands on the bottom of the steering wheel now. "But it's definitely my place."

"What are you . . ." The words stick in my throat, rasping it dry like sandpaper. "What are you talking about?"

LeAnne's dark eyes, big and brown just like Blake's, move to me. She doesn't turn her head, just stares at me with a look that sends a chill down my spine. "I knew your father when I was young. In fact, I knew him *really* well. I knew Everett Harding before the world did."

"Well, sure. You must have attended Fairview High too," I say in a weak voice, as I try to make sense of this exchange. Where is this going? What is she about to tell me? The coldness in her eyes tells me I do not want to know.

LeAnne tuts at my naive innocence. "Mila . . . Sweetie. Your father and I . . ." she says, turning her head to look at me through narrowed eyes. Then she takes a deep gulp of air and looks away. "We were engaged."

I stare at LeAnne with an expression so blank it's as though her words have gone straight over my head. They don't hit me in the way they should, they don't sink in. I don't understand. My Dad? Engaged? To Blake's *mom*?

"That's a surprise to you, isn't it?" LeAnne continues over my silence. She presses her lips together into forced pity. "It's no surprise to me, though, that your parents wouldn't tell you about their own infidelity."

The heat across my face turns to ice and I feel deathly sick all of a sudden. All the oxygen seems to have been vacuumed out of the car – my breaths grow labored. "What are . . . What are you saying?" I whisper, shaking my head in disbelief. Why is she telling me these nasty lies? What did I do to make her treat me like this?

"Oh, this is such a shame that I have to be the one to tell you," she sighs, but the undertow of glee in her voice implies that this is anything *but* a shame for her to be the one to tell me. With a gentle cough to clear her throat, she sits up and clasps her hands together in front of her the same way I imagine she does when delivering a speech. "Everett and I were high school sweethearts," she begins. "We started dating in our sophomore year and got engaged the summer after graduation. We were so young; I should have known it was a silly, silly idea. And then we went off to college. Your father went to Belmont to study theater arts; I ventured further, to Yale to study political science. The creative arts are such a flimsy option . . . No stability in those careers. I had my head screwed on too tight for your father, and it pushed us apart when he met someone at Belmont who showed enthusiasm for his *acting* in a way that I didn't."

"My mom," I whisper.

I've always known exactly how my parents met. They met in college, at Belmont University here in Nashville. Mom had moved from South Carolina to study in a city that she believed was expressive and full of life, and it was at school that she met Dad. She loved that he wanted to pursue acting, and he loved that she supported his dream despite how out of reach it may have seemed. They got married after they graduated and settled in Fairview together in the house where I lived the first six years of my life in. That's their story. *That's* how they met.

Except right now LeAnne is retelling the story in an entirely different light.

"Yes, your mom," she says bitterly. "You'd think, having met someone else, that Everett would have the courtesy to call off the engagement. Your parents snuck around behind my back for two months, all because I was at school a few hours away and your dad claims that he wanted to wait until he next saw me – *face to face* – before calling it quits. I'd have rather heard the truth over a phone call – hell, a text would've been fine – on day one than be told the truth to my face months down the line. But no, Everett chose to cheat."

"You're lying," I gasp through clenched teeth. "None of this is true!"

I mean, it can't be . . . The Mayor of Nashville is telling me that my dad cheated on her – with my mom? My dad was supposed to be *married* to LeAnne? This is all a bizarre fantasy. There's no way it can be true. My parents have told me how they met, and their version of events did not involve an engagement to someone else. There's a dirty taste of grit in my mouth at the thought.

"Mila, what possible reason could I have to lie about something like this?" LeAnne says in a voice seemingly full of pity, cocking her head to one side to observe me. She can tell that I don't believe a word she says. "We called off the engagement and I took a few years to find myself while your parents got married instead. I met someone else, I became a mother, and I threw myself into my work with the council. But then your father made his Hollywood debut."

As I look at her, the only thing flashing through my mind

is my parents' reactions when I mentioned her name over video call earlier this week. Mom became wide-eyed and quiet; Dad filled with a rage so intense he slammed his laptop screen shut . . . There *is* obviously something there between my parents and LeAnne Avery, but it can't be . . .

It can't be *this*.

"What does his Hollywood debut have to do with anything?" I force out, despite the tremor in my voice.

"Because it meant he would now be in the spotlight," LeAnne says. "He was worried I would speak to the press and sell them the story of how the heartthrob that is Everett Harding once cheated on his faithful, hardworking fiancée. No one likes a cheater, do they? Such negativity. Imagine . . ." She relaxes back against her seat again, and for the first time tonight, her energy shifts from offense to defeat, mixed in with a tinge of sadness. "Your parents tried to pay me off, Mila. A man by the name of Ruben Fisher wanted to send me a big fat check in exchange for a non-disclosure agreement. Naturally, I have more dignity than that, and for the sake of my own career I have no intention of making my history with Everett Harding public."

"This isn't . . ." I shake my head fast and rub my eyes, hoping that when I open them again I'll be anywhere else but here. "I can't make sense of anything you're saying."

"I think you can. Mila, I'm not telling you this to upset you. I'm telling you this because it's the kind of backstory that means our families really shouldn't mix, and I'm sure your parents would agree with me," LeAnne says softly. She pushes a button, and the passenger door opens, signaling that it's time for me to get out. Then, gripping the wheel, eyes set firmly on the road ahead, never quite looking at me again, she adds, "I hope for everyone's sake, Mila, that you'll get to go home soon."

And I step out of the car, defeated.

19

We don't go to church that Sunday morning.

Popeye is tired, so Sheri decides it's best if the three of us stay home today. She doesn't realize how much of a relief this is – I don't think I could face the Averys so soon after last night's bombshell revelation.

It's mid-afternoon and I'm back in my room after washing the dishes after lunch, sprawled out on my bed, and staring blankly at the ceiling. My phone is turned off and shut away in a drawer. The whir of the rotating fan on my wall is oddly soothing as the cool air brushes over my skin every five seconds. I don't have the energy to move. Even just *thinking* feels like too much effort. It feels as though I'm carrying the weight of a thousand bricks inside my head.

All my life, I thought my parents connected naturally at school and fell in love in that perfect, old-fashioned sort of way. But how could LeAnne know that my parents met at Belmont if what she told me wasn't true? How could she know Ruben's name?

Well, all that information can be easily found on the internet, I tell myself. But yet, I know somewhere deep within me, in that same part of me where I hold on to the resentment of feeling second-best to Dad's career, that LeAnne's words aren't vicious lies.

I feel shaken to the core by the idea of Dad cheating on someone, not even on an early girlfriend, but on his *fiancée*, and that Mom was complicit. And then Dad was so worried about his career, about the consequences of what he'd done, that he attempted to buy LeAnne's silence, even though she didn't need any convincing to be quiet. If the past month has taught me anything, it's that there are seemingly no limits to the lengths to which Dad will go to remain adored by Hollywood – and squeaky clean in the eyes of the public.

"Mila?" Sheri says, knocking on my door and then pushing it open anyway.

"What?" I say without bothering to tear my eyes from the ceiling.

I don't mean to be abrupt or cold with Sheri and Popeye, but today I can't help it. It's obvious they know the truth – how could they not? – that's why Sheri was clearly uncomfortable and encouraged me to speak to my parents, not her, about LeAnne Avery. I don't want to tell them that it was, in fact, LeAnne herself who told me the truth as to why us Hardings and the Averys can't be friends. If I discuss this with Sheri . . . It would be like I'm admitting that I believe LeAnne's story. Admitting that my parents have lied to me about how they met. And admitting that I honestly don't know who Dad is anymore.

"You have a visitor," says Sheri, flipping a dish towel over her shoulder and folding her arms. She leans back against the door frame with a sigh. "Blake buzzed the gate. I let him in."

"You did?" I pull myself upright and blink at her in surprise. "Why? I thought you told me you didn't think it was a good idea for Blake and me to hang out together."

"Well, it's *not* a good idea," she says, and then she smiles in her usual soft, warm way that lets me know she's on my side. "But I'm not going to stop you from seeing a boy you like."

I rise from my bed and slip on a pair of flip flops, then brush past Sheri with an embarrassed grin. And as I run downstairs, I realize that for the first time I didn't argue the point of Blake being a boy who I like.

Outside in the blistering heat, he waits.

The gate is shut again, but Blake's truck is parked next to Sheri's van, and at the foot of the porch steps Blake stands with Bailey's leash wrapped tightly around one hand and the other slid into the pocket of his shorts. Bailey sits on his haunches, tail wagging and tongue hanging out. The sight of the two of them immediately eases the tightness I've felt in my chest since last night. They are *so cute*.

"You weren't at church, and you weren't replying to my texts," Blake says as I skip down the porch steps to meet them. "I got worried. I thought . . ."

I kneel down to rake my hands through Bailey's fur. "You thought . . .?"

"I thought you packed up and went home," Blake says, looking down. He's changed from his church slacks to a

Tennessee Titans jersey, and he fiddles anxiously with the hem. "After what my mom told you."

Oh. He knows.

I mean, he already *knew* about his mom's history with my dad. But I didn't expect him to know that LeAnne told me the truth last night. It's a relief, I guess. It saves me the discomfort of having to tell him what happened.

Still, I have no idea what to say in response. I just stare into Bailey's huge glossy eyes and continue scratching behind his ears in silence. My face burns.

"How about a walk?" Blake suggests after a minute.

I hesitantly nod. After our kiss last night, I should be thrilled to see Blake again. We should be giddy and shy, but LeAnne's revelations have ruined everything. How am I supposed to feel excited and flirty around Blake when I feel like my head might just combust from the pressure that's mounting inside it? This isn't how the morning after is supposed to be.

I straighten up and follow Blake back to the gate where I let us out. We head out onto the empty country roads together, the two of us side-by-side, while Bailey tugs on the leash to sniff at the grass overgrowing from the surrounding fields. Our steps are slow, and neither of us says anything for the first few minutes. We just stare ahead, squinting into the sunlight and mulling over the different thoughts inside our heads.

Finally, Blake says, "I'm sorry."

"Yeah," is all I respond in a quiet voice. I hug my arms around me and fight the burning at the corners of my eyes.

Here they come again, all these thoughts about Dad . . . A cheater . . . A liar . . . A fraud.

"Have you spoken to your parents?"

"No. I don't think . . ." I take a deep breath and squeeze my eyes shut. "I don't think I can face them. Not yet. I need to process all of this first."

"My mom shouldn't have told you," Blake says, shaking his head. He glares up at the clear blue sky. "That was so wrong to ambush you last night like that. It's something you should have only ever found out from your parents themselves."

"I don't think my parents would have ever told me," I mumble. When I questioned them about LeAnne Avery, that was their opening. That was their opportunity to tell me the truth, but they chose to keep silent. I don't believe for a second that this was a secret of theirs they ever intended on sharing.

"Probably because it's not something you needed to know," Blake says. We stop walking to wait for Bailey to finish exploring a patch of thorn bushes, and Blake rubs his hand over the back of his neck in his usual frustrated way. "Me and my mom aren't talking anymore. Not that things were exactly great between us. I didn't get home until two last night because I stayed until the fire was out and the ash had cooled, and she was in the kitchen waiting for me. She told me what happened when she dropped you off."

"Does she know you're here right now?" I ask as we begin to walk again. Our pace feels slower and slower with each step we take. We have barely made any progress; the walls of the Harding Estate still run parallel to us.

"No, she thinks I took Bailey to the park," he says. Then, with a faint smile, he adds, "And I blocked her from checking my location, which is something I should have done forever ago."

The frown on my face doesn't waver. My head feels even heavier as if it really is weighed down by bricks. I am learning too many secrets recently, and there's no room left to deal with all of these conflicting emotions of hurt and betrayal and confusion.

"She doesn't want you to see me," I say.

"I know."

"Then why did you come?"

Blake halts and turns to face me. His eyes narrow as they run over me, taking me in. "Why wouldn't I?"

"But—"

"No. Listen," he says abruptly. He steps forward and places his hand on my hip, bowing his head to look at me solemnly from beneath his eyelashes. "I don't care, not one bit, about what happened in the past. That's between my mom and your parents. Not us. So please don't think for even a second that I'm going to lose interest in you simply because my mom is holding a grudge."

I only absorb a couple of his words, but they are the most important ones. "So . . ." I can't help but tease, "you're interested in me?"

"Oh, c'mon, Mila," he says, kicking self-consciously at the dirt. "You should know by now that I was interested as soon as you opened my truck door that first weekend. Catching your eye in the rearview and you giving me this shy, timid smile while you blushed. Yeah, exactly like that!"

My hands fly to my face to hide the color that has risen in my cheeks. Honestly, I have zero hope of ever hiding how Blake makes me feel. It's so uncontrollable, and it gets one hundred times worse once I become aware of it.

"Miss Mila, let me see that cute blushing of yours," Blake says. His hands reach for mine, Bailey's leash around his wrist, and he pulls them away from my face, revealing my burning, freckled cheeks again. He beams, his dimples flashing. "There we go. You'd miss me making you blush if we stopped seeing each other, right?"

I nod, biting my lip to stop myself from grinning too wide. My hands are still in his. "Maybe."

"Then stop worrying about what my mom said, because I'm not going anywhere."

Our gazes lock on to one another a little stronger. Our hands are held together between our chests, and Blake ignores Bailey tugging on his leash. We are standing in the road with the sun shining down upon us and no cars in sight, just Blake and me in the Middle of Nowhere, Tennessee. The Nashville-dreaming musician and the girl who one day wants to be more than just Everett Harding's daughter. Two people trying to live in their parents' shadows; two people who aren't going to be told what to do.

Blake edges closer.

"Wait," I whisper. "Not right now."

I would love to kiss Blake again, but my head is a mess.

I want the next time I kiss him to be perfect and with no random interruptions; I want to be able to focus entirely on only him. This isn't the right moment; not when the ground has just been knocked out from under me and I have so many questions that still need answers.

"Okay, Miss Mila," Blake murmurs, and he lightly presses his soft lips against my cheek instead.

20

On Wednesday, Sheri reluctantly agrees to take some time away from the ranch to do something for herself. It took a lot of convincing for her to accept Patsy's offer of simply heading out for coffee together, because I'm starting to realize that Sheri hasn't done anything for herself in a long time. She works too hard.

I promised to keep Popeye company for the afternoon and I even offered to cook dinner tonight, and finally Sheri left the ranch with her hair and makeup styled to perfection by none other than me. It helps having a mom who's a professional artist – I've picked up some tips over the years.

She's been gone for a few hours now, and Popeye and I have been left to our own devices. We've played Scrabble, because Popeye says it was his favorite board game when he was younger, and now I'm in the kitchen peeling fresh vegetables because it's nearing dinner.

"Do you want me to refill your tea?" I call through the kitchen to the living room where Popeye watches TV. I chuck a bunch of chopped carrots into the crock pot, then pause when I realize Popeye hasn't replied. His hearing isn't the greatest anymore. I wipe my hands on a towel and cross to the living room. "Popeye, would you like . . ."

My words die in my throat when I realize why Popeye is ignoring me – he's engrossed in the TV, visibly aggrieved. He has switched the channel over from the old black-and-white movie I left him watching earlier to the showbiz entertainment channels.

The host of a gossip show is gesturing at a picture of Dad and his co-star, Laurel Peyton, at one of their press conferences, his hand around her waist and their eyes bright from the flashing of a thousand cameras.

"*Everett Harding and Laurel Peyton are gearing up for their biggest box office success yet. The long-awaited third installment of the Flash Point series hits movie theaters across the country this weekend, and we have our leading couple here now!*"

The live audience erupts with applause as Dad and Laurel emerge from backstage. Dad's in black slacks and a white shirt with too many of the top buttons undone – at the orders of his stylist, no doubt – and Laurel wears a butter-yellow summer dress that floats around her slim legs as she struts across the stage. They both have their dazzling Hollywood smiles plastered upon their faces. They wave to the appreciative audience, then sit down on a couch opposite the host, ready to respond to questions with charm and wit.

"He thinks this is real work," Popeye mutters under his breath. "Smiling to a camera . . ."

I step in front of the TV and stare down into Popeye's gaze. "Why are you watching this?"

Popeye only stares straight ahead, as though he can still

see the TV through my body. I grab the remote out of his lap and turn off the show, zapping the living room into an intense silence.

Popeye grumbles in annoyance and fixes his eyes stubbornly ahead. "What – I can't keep tabs on my own son every now and again? How else will I ever know what's going on in his life? It's not like I ever hear from him."

"Oh," I say, unsure. Popeye has never spoken to me in such a sharp tone, so honest and so open, and I'm taken aback by how agitated he looks. "I'm ... I'm sorry that he doesn't call enough."

I'm not oblivious to reality. Dad's life these days is far too glamorous and hectic; there's no time for visits to the childhood ranch. I sensed the moment I arrived in Fairview that Sheri and Popeye feel a bit abandoned, relegated to pieces in the puzzle of Everett Harding's former life, but I didn't know how that must feel until recently. I know now how badly it hurts to feel second-best. And Sheri and Popeye ... They are much further down Dad's list of priorities than I am.

"Doesn't call. Doesn't visit," Popeye growls with an anger I wasn't expecting my words to trigger. "How difficult is it to pick up the phone? Are we really that forgettable? Not good enough for him?"

This is the most emotion I have seen Popeye show this summer. He is usually so warm and kind, but now he seems angry and wounded, his feelings raw. I wish I could fix this, but I have no control over Dad's choices or his behavior. I barely have any control over my own.

I sit down on the couch next to Popeye and reach for his

hand, holding it tight in mine. "I'm sorry, Popeye. Of course you're good enough for him. He loves you. He just lives a busy life."

Neither of us says anything more, because what else is there? Popeye doesn't have to tell me how he feels – I know.

After a while, he asks, "Can you play a song for me?"

I lift my head to look at him. I nod and cross the living room to the polished wood record player that sits on a table by the window. This player is so old – beyond vintage – that I'm always amazed when I hear the tinkle of music streaming through the house.

"What song, Popeye?"

Popeye closes his eyes and inhales. "Play me 'Close To You' by the Carpenters."

I flick through the box of vinyls, which is Popeye's treasured collection from when he and Mamaw were first married back at the start of the '70s. Most of these songs I've never even heard of. Their sleeves are a little tattered and slightly faded, but that just means they've been well-loved over the decades. Finally, I find the album Popeye has requested and I carefully slide the vinyl out, lift the tinted clear cover and place it on the player. I move the needle into place and then stand back as the opening beats of the song ring out around the living room, and although I don't recognize the song title, I quickly realize that I *have* heard this before. It's so old, so slow, so '70s.

Popeye keeps his eyes shut as he nods appreciatively in unison with the agonizingly drawn-out rhythm, and then he asks, "Can you dance with me, Mila?"

Dancing to golden oldies is *not* my forte, but Popeye needs some cheering up. This is what loving granddaughters do – slow dance to '70s hits they only vaguely know.

I move back to Popeye and gently help him up from the couch. We are unsteady at first, toppling awkwardly, but then he wraps an arm around my back, and we balance ourselves out. Popeye's much shorter than I remember him being when I was younger – I think he has shrunk. He clasps one of my hands in his, and we begin to sway. Then, after a moment or two, we hit the beat nicely together and move along smoothly as the record plays, and Popeye rests his head on my shoulder.

"I know you didn't choose to come here," he murmurs, "but I'm really glad that you've spent some time with us. It's been wonderful watching you live the life you could have always had."

His words hit me hard.

The life you could have always had . . .

If Dad had never gotten his big Hollywood break, we might have never left Fairview. I would have continued growing up here. I would have my own southern drawl, I would have been best friends with Savannah all through school, I would have met Blake a decade ago. Tailgate parties and singsongs around campfires would be a regular occurrence, and trips to Nashville to eat meat smothered in barbecue sauce at Honky Tonk Central would be normal rather than outlandish. I might have gone skinny-dipping in the lake, and who knows, I would probably even know how to ride a horse properly.

Dad wouldn't have adoring fans who stalk his every move, we wouldn't have Ruben controlling our lives, and Mom would be able to step out in public in sweatpants with her hair tied back without worrying about letting Dad down – or having the media pick over the "faults" in her appearance like carrion crows. We would maybe even live here, on this ranch. That was the plan, after all – for Dad to eventually take over once Popeye was no longer able to run this place by himself. Maybe by now we would have sold that house of ours on the other side of town and would be living here instead. Sheri would be out making the most of her life, enjoying her own adventures, and Popeye wouldn't feel so estranged from his son.

I can't regret the life I've had in LA ... but growing up here is the life I could have lived. Not this one – which I'm suddenly learning is jampacked with secrets and lies.

A voice from the kitchen breaks into my thoughts. "What's going on?"

I didn't even hear Sheri arrive home, but here she is right in front of us, reaching for Popeye to untangle him from me. Her expression is one of exasperation and something like fear.

"He wanted to dance," I say. I stand back, confused. Have I done something wrong? Why can't we have an easy little dance?

"Oh, Sheri, c'mon!" Popeye protests as he swats her hands away. "You act like that ol' Grim Reaper is going to come knocking any day! Stop coddling me."

Sheri shepherds him back to the couch, though Popeye

moves reluctantly while tutting in disagreement. "I just don't want you losing your balance again, Dad," she says, her tone worried.

"I'm sorry," I murmur from the sideline, twisting my fingers over and over again, unsure of what exactly is going on.

Popeye losing balance? Again?

"Don't apologize, Mila," Popeye says just as the needle lifts up off the end of the vinyl. "Thank you. You always were a sweet girl when it came to dancing."

I am really, really lost. My brows knit together as my gaze flickers back and forth between Popeye and Sheri, trying to read their unfamiliar expressions. "What's going on?"

"Nothing, Mila," says Sheri at the exact same time as Popeye says, "Let me tell you something, Mila."

Sheri parts her lips in protest and shakes her head fast. "Dad!"

"She'll figure it out eventually. Things aren't getting any better."

"What isn't getting any better?" I urge.

Popeye moves his stern gaze from Sheri to me. He forces a smile and his cheeks crease with deep wrinkles. "Sweet Mila, sit down," he says.

Sheri rubs at her temples as I sit down on the couch next to Popeye. I can't get comfortable – I sit on the very edge, my knees knocking together. I think I know what Popeye is about to say, but I don't want to believe it yet. I can't handle any more secrets.

"I am so glad that you're here," he says, reaching out for my hand, "because I'm slowing down."

"You're not *that* slow, Popeye," I say, looking at him askance. Popeye is only in his early seventies. It's not like he's a hundred and six.

"Maybe not," he says with a twitch of a smile, "but we think there's something wrong with me."

"How—" I swallow the lump in my throat and blink back the resurgence of tears from earlier, then I jump up and point at him in anger. "What do you mean, there's something wrong? You're fine, Popeye. You could have danced with me all afternoon!"

"We don't know yet, exactly," he hedges, but as he says this, there's no denying the fear that flashes in his eye. "We're running tests. I haven't been great for a while. Lots of little things. Oh, Mila, don't look at me like that!"

My heart shatters and the splices cut through me, leaving a burning wound in the middle of my chest. All of a sudden I can only imagine the worst. Hot tears spill down my cheeks, blurring my vision and making Popeye unrecognizable in front of me. I feel Sheri move closer to place a comforting hand on my shoulder. I don't mean to cry, but the thought of something being wrong with Popeye, the grandfather I haven't spent nearly enough time with, is too dizzying to bear.

"Does my dad know?" I force out, struggling to keep my breath steady. Dad has never mentioned *anything* about Popeye being ill.

"No," Sheri answers, squeezing my shoulder harder and guiding me back down onto the couch. She sits next to me and wipes away a tear. "I really do think we should tell him."

"No!" Popeye fiercely interjects. "Don't you dare, Sheri. This may be nothing."

"Dad should know that you aren't feeling well, Popeye," I say. "He'd come and visit you."

Now Popeye turns his angered frustration toward me, a strong tremor in his jaw. "I don't want him to visit out of sympathy!" he snaps, then shakes his head at Sheri and me. "Both of you stop looking at me like that! Stop! I'm not at death's door! Nowhere near it, in fact."

"We're just worried about you, Dad," Sheri says.

But Popeye is fed up of the concern, too stubborn to allow any pity for himself. Grumbling unintelligible words in a low voice, he rises from the couch and slinks off through the house, though now that I watch him with intense focus, I realize just how awkward his movements are, signs of the pain in his body.

Sheri collapses back against the couch, her hands pressed to her face, groaning a sigh. "There are a lot of things you don't know, Mila," she says quietly, but her voice is both apologetic and full of sympathy. She wraps an arm around me and pulls me in close, and, as she rests her chin on my head and hugs me tight, I sense that I am as much of a comfort to my aunt as she is to me.

21

That evening, I really feel like I can't stay at the ranch any longer. It's unbearable being alone in my room with a million different worries building up around me, and every time I go downstairs to fetch a drink, I can't even glance at Popeye without my chest heaving. Sheri is awfully muted, too.

I need fresh air, so I slip on my Nikes, pull a cap over my hair, then head out of the gate. I turn right and stride down the country road in the heat, southbound in the direction of downtown Fairview. It's an odd feeling, not quite knowing if you want to be alone or are desperate for someone to talk to. Not a single car passes me until thirty minutes later when I'm trudging through the overgrowth at the side of the main road. The people who do drive by all give me a friendly wave, but I don't return the gesture. I am not in the mood for small-town pleasantries.

Further down the road, it dawns on me that I *don't* want to be alone. I kind of want my mom. I want her to hop on the first flight to Nashville to come here, right now, and hug me. Her reassurances would mean the world, even though I don't know where my emotions sit in regard to her part in

254

all of this. The way LeAnne phrased it, it seems like Mom knew Dad already had a fiancée when she started seeing him, which makes her entangled in the betrayal ... Sure, Dad may have told LeAnne the truth eventually, but why did Mom continue seeing him until then? It just seems so massively ... disrespectful. And if Dad doesn't know about Popeye, then neither does she.

I pause beneath a tree to catch some shade from the relentless sun, and then pull out my phone. With an exhausted sigh, I call a number – that of the first person I think of – and wait patiently as the dial tone echoes across the line.

"Mila, hey," comes an answer, just before the call is about to go to voicemail.

"Blake," I stutter. "Uh-huh. Hi."

"Are you okay?" he asks, concern evident in his voice.

"Yeah, I'm just ... I needed to get out of the house," I say, rubbing at my eyes and sinking back against the tree. I feel so ... *Tired.* Tired of all these secrets. "Are you home?"

"Sure am."

I pause for a beat. "Your mom?"

"In the city," answers Blake. "Are you coming over? Do you want me to pick you up?"

"I'm walking. Can you text me your location? I don't really know where I am."

"Damn. Okay." Blake laughs. "Don't get lost."

I hang up and stare at my screen, waiting for Blake's message to arrive. A few seconds later and there's a text containing his live location. I pull up the directions, see that it's only two miles from here, and get back on the move.

It's not that late; just after six thirty. It's also the first time I've really taken the time to look at Fairview. I've explored a bit of the downtown area with Savannah and Tori, and I've seen all these quiet streets when driving through, but I've never just *walked*. It's so peaceful and the air feels fresh, so much cleaner here than back home. It also feels crazy to walk for thirty minutes without ever brushing shoulders with another person. Here in Fairview, with its quiet streets and mass of clear space, there is no pressure.

I cross over Fairview Boulevard, the only street around here that shows signs of civilization, with traffic and some pedestrians, and I continue south into residential neighborhoods. My phone guides me all the way to Blake's home. The stars and stripes above the porch blows in the breeze and his truck looks glossy and freshly waxed under the dusk sun. Although Blake already told me his mom is in Nashville, it's still a relief to see that her Tesla is gone. If she were here, I think I would back away right now.

Putting my phone away, I head around the side of the house and as soon as I brush my hand against the gate, the yelps of an excited Bailey fill the air. He catapults across the lawn and tangles himself around my legs the second I step foot in the yard, so pleased to see another human being that he doesn't quite know what to do with himself.

"You made it," says Blake.

I glance up from ruffling Bailey's golden fur and a smile spreads over my face at the sight of Blake walking over. It could be because I'm happy to see him again, but it could also be because he's wearing gray sweatpants ... *Only* sweatpants.

Blake is shirtless. It's not the first time I've seen his body – I could barely get a word out that day at the Bennetts' pool – but right now, as he strolls toward me in the hazy glow of the sunset, he looks even more perfectly sculpted. His tanned, toned skin shimmers with trickles of sweat and there's a very prominent V-line that disappears under the hem of his boxers. A silver chain around his neck catches the sunlight as he walks, and he pushes his damp hair back out of his eyes.

"What have you been ... doing?" I manage to force out.

"Oh, just some bar pull-ups in between jamming," he says with a laugh, then changes direction toward the house instead. "I'll grab a shirt. Back in a sec."

"No!" I blurt, then instantly want to *die*. Blake stops and looks back at me with a raised eyebrow, his eyes flashing and a smirk forming. "I can't believe I just said that."

Blake chuckles and swaggers his chest a little at me, then continues into the house.

"Oh, Bailey ..." I mumble, shaking my head at myself, mortified. Bailey gazes up at me with shining eyes, his head tilted fully to the side. "When will I ever act cool in front of him?"

With Bailey on my heels, I cross the yard to Blake's cabin. The glass doors are propped open wide and there's music playing at a muted volume from a speaker beneath the TV. Some weighted plates are scattered on the ground next to the gym equipment, not yet packed away. On the couch, Blake's Gibson Hummingbird sits surrounded by notebooks with scrawled handwriting covering the paper. Despite my curiosity, I refrain from being intrusive and tear my eyes away from his words.

"Let me move that," Blake says, appearing behind me. He's wearing a baby blue T-shirt now that matches surprisingly well with his dark hair and eyes, and I smell the fresh spritz of deodorant.

Blake gathers up his notebooks at speed and stuffs them away into the drawer of a side table, then picks up his guitar and gestures for me to take its place on the couch instead. I do.

"Don't put it away," I say, when he moves to put his guitar back in its case.

Blake pauses, his guitar hovering mid-air. "No?"

"I might need you to play for me," I admit, then hunch forward over my knees and press my hands to my face. Groaning, I tell him, "I'm having a rough day."

I sense Blake rest the guitar into its upright stand, then head back around the couch to sit down next to me. His knee bumps mine, accidentally for once, and he presses a comforting hand to my back. "What's up, Mila?"

"Popeye . . ."

"Popeye?"

"My grandpa," I say, dropping my hands from my face. I peer at Blake out of the corner of my eye and feel at ease seeing his guitar resting on its stand. Maybe he *will* play some music for me so that I can focus on anything but the Harding family secrets. "Something is wrong with him."

"Oh." Blake inhales sharply. "I'm sorry."

My eyes are fixed straight ahead, locked on nothing in particular, my shoulders swaying. It makes me feel dizzy, knowing that one day Popeye won't be around anymore and that I missed out on so many memories with him that I would have had if circumstances had been different. I know Popeye is aging, that much is guaranteed, but what if something really is *seriously* wrong? Something that'll take him from us sooner?

I manage to gather my thoughts enough to speak. "He seems okay for now, but it sounds like they're trying to figure out what the problem is. He doesn't want my dad to know. My dad, who doesn't even visit . . . Maybe if he did, he would notice for himself."

Blake rubs soft circles on my back with his palm. "You seem pretty angry at your dad," he says gently.

"Of course I'm angry!" I snap, tearing my eyes away from the wall and setting them on Blake. Exasperated, I fling my hands up in the air, daring the world to throw me one more curveball. "Dad ships me over here for the summer and sets secret orders for me to essentially be held captive at the ranch. And then I find out there's something wrong with my grandpa and my dad is off living his glamorous life, totally oblivious, because he doesn't ever bother to go call. Oh, and how could I forget – I find out he was once engaged to your mom! But he cheated on her! With *my* mom!"

Blake winces. "Uh, yeah. Not exactly the greatest guy on earth, is he?" he says awkwardly, then reaches for my hand. He intertwines our fingers. "Have you spoken to him about *any* of this?"

"What is there to say? *You may have the rest of the world fooled into thinking you're some charming, family-focused man, but you're really just a selfish phony who cares about no one but yourself?*"

Blake pulls a face. "Damn. That's harsh." He smiles softly at me. "Even though I have to agree."

I sink my head forward again and rub my temple, feeling the stress pulsing from me. "I don't really . . . I mean, he's my dad. I love him. Of *course* I do." I straighten up and look at mine and Blake's interlocked hands. All of the anger pent up inside of me deflates a little, leaving my shoulders to slump in defeat. "I just don't think I know who he is anymore."

"Do you want to call him?" Blake asks. "Maybe he'll have some answers for you."

"Well, yeah. I just keep putting it off because . . ."

I take a deep breath. I have never – not once – in my entire life confronted my father about *anything*. We have never really fought all that much besides petty disagreements where I slam a door in his face for not letting me stay out later than curfew or something equally as trivial. This though? This is *huge*. This is serious. It could ruin both our worlds, and it's the kind of drama Dad really *doesn't* love. Something in my gut tells me that if I go through with this, if I question Dad about all of these secrets I've discovered, then things might change between us. And it might be a change that I don't have the ability to fix again.

"I guess I don't want a fight," I finally finish, my frown deepening. "I've gotten used to staying quiet unless told otherwise."

"You could call him now when you aren't alone. It might help if I'm here." Blake's tone rises to end on a hopeful note. "And if it doesn't go well, then I'll sing to you all night until you're smiling again."

His goofy words are enough for me to smile right then and there.

"Okay," I say, then nod several times in affirmation. "Okay."

"I'll be right outside. If you need me, just shoot me a hand signal, all right?" Blake says, letting go of my hand and standing up. Then he does the most surprising thing – he clasps my face in both hands and lowers his head to mine, gazing into my eyes with supportive reassurance. "It'll be cool. Stand firm, say what you need to say, and if you feel like you're going to cry, do some math in your head as a distraction technique." He smiles. "Or just – you know – imagine me naked."

"Blake!" I gasp, but the sound of his name has barely filled the air before he pecks his lips against mine. Then his smile widens and that knot in my stomach becomes undone.

"C'mon, Bails," he instructs.

With Bailey curiously following, Blake heads out of the cabin. He fetches a rubber ball from inside a pot plant and erratically squeezes it, driving Bailey wild. While the two of them mess around, I pull out my phone.

Dad's name is quite far down in my list of recent contacts. Most of my calls have been to Mom and my friends, but with the occasional call from Ruben to check in on "life at the farm". It makes me nervous to pull up Dad's number now. I should know better than to contact him unsolicited and without warning.

But he should know better than to keep secrets from his daughter.

I dial the number before I can change my mind, then instantly begin pacing the length of the cabin, dodging weighted plates, and nearly tripping over Bailey's water bowl. It feels like my lower lip is nearly bitten to shreds by the time the call is answered.

"Mila, honey!" Ruben's artificially sweet voice shrills across the line. His pleasure to hear from me is so forced, so fake, that it makes me hate him a thousand times more than I already did.

"I need to talk to my dad," I state clearly, calmly. "Give him his phone."

"Oh, Mila, not right now. Everett is busy. He's just about to do a live interview with –"

"Put – my dad – on – the phone," I demand, vehemently spitting each word.

"Wow. Where did this attitude come from?" Ruben asks loftily, chuckling to himself. "Doesn't sound like you've learned much about that famous southern hospitality!"

"I need to talk to my dad," I repeat, calm again before my killer punch. "And that means right now, or I'll let your favorite gossip columnists know that Everett Harding has locked his daughter away for the summer in case she *embarrasses* him."

Ruben quits laughing. He is momentarily silenced, perhaps in shock that I seem to have suddenly grown a backbone. "Mila ... C'mon now ..." he says warily in an attempt to de-escalate my rage. "Let's not make threats—"

"NOW, RUBEN!"

"Keep your hair on," Ruben huffs. "I'll see what I can do."

I hear him cussing under his breath, and then there's the muffled sound of Dad's phone being passed around. A few moments where I think I can hear hushed voices speaking fast, and then the call is picked up again. It's not Ruben anymore.

"Mila," Dad says. There is no warmth in his clipped tone. "This is really not a good time. What are you doing making wild threats to Ruben?"

"Hi, Dad," I reply, as falsely cheerful as Ruben. Then, no preamble, I tell him, "I – know – everything."

Silence again. I can hear a lot of commotion in the background, most likely Dad and Ruben are backstage of some TV talk show, but then a door clicks shut, and the noise disappears. I think Dad is alone now.

"You know *what*, Mila?" he prompts, his voice a steely calm.

"I know it was your decision to lock me up on the ranch," I say, still pacing the cabin. I freeze on the spot for a second and stare outside into the yard where Blake is wrestling the ball out of Bailey's mouth, but his eyes are on me, watching. In an even harder, colder voice, I add, "And I know you cheated on LeAnne Avery with Mom."

The weight crushing down on my chest lifts. It feels like such a relief to finally face up to Dad, even though I know this conversation isn't over yet. The old Mila knows she should be afraid of Dad's reaction, but the Mila I'm becoming? She's different. She needs more than to be a prop in Everett Harding's life, picked up and put down in her place by Ruben. She needs her own life.

Dad is quiet for an awfully long time. All I hear across the line is his shallow breathing, and I imagine him pacing back and forth the same way I have been, his mind racing to calculate the most effective method of damage-control. At last, he heavily exhales and says, "I can't do this right now, Mila. Really. I'm working."

"Sorry, I forgot – everything is about *work*, right?" I sneer. "You'd rather get rid of your daughter than risk her daring to do anything that embarrasses you." I pause, gathering my strength. "And you had an *affair*! Does it make you nervous that LeAnne Avery never signed that non-disclosure agreement? Are you worried one day she'll tell the world that you're a cheater? Now *that* would be embarrassing."

My name sticks in Dad's throat, like his airways are tightening. "Mila," he rasps.

"*Dad*," I mimic.

"Why are you doing this right now? What exactly do you want?" he questions in a small voice, a trace of panic lacing his words. "Do you want to come home? Is that it? I'll get Ruben to book you a flight first thing tomorrow."

"No. You can tell Ruben not to book me a flight until the day before school starts, because maybe I don't *want* to come home," I say. "At least the people here are *real*. Oh, by the way, there's something wrong with Popeye's health, but you would know that already if you actually paid attention to your family."

"What?" he whispers.

A deranged laugh escapes me and bounces around the cabin, and Blake shoots me a wary look. "Dad, please don't bother acting like you care now. You should call him more! You should visit! Not because there might be something wrong with him, but because you *love* him. He's your father, remember?"

"Mila, you should come home," Dad mumbles, uneasy. For once, he doesn't have the upper hand. I am the one with all the power right now, because I *know*. And Dad seems – and I can hardly blame him – afraid of what I may do with all of this newly discovered information. "You shouldn't be out there in Fairview."

"Maybe before you shipped me out here," I hiss, "you should have thought more carefully about which of your lies I'd uncover."

And then, without another word, I do something I have never done before – I hang up on my father. I want the final say. There are no excuses for what he's done, and I don't want to hear him attempt to conjure up some. All I want is for him to know that I'm not in the dark anymore. I'm old enough now to know these secrets – they are about my family, my past, the future of the people I love – and I don't want to be lied to. It's as simple as that.

Blake notices me end the call, and jogs over to join me inside the cabin while Bailey remains scampering outside. "No tears. That's good. How did it go?"

I release a long, deep breath that I've been holding on to and collapse onto the couch, letting my phone slip through my fingers to land on the floor. Did I seriously just talk to Dad in such an assertive, confrontational way? Adrenaline is pumping so fast through my veins that I feel lightheaded.

"He's unsettled. I threatened I'd talk to the press." I sit up and widen my eyes at Blake, wishing to reassure him that I'm not the kind of person who would betray my family in such a way. "But, honestly, I would never, *ever* speak to anyone about him. Dad should know that I wouldn't do that, no matter what."

"Still. You did it, Mila," Blake says with a growing smile as he sits down next to me. "You spoke to him on your terms. Not so behind the scenes anymore, are you?"

Without thinking, I rest my head on his arm and sigh, full of mixed feelings. My body is in a tumult. A distraction wouldn't go amiss. I look up at him from beneath my lashes. "Can you play for me now?"

Blake nods and reaches for his guitar that's still propped up in its stand. My head falls back against his bicep as he pulls the guitar onto his lap and positions his hands. Just before his fingers touch the strings, I ask, "Do you write your own songs?"

"I try," he admits, "but I've never finished anything yet. I'm not great at putting my thoughts into words. That's why I always fail my English Lit assignments." He gazes at his guitar in concentration again, lining up his fingers. He isn't using a pick this time, which probably explains those callouses on the pads of his fingers. He strums once, letting the note hang in the air, then suddenly flattens his hand against the strings, silencing the noise. "Before I start, let me ask you something before I forget. My friends have managed to get tickets to your dad's movie this weekend. They got a ticket for me. And they – uh – got one for you, too."

I sit up and my brows knit together. "I thought you weren't a fan."

"I'm not, but we were gonna get food after. I don't wanna miss out," Blake confesses with a laugh. "I told Barney you probably don't want to go. I don't know. Is it crazy for you to watch your dad on screen? I'm not sure how you feel about these things, especially after that phone call . . ." He speaks faster than usual, like he's worried he's going to offend me and would rather get the words out as quickly as possible.

"It's okay," I say. "I'll come."

It's not something I've ever done before. I watch Dad's movies at exclusive early screenings, and never at the movie theater with everyone else. It makes me uncomfortable, honestly, to see Dad on screen, so it always seemed too weird to *choose* to watch his movies. But if Blake's friends have gone to the effort to include me, someone they barely even know, then it feels rude not to take up the offer. It would even feel over-dramatic *not* to go, like, *Mila Harding thinks she's much too special to watch her dad's movies with mere civilians.* They probably wouldn't think that, but still. I just want to be like everyone else. And Blake will be there, so it means spending more time with him, too.

"You'll go?" Blake says, surprised.

"Sure. I've already seen it, anyway. The ending is a huge let-down, and the second movie is still the best one, but don't let the critics hear me admit that," I joke, managing to laugh for the first time today.

Blake grins and says, "Looks like you and I are going to catch Everett Harding's new movie on Sunday."

"I can't wait," I say with an overly dramatic roll of my eyes, and then I rest my head back against him and wrap my arms around his. On purpose this time.

Blake returns his focus to his guitar, once again positioning a hand on the fretboard and the other by the strings, and then he plays. My eyes close as I listen to the acoustic rhythm fill the cabin, drifting gently into my body, and I slowly start to feel calmer as Blake's smooth voice dances in my ears, and I think my heart grows a little bigger.

22

"Look, if commercial first class won't convince you, how about I ask your father to send out a private jet? I'm sure in these circumstances there are no financial limits."

"You are beyond hilarious, Ruben," I say nonchalantly as I slip on my shoes, not exactly listening. My phone is on speaker on the nightstand as I've been getting ready and rolling my eyes every ten seconds at the absurdity of Ruben's pleas. "Go ahead. Send a private jet to come get me, but the pilot will have a wasted journey. I already told you a thousand times – I'm not coming home until the day before school starts, and that's only because I have to."

"When did you get *so* difficult?" Ruben grumbles. After days of blowing up my phone to convince me to come back to LA now that he and Dad have realized sending me off to Fairview was a terrible idea, Ruben is at the point where he doesn't even try to mask his annoyance at me with fake pleasantries and artificially sweet tones. "You were much easier to handle before you decided you have a say in any of these matters."

"Well, Ruben, *these matters* are my life," I retort breezily, getting to my feet. I grab my phone from the nightstand and press it to my ear. "And that sort of means that I should be the one who decides how to live it."

"Mila—"

"So sorry, Ruben, but I really do have to end this call now. I'm out," I interrupt, my voice rife with sadistic pleasure because I know how much this will aggravate him. And then, with extra sarcasm, I add, "Fingers crossed I don't cause too much trouble," before hanging up.

Honestly, if I had a couple more ounces of bravery, I may have blocked Ruben's number by now. But I don't want to deal with that fallout, and it's fun to torture him instead. I imagine him and Dad huddled close together in our lavish kitchen back home, conferring over how to deal with me, knowing all this information that shines a negative light on Dad's character. It's not very kind of me, but, hell, they deserve to feel unsettled.

My phone buzzes in my hand. No, it's not Ruben harassing me again.

It's a message from Blake that reads: *Hey, Mila. Get your sweet self outside. I'm waiting.*

With a grin of anticipation, I leave my room and head downstairs to where Popeye and Sheri are eating together at the dining table. We're all going for food after the movie, so I've had to skip dinner tonight.

"Blake's here," I announce, stopping behind Popeye and placing a hand on his shoulder.

Sheri sets down her fork and breaks into a laugh. "When you confronted your dad about Mayor Avery, did you remember to mention that you're dating her son?" she asks, wiggling her brows at me. She seems more at ease now I've confessed to her that I know all about how my parents' relationship started, that they have a history of infidelity. Now Sheri can relax and not have to worry about letting that particular secret slip.

"This isn't a *date*, Aunt Sheri. Blake's friends are going to be there," I say, because I'm not really sure that Blake and I could even be considered as *dating* in the first place. It's not like we've had an official date, but at least I am no longer denying that I like the boy. And I'm okay with that for now. We're still getting to know one another.

"And you wear perfectly applied red lipstick every time you hang out with friends?"

I purse those red lips of mine to blow her a pouty kiss. "Ha ha. Okay, I'm going now. Bye, Popeye."

"You are the image of your grandmother. Beautiful," he says. "Enjoy your evening, Mila."

With a small wave, I slip through the door and out into the evening sun. It's been another gorgeous day, but I'm realizing now that every day in Tennessee is a beautiful one. For once, though, I've remembered to bring my sunglasses with me, and I push them down over my eyes and trek toward the gate where Blake awaits on the other side.

We saw each other earlier at church. But he was with his mom, and with a flickering moment of eye contact across the pews, we exchanged an unspoken agreement to stay clear of each other. When the service wrapped up, we didn't search for the other in the parking lot. Blake remained firmly by

LeAnne's side while she nodded enthusiastically along to the church elders, and I didn't attempt to pull him over for a chat by our favorite shrubs, so instead I hung out with Savannah. When it comes to LeAnne's approval, I don't think we're going to get it. That just means Blake and I may have to be a little more discreet.

I reach the gate's control panel, hit my fist against the bright green button, and wait while the gate peels open to reveal Blake hanging casually out the rolled down window of his truck. His hair is styled with gel, tousled to one side, and he beams when he sees me.

"C'mon, girl, we've got a movie to get to!" he calls, rapping his hand against the truck door. "I heard from a reliable source that the ending *sucks!*"

With a snort of amusement, I climb into the passenger seat as he contorts himself back through his window, and we look at each for a long moment, our gazes bright and our smiles identical. For two people who don't particularly want to catch Everett Harding's new movie, we're both in a spectacularly good mood. Maybe because it's the weekend, or maybe because we can finally hang out together after having to act like strangers at church.

"Ready for our second Nashville adventure?" Blake asks, dimples flashing.

"Hopefully this one doesn't result in me yelling at you on a street corner," I say between nervous giggles as I pull on my seatbelt. As always, there's music playing, but the volume is down low. All these country albums have really grown on me and I've become accustomed to listening to them on full volume whenever I've been in Blake's truck, so I reach over and flick the volume straight up. "Better."

Blake stares at me slack-jawed in complete and utter fascination. "A girl who turns up Kelsea Ballerini? Damn."

He puts the truck in drive and places a hand on my thigh. I immediately rest my hand over his, leaning my head back against the headrest, closing my eyes and feeling the warmth of the sun against my summer-freckled face.

And as we head off along these same old quiet roads with the sun lowering in the sky ahead, with the bitter-sweetness of a country melody playing and the breeze from the open windows rustling my hair, I think that maybe tonight we can't stop smiling because I like Blake and Blake likes me.

23

The movie theater is at a mall in a neighborhood south of downtown Nashville, and it – is – packed. *Flash Point* movie posters dominate every wall, stealing all of the glory from other new releases, and there's even a huge cardboard stand at the entrance which is essentially one giant cast photo. A bigger-than-life-sized Dad and Laurel Peyton are front and center, flanked by the supporting cast. When we passed, fans were posing in front of the stand, and I shot Dad the fiercest glower I could manage. It's the closest I'll get to the real-life version of him for now.

There's a buzz around the theater's foyer, the clash of hundreds of voices musing in anticipation. The thing about the *Flash Point* movies is that they appeal to every age group, from elderly couples to groups of friends younger than me. There's all sorts of people standing in the same line as we are, waiting to have our tickets checked for one of the two screens showing the movie in fifteen minutes. I imagine the production company executives rubbing their hands together with glee, knowing these double screenings are happening all over the country this weekend.

It's also a little . . . awkward.

For the most part, no one ever knows who I am. It's not *me* who's the actor, so only Dad's most devoted of fans would recognize me if they passed me in the street. I can get by under the radar pretty easily unless someone mentions my full name and others piece two and two together. But luckily tonight I am blending in. I am making the conscious effort to do so – I keep my head slightly lowered and ensure I'm circled by Blake's friends at all times. Ruben is already at the end of his tether with me, and if he knew I was attending a movie screening in Nashville where one of Dad's super fans could spot me at any second I think he would fly that private jet here solo just to drag me back home.

"Hey, Mila," Barney calls in a voice that's a little too loud. "Is this weird for you?"

"Yup," I murmur, while Blake helpfully kicks him in the shin.

I'm trying to block out the group of girls waiting in line in front of us who are gushing about how *sexy* Everett Harding is. Bile churns in my stomach. These girls aren't even that much older than me, and they're talking like that about my *dad*.

Gross.

Blake brushes his pinky finger against mine as a sign of solidarity and I fight the urge to take his hand, not because we're trying to hide whatever this is between us but because we're in the middle of a movie theater with his friends. It seems kind of inappropriate to be all touchy around one another, even though I get the sense his friends wouldn't be so surprised if they did spot us getting a little close. They *did* get me a ticket tonight, so it seems they've accepted the fact that I should be counted as Blake's plus one for things like this.

We're here with his friendship circle, and it's nice for me to get to know who Blake tends to hang around with when he isn't hosting his big get-togethers. Blake and his friends are entering their senior year at Fairview High together in the fall, so they are all a year older than me. That's why Savannah and Tori aren't here, but Barney and Lacey are. Myles is here too with the girl he seems to be in a casual fling with, Cindy. The guy Savannah has a crush on, Nathan Hunt, is also one of Blake's closer friends, along with some guy by the name of Travis who I vaguely recognize as one of the guys who helped Blake out with the fire last weekend. So far, they have been welcoming, except Lacey didn't quite smile when Blake and I met up with the group in the parking lot. And although Barney was the one to steal my phone and call Dad that very first weekend I arrived, I am starting to relax a bit more around him, but only because he hasn't pulled anymore stunts since then.

Those girls in front of us are still talking about Dad in great detail. No matter how hard I focus on trying to tune out their conversation, I can't bear it anymore when they start wondering out loud how many scenes there'll be that feature Dad stripping off.

"You know he already turned forty, right? He's double your age," I remark in a loud, clear voice without even thinking. As soon as the words leave my mouth, I want to shove them back in. I shouldn't be drawing attention to myself. Especially not like that.

All three girls turn around to stare at me in surprise, taken aback by such negativity in a line that's supposed to be full of fellow enthusiasts.

"Sorry," Blake says, stepping around me to block me from their view. "She's just a friend we've dragged along with us. She *hates* Everett Harding."

"Yeah, she absolutely should have stayed home," Lacey mumbles. Her blue eyes meet mine, and I have a strong sense that she isn't just playing along with Blake.

The girls shoot our group strange looks, but turn back around and resume their conversation at a much lower volume. I press my hand over my eyes in embarrassment. I really shouldn't have said anything, but it's so hard not to. I live a life full of rules that other people aren't even aware of, and one of those rules is to remain silent and allow strangers to fantasize about your dad.

"Lucky for you, Mila," Barney says, "it's Laurel Peyton I have the soft spot for and not" – he lowers his voice to a whisper and cups his hand around his mouth – "*your hot-as-hell father.*"

We share a laugh, and I relax slightly as the line lurches forward. The screen doors have opened, and excitement flows down the line in a wave. We work our way down to the screen, have our tickets checked, and then head in through the heavy doors.

The seats are filling up fast, but that's to be expected – it's a sold-out screening. Everyone floods up the aisles in a stampede as though there won't be what will feel like hours of trailers to sit through first. Our seats are way at the back, which I quickly realize are actually the *worst* possible seats for me. I have a full view of the theater, of all these rows and rows of fans, of women (and probably some of the guys too) who are completely star-struck with my dad.

"I can't believe people love these movies so much," I murmur as we get comfortable, reclining back.

"I don't get it either," Blake says from my left.

"It's because they have a mixture of everything!" Cindy says. She's sitting on my right, a huge bag of popcorn in her lap, and she sits up and nearly jumps over the armrest to get closer to me. "Action. Adventure. *Romance.*"

"Well," I say with a forced smile, shrinking back further into my seat, "I hope you like the movie." Even though I know already that she won't.

Dad and Laurel Peyton's characters have been gradually falling in love over the course of the first two movies, but in this third installment they don't end up together. Two hours from now, this room will be filled with disappointed groans. At least I have the scene where Dad's character takes a bullet to the chest to look forward to.

"You okay?" Blake asks quietly, his head turned, and his gaze focused on me.

"Mmhmm," I respond unconvincingly.

I'm relieved when the lights dim and the trailers begin, because it shuts up the audience and I no longer have to listen to endless discussions around people's predictions for what this movie has in store. Next to me, it sounds as if Cindy isn't even breathing when the movie's opening sequence rolls; around us, the theater is in complete and utter silence.

Because I've already seen the movie once before, it's not that bad watching it a second time. Dad *is* an amazing actor and there is no denying that he was born to be on screen, but it's always so strange to see him act in ways he doesn't in real life. There are certain facial expressions that belong to the character, and not Everett Harding. Mannerisms that I know aren't Dad's. It makes for an odd experience, watching someone you *know*, your own dad, as someone you don't recognize. But lately, it's not just on screen that I don't recognize him.

I physically cringe whenever Dad whispers some cheesy line in a husky tone, and I flat out close my eyes and will myself to fall asleep whenever he and Laurel share an on-screen kiss. *This* is always the weirdest part. I think it's pretty gross seeing Dad kiss my own mom, let alone smooching with his co-stars on a massive screen in HD.

"Hey," Blake whispers during the third of these sickly romantic scenes, nudging my knee, "do you want to get out of here?"

I peel open one eye and look at him through the darkness, his face illuminated by the screen, the movie flashing across his eyes. Obviously, Blake has picked up on my discomfort.

"Please," I whisper.

Blake finds my hand in the dark, pulling me up with him. We shuffle along the row together, him guiding the way, but then I trip over the outstretched foot of Lacey.

"Sorry!" she hisses, but her tone isn't that apologetic.

Blake and I continue hastily along the row, trying our best not to disrupt the movie (even though – childishly, I admit – I would love to call out the ending and spoil it for everyone), and then dash down the aisle, taking two steps at a time with our hands still interlocked. I hear a low wolf-whistle that I imagine is from Barney, and before we round the corner to leave the screen I steal a look back at the audience. They are all truly captivated, their eyes glued to the screen, no one so much as daring to rustle a bucket of popcorn.

We push our way out through the heavy doors and into the now empty foyer, and I breathe a huge sigh of relief. There's no one here except an employee sweeping up, but I can hear the rumble of sound from movies playing in all of the screens.

"You were right," Blake says, laughing like we've just escaped a fate worse than death. "That movie really does suck, and I'm making that judgment after only sitting through forty minutes of it."

"I don't want to go back in there," I tell him, staring back at the screen doors with a sense of dread.

"We don't have to," he says. "C'mon."

We head back toward the ticket desks and concession stands, but I have a feeling they won't get busy again until the crowds for the next showing of the latest *Flash Point* movie arrive, bringing with them a new buzz of noise and commotion. When we walk past that cardboard stand of the cast by the entrance again, I'm in half a mind to punch a hole through it exactly where Dad's ridiculous grin is. But I don't want to be escorted out of the movie theater for assaulting a photograph, so I leave it be and make my way outside with Blake.

We've just missed sunset. The sun has disappeared behind the horizon for the day, but it's still light out and the air is thick with lingering heat that radiates up from the concrete sidewalks. It's a Sunday evening, so the plaza is pretty busy. People are disappearing into restaurants and bars, but Blake leads me back to his truck.

He leans back against the tailgate and gazes down at my hand, aimlessly touching my bracelet and playing with my fingers. "We don't have to wait for the others to get out of the movie," he says. "We can grab food ourselves. There's a Cheesecake Factory over there –"

"Or," I say, cutting him off, "we can do this."

And for the first time in my life, I pluck up the courage to make the first move. I grasp Blake's hand and move it to my hip, then step forward to close the distance between us. Against his truck, I press my lips to his.

We may be in the middle of a parking lot, but Blake kisses me as though we are alone in the world. That first kiss of ours on the night of the bonfire was tentative and careful, but this time we know the other won't pull away. That's why we don't hold back; we lose ourselves completely. Blake's free hand is in my hair as he kisses me deeply, holding me close, and I forget all about the movie.

"Yeah, this is way better," he murmurs, smiling against my lips.

We pull apart for only a moment, our foreheads together, my thumb brushing the dimple in his left cheek. We stare at each other, breathing more heavily than before. I'm not sure whose smile is the brightest.

"We're in Nashville," I murmur in between breaths, "and I think we should take advantage of that. How about a detour to Honky Tonk Central?"

And then I have my answer – the brightest smile from Blake.

24

Late Tuesday afternoon, I am parading the aisles of Walmart with Savannah and Tori on the hunt for a new hair dryer after Savannah's blew up, but we've gotten distracted and now have a cart full of random unnecessary junk. We only popped in here after grabbing iced coffees from Dunkin' Donuts down the street, but have now been wandering the aisles for almost an hour.

"Imagine having the nerve to walk out of your dad's movie," Tori says, posing in front of a mirror with a pair of bright red sunglasses that I believe are now the hundredth pair she's tried on. "That's bold, Mila. You literally give *zero* shits about who your dad is, and for that you have my utmost respect."

"We're going to see the movie on Friday," Savannah says as she rounds a clothes rack with the overflowing cart, "but Myles said not to get my hopes up." There's a bag of Cheetos propped up in the kid's seat – yeah, strapped in – which she has opened and is munching her way through as she continues to browse.

"Myles is right," I agree with a laugh.

Although the opening weekend has racked in big bucks at the box office, the reviews have been less than stellar. Once upon a time there were rumors among the production executives of a fourth installment, but I imagine they'll need to rethink how well a fourth movie would be received after the disaster that is the third.

Months ago, I would have been feeling disappointment, but now? I don't really care. Dad is already so successful, he doesn't need to be thrust even further into the stars. In fact, he could do with a reality check every once in a while.

Tori finally decides which three-dollar sunglasses are the most likely to last for more than a week (round, edged with diamante daisies), then tosses them into the cart. "Okay, but I still can't believe you went to Honky Tonk Central and *didn't get kicked out*. Is this what happens when you're the kids of Everett Harding and the Mayor of Nashville? People make special exceptions, like letting minors stay *illegally* in their bars?"

"No one made any exceptions," I say, playfully shoving a pouting Tori away from me. "We just hid ourselves at a table right at the back when it turned eight, and the bouncers walked right on by. We didn't stay that late."

"You stayed until one," Savannah points out, cocking a brow at me and shoving another Cheeto in her mouth. Her earrings today, surprisingly, are plain studs. "That sounds like a pretty fun night to me."

My thoughts drift off to scenes of last night, of Blake and I together at Honky Tonk Central. We shared the same platter of appetizers again that we had on my first visit, and because it was the weekend all three floors of the bar were packed from wall to wall with people having a good time. The music blared loud all night, and I couldn't stop the rhythm from taking over my body. I left Blake behind at the table, shimmied my way over to the squashed dance floor, and lost myself in the music of the live band smashing out country hits. I blended straight in – not Everett Harding's daughter, just Mila putting her dance classes to good use. I felt free and alive, dancing all night among strangers in the city I'm falling in love with, and Blake watched me for a while with an odd twinkle in his eye. Soon he joined me on the dance floor, spun me into his arms, and kissed me right there and then.

"We just listened to the music and danced a little," I say, keeping my head tilted down.

"Oh, is that all?" Savannah says, raising an eyebrow.

"Let me think..." Tori grins. "And stuck your tongue down his throat?"

My face heats a bit and I grin sheepishly as Savannah and Tori squeal with delight, bouncing on the balls of their feet. Savannah rams the cart out of the way, nearly knocking a mannequin to the floor, and shakes me by the shoulders.

"See? I knew it. I am *psychic* when it comes to these things!"

"Oh, shut up, you mystic weirdo," Tori says, shoving Savannah to the side and stepping in front of me. "You are now officially my idol. Not only did you waltz out of your dad's movie, you did it so you could spend the night *kissing Blake Avery*. You are living my eighth-grade dream!"

"Tori! We're talking about my cousin here, remember?"

"You don't care that he's your cousin when Mila is the one who gets to kiss him!"

"Guys," I say, holding my arm out between them, a grin still spread wide across my face. "Chill."

"Let's go back to the ice cream," Tori decides with a dramatic flourish. "I need to drown my sorrows."

We finally finish up at Walmart fifteen minutes later and we head out into the parking lot where Tori's older brother, Jacob, waits for us. We are laden with bags full of ice cream, snacks, sunglasses, a disposable grill, and of course a hair dryer, among a thousand other things. As we haphazardly stack the bags into the trunk of the car, I receive a text from Blake Avery himself that reads:

Hey honky-tonk-loving Mila who knocked out the killer dance moves last night. Where are you?

I hope he's not looking for me back at the Harding Estate. I quickly text back:

Walmart with a cart load of crap. You?

Our responses become pretty instant as we fire them back and forth.

BLAKE: Home. Wanna come over?
MILA: Is your mom there?
BLAKE: All clear at the Avery abode.
MILA: See you soon!

I climb into the backseat of the car and, as Jacob navigates out onto the highway, I clear my throat and say, "I was wondering if maybe you guys could take me to Blake's."

"Okay, now *that* stings, Mila," Tori huffs, but her eye roll reassures me that there's no hard feelings. "Jacob, head over to the mayor's house."

As we drive down Fairview Boulevard, Savannah analyzes me with an inquisitive gaze. "What does my aunt think of the two of you?"

My smile fades and I turn my attention to the passing stores outside the window. "Oh – um – I've only met her a few times. I don't think she's picked up on it yet," I lie, adopting a clear voice and utilizing those acting genes of mine again.

From what Blake has told me, Savannah and Myles have no idea that once upon a time Everett Harding was destined to be their uncle. After all, Dad's engagement to LeAnne happened before any of us were ever born, and it's not the kind of history you bring up out of nowhere. Plus, they don't ever need to know ... The fewer people who do, the better. That's why I can't talk about the fact that LeAnne does not like me. At all.

Fairview becomes more familiar to me with each week that passes, so I know Blake's house isn't far when I recognize the outskirts of his neighborhood. Butterflies build in my stomach the way they always do whenever I'm around him and my body tingles with nervous excitement, even though I know by now that I should be over these nerves. *You know him, Mila. He's not a stranger anymore.*

But I can't help thinking that maybe it's a good thing that he still makes me nervous even now.

As we pull up outside his house, the butterflies in my stomach die. LeAnne's Tesla is parked on the driveway alongside Blake's truck. He said she wasn't home, but that was ten minutes ago. Maybe she returned home from her office in Nashville early, maybe a meeting was cut short . . . All I know is that she's here, but so am I now. I can't just ask Jacob to keep on driving.

"Have fun!" Savannah says cheerfully.

"But not too much!" Tori adds with a saucy wink.

Swallowing, I step out and wave them goodbye as the car disappears down the street, and then I turn for the house. I know by now not to use the front door and to head around the back, but I'm only halfway up the driveway when I hear the gate swinging open.

Blake rushes toward me, but rather than flashing me his usual gorgeous smile, he is wide-eyed and shaking his head fast. When he reaches me, he grasps my wrists and pants, "Mila, hell, I'm so sorry."

"What?"

"I don't even know what to – wait." Blake cuts himself off and the color instantly drains from his face, leaving him pale and unrecognizable. "What?"

My heart skips a few beats, sending my heartbeat out of sync. Palpitations throb painfully in my chest as I look down at his clenched hands around my wrists. "What are you talking about?"

Blake stares at me in absolute horror. "I just saw it . . . But you don't . . . You don't know."

"Know what?" I whisper in fear. I don't want to hear

his answer, because I know already that whatever it is I don't know, it is something *bad*. My stomach twists with agonizing dread. The sudden change from excitement to terror has sent me lightheaded and I feel utterly blank until my phone vibrates.

Blake lets go of my wrists, but still I don't reach for my phone as he runs his hands through his hair, gripping the ends and pulling hard. "Hell, Mila. I shouldn't be the one who tells you. I don't know how to."

"Oh, Blake. Put the poor girl out of her misery."

Blake and I flinch at the sound of LeAnne's voice. We turn to the porch where she has appeared, her hands on the porch railing as though she has been leaning out to listen. She tuts under her breath, then descends the porch steps and approaches us on the driveway.

"Mila, have you really not heard yet?" she asks, eyes flashing the same way they did that night after the bonfire. She stops a mere two feet away from me and looks me up and down with a pitying frown. "Do you really not know? I would have thought you'd be the first."

"Mom. Don't you – don't you fucking *dare*," Blake hisses, taking a threatening step toward his mother. He blocks me off from her as though to shield me, and I notice his hands are balled into fists by his side.

LeAnne sighs as though this is all merely an inconvenience to her. She flips her hair over her shoulder and fixes Blake with a glare as equally threatening as his, the animosity intensifying. "What have I told you about using that language with me?"

"Mila, get in the truck," Blake orders, reaching behind him in search of my hand. He doesn't look away from his mom as he says, "We're leaving."

Blake pulls me away from her, his steps quick and desperate as he fumbles for his keys. His grip is tight around my hand, like he's terrified of letting go. My head spins even faster, as if in time with my phone as it vibrates more persistently.

"Mila, don't you think you deserve to know?" LeAnne calls out, the cruel edge to her voice unmistakable. "It seems only fair – apparently your father hasn't changed much over the years."

I dig my heels into the ground and root myself to the spot, pulling my hand free from Blake's. I need to know what the hell is going on, and I need to know *now*. My heart is slamming around inside my chest so hard that I worry I may go into cardiac arrest if I am kept in this state for a second longer.

I march back over to LeAnne, my chin tilted up to face her and my teeth clenched tight. I stare unflinchingly into her dark eyes that so resemble Blake's. "Tell me," I demand. "Right now."

"*Mom!*" Blake pleads, and I hear him slam his hand against his truck. The ding of metal rings out around the street. "Don't. She shouldn't hear it from you. Let me be the one to tell her."

"I don't have to tell Mila anything," LeAnne says coolly. "I can just show her. *Share* it with her." She steps back, breaking our intense eye contact, and pulls out her phone from her purse. Unlocking the device, she taps at her screen for the longest few seconds of my life, then turns it around and holds it up in front of my eyes. "There, Mila."

I don't know what I expected, but it wasn't this.

Shock grips me like a vice and my blood runs cold so fast that my legs go weak and I nearly topple over from the sudden disorientation. But I catch the meaning of the words on the screen before it blurs and the headline distorts until it no longer makes sense.

EVERETT HARDING AND LAUREL PEYTON
TAKE THEIR AFFAIR OFF-SCREEN

I press my fingertips into my eyes until I can focus again. Then, I home in on the photograph beneath the headline. A shot so zoomed in that it's fuzzily pixelated, but there is no denying the truth it shows – in the shadowy, dim corner of a restaurant, Dad has Laurel pulled in close against him, his hands around her body and his mouth against hers. They aren't in costume. They aren't on set. This isn't a scene rehearsal.

This is my dad passionately kissing another woman.

In real life.

"Looks like the old adage is true," LeAnne says, lowering her phone. "Once a cheater, always a cheater."

Blake has rushed to my side, but my body no longer feels like something I have any control of. His voice sounds muffled, my vision is nothing but a blur, my hands are trembling and numb. I vaguely feel him pulling at me, trying to guide me away from LeAnne, but my legs have turned to lead.

"Mila. Mila, c'mon," he pleads, his voice breaking in sympathy. "Let's go somewhere. Anywhere."

"I ... I need to go home," I croak, blinking hard in an attempt to regain my focus. The world is spilling out of control, stretching and expanding, leaving me unbalanced and wrecked. I can make out LeAnne's outline still standing over me, watching. The buzzing of my phone seems to grow louder and louder.

"I'll drive you home!" Blake says determinedly, interlocking our hands and pulling me even harder. "C'mon, get in the truck."

"Mila, Blake is right," LeAnne says, and her voice softens as though she may genuinely feel sorry for me, despite everything. "Go with him. Let him take you home."

"No," I whisper, shaking my head. They don't understand. "I need to go *home*."

My world has shattered. I can't stay here in Fairview right now – I need to go home; I need to go back to California. Have Sheri and Popeye seen this breaking headline yet? Has *Mom*? Oh, Mom ... Tears erupt all at once, spilling down my cheeks in hot waves. This will blow my family apart. I need to go. I need to leave.

Tearing myself free from Blake's grip, I back away from him and LeAnne slowly, willing my strength to return. Through my tears, a semblance of vision forms, and I see their expressions. LeAnne's arms are folded across her chest, but she bites down hard on her lower lip as her gaze is filled with what I can only assume is empathy from someone who fully understands the price of betrayal. By her side, her son stares at me, open-mouthed. His expression is different – his dark eyes flooded with panic, for we both know what it means if I go home.

"Mila, wait!" Blake calls out, his voice cracking. Then, louder, he begs, "Don't go! Not like this!"

But I turn my back on him, and I run.

Thank You

Thank you a million times over to my readers for being such amazing champions of Mila and Blake even before ever reading their story, and for supporting every step forward I take in my writing journey.

Thank you so, so, so much to all of the team at Black & White Publishing for being the greatest publishing team I could ever wish to have behind me since the very beginning. Thank you to my editors, Emma Hargrave, Janne Moller and Alice Latchford, for your guidance and expertise. Special thanks to Campbell Brown and Alison McBride for continuing to make possible my dream of having my name on bookshelves.

So much love for my closest friends for keeping me sane. Rachael Lamb, Heather Allen, Rhea Forman and Bethany Stapley: thanks for the road trips for ice cream, endless cups of tea, and true friendships that I cherish.

But most importantly, thank you to those who make my world shine brighter:

My mum, Fenella, for all of the amazing memories we continue to make together.

My dad, Stuart, for always reminding me that I can achieve anything I set my mind to.

My sidekick, Bear, for filling me with joy whenever you look at me with your little puppy eyes.

My best friend, Rachael, for being the person I laugh the hardest with.

My granda, George, for being equally as stubborn as me, but who I wouldn't change for the world.

My grandma, Fenella, for always being so full of warmth and love.

My sister, Sherilyn, for being the strongest person I've ever known.

And my nephew, Anders, for always being the shining light at the end of every tunnel.

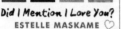

JUST DON'T MENTION IT

The one all DIMILY readers have been shouting for ... Tyler's story!

As irresistible and dazzling as its Californian backdrop, here is Tyler's story – his heart-stopping tale of past hurt, finding hope and figuring out who the hell he wants to be.

DARE TO FALL

A new take on teen romance that explores how loss affects young lives and relationships.

In Windsor, Colorado, two teenagers experience bereavement much too young. It's left MacKenzie terrified, but Jaden refuses to dwell on the past. Will MacKenzie dare to fall for the person she's most afraid of growing close to?

THE WRONG SIDE OF KAI

A story of broken hearts, forgiveness, vulnerability – and the exhilaration of falling in love.

Vanessa doesn't believe in serious relationships. In fact, she doesn't believe in any kind of relationship. But when her casual fling with Harrison ends in the ultimate betrayal, she's out for revenge. Enter Kai.

THE JOURNEY STARTS HERE

@inkroadbooks

Playlist

Check out the music that kept me inspired while working on *Becoming Mila*.

la	*Kelsea Ballerini*
Nothing To Do Town	*Dylan Scott*
Same Dirt Road	*Eric Lee*
Setting the Night on Fire	*Kane Brown (with Chris Young)*
Mgno	*Russell Dickerson*
Unforgettable	*Thomas Rhett*
Leave the Night on	*Sam Hunt*
Fearless	*Taylor Swift*
Chance Worth Taking	*Mitchell Tenpenny*
Cortado, Pt. 2	*anton*